Meliss

A Diamond from Tiffany's

and Other Stories

SIMON &
SCHUSTER

London · New York · Sydney · Toronto · New Delhi

A CBS COMPANY

First published in Great Britain by Simon & Schuster UK Ltd, 2015
A CBS COMPANY

Copyright © Melissa Hill, 2015

This book is copyright under the Berne Convention.
No reproduction without permission.
® and © 1997 Simon & Schuster, Inc. All rights reserved.

The rights of Melissa Hill to be identified as author of this work
have been asserted in accordance with sections 77 and 78
of the Copyright, Designs and Patents Act, 1988.

3 5 7 9 10 8 6 4 2

Simon & Schuster UK Ltd
1st Floor
222 Gray's Inn Road
London WC1X 8HB

www.simonandschuster.co.uk

Simon & Schuster Australia, Sydney
Simon & Schuster India, New Delhi

A CIP catalogue record for this book
is available from the British Library

Paperback ISBN: 978-1-47115-370-9
eBook ISBN: 978-1-47115-371-6

This book is a work of fiction. Names, characters, places
and incidents are either a product of the author's imagination or
are used fictitiously. Any resemblance to actual people living
or dead, events or locales is entirely coincidental.

Typeset in the UK by M Rules
Printed and bound by CPI Group (UK) Ltd, Croydon, CR0 4YY

Simon & Schuster UK Ltd are committed to sourcing paper
that is made from wood grown in sustainable forests and supports the Forest
Stewardship Council, the leading international forest certification organisation.
Our books displaying the FSC logo are printed on FSC certified paper.

In loving memory of Homer –
this girl's best friend.

A Diamond from Tiffany's

Chapter 1

Rachel Conti's eyes sparkled almost as brightly as the diamond ring she had just removed from her finger.

Even now, two years on since Gary had proposed, the sight of it twinkling majestically under the lights sent a little shiver of delight down her spine. A diamond from Tiffany's could do that.

Placing the ring in its designated safe spot above the restaurant kitchen sink, she smiled fondly at the realisation that this was one of *two* engagement rings from the world-famous store she'd been lucky enough to wear – how many women could say that?

Thankfully the sentiment behind this one was the real thing. The other ... well that had been a completely different story, but a great adventure just the same.

An unfortunate mix up with a pair of Tiffany bags in New York two years before had resulted in Rachel ending up with a ring that was actually meant for someone else entirely. It had taken some time and quite a lot of drama for that particular misunderstanding to be sorted out but ...

'Rachel ... *Rachel*?'

Her best friend Terri's voice surprised her out of her daydreams, and she blinked, trying to clear her thoughts. 'Sorry ... I was miles away.'

Terri shook her head indulgently — it certainly wasn't the first time Rachel had completely zoned out, no doubt lost in a daydream about potential new recipes for menu items, or more likely, about her forthcoming wedding.

It was Terri's job to keep her friend and business partner on her toes, especially when dinner tables at their busy Dublin restaurant, Stromboli, were filling up quickly with hungry customers.

'Do I have to remind you again about tonight?' Terri rapped her bare knuckles on the prep table's metal edges. She knew she was being stern, but Rachel responded best when she took action. Following Rachel's line of vision, her gaze automatically rested on the twinkling engagement ring her friend had popped in a saucer above the sink.

Case in point, she thought, recalling another crisis involving Rachel she'd had to avert, and once again she felt a jolt when confronted by a memory involving Ethan Greene.

'Yes, of course, tonight,' Rachel muttered, standing up straight. 'So the specials are aubergine tart and—'

Shaking her head, Terri cut her off. 'The *critic*, Rachel. From *Culinary Connect*, remember? This could be massive for us.'

2

Rachel had known about the critic but it had been buried in her memory.

Practically all she could think about these days was her dancing slowly with Gary under shimmering New York City lights ...

'Oh yes, of course. Sorry, I really was a million miles away. Has he arrived yet?'

She stood up and walked to the larger wooden swing door that divided the kitchen from the dining area. Peering out of the metal and glass porthole window, she struggled to make out the faces of the diners.

Their shared business venture, Stromboli, was everything Rachel had imagined it to be when her best friend and fellow catering college graduate, Terri, first proposed the idea of a Mediterranean eatery a few years before.

A combination of art, furniture and ethnic recipes fused with age-old Irish favourites, the restaurant had in its three short years in business become a huge hit with the local foodie crowd, and the artisan bakery section was in itself a popular Dublin tourist destination.

The wood-panelled and stained-glass interior of the dining area was then just dimly lit with candles, serenading music, and full of happy patrons, and it always put Rachel in the mind of big bustling family gatherings of the kind her Sicilian ancestors must have experienced.

For her, this place and its crew were the closest thing she'd had to a family since she'd lost her parents as a teenager.

Though that would all change soon, she thought, smiling, as her upcoming wedding pushed its way back into her consciousness, as it did so often these days.

Groaning, Terri grasped Rachel's white-clothed shoulders and swung her determinedly round, past the staff that were peeling vegetables and boiling water. She steered her back into the centre of the prep area.

'It's an anonymous visit,' she said, referring to the food critic. 'We have no idea what this guy looks like, what his name is or even if he's coming tonight. What I do know is that he's highly respected on the ethnic restaurant scene, and a good review from the magazine could take us to a whole new level.'

Rachel was used to being scolded. She and Terri might have been best friends since college, but her friend was much more to her than that. The fiery redhead was her sister, her mother, her grandmother, and her personal life-planner wrapped into one tiny (but deadly) package. She knew that Terri was only being firm out of love and obligation to her and their business.

Just then a finger poked Rachel's shoulder.

'Um, sweetheart?' Justin, their sous-chef pointed out. 'The lasagne.'

'What about it?' she replied absently. 'I put it on about thirty minutes ago.' Rachel's favourite recipe was her father's vegetable lasagne. She served it at Stromboli in his memory with the utmost pride and respect once a week every single week.

'It's burnt,' Justin said bluntly, keeping his eyes on the ground as he prepared for the response.

'*What?*' Terri reacted first, as she led the sprint to the metal, industrial-sized ovens, where Jen, one of the waitresses was pulling out a large metal tray.

Rachel took one quick look at the pasta dish and stood back in dismay.

It was unrecognisable. A nasty mix of black and browns, the dish was nowhere near customer-ready, let alone critic-ready.

She had Jen set the tray down on the prep table so she could examine it further, while Terri paced back and forth behind her.

After a long, horrible half-minute of silence, Rachel stood up straight and turned to face her business partner. 'Looks like I was wrong. It may have been in there for a teeny bit longer than thirty minutes.'

'Rachel ...' Terri wanted to begin a lecture about the critic again, but Rachel held up her hand to stop her before she could even begin. Instead, she took a deep breath, and assuming a state of almost Zen-like calm, suddenly transformed into the skilled and focused chef that she was.

'Justin, start chopping more onions and tomatoes. I'll start another round of pasta for the lasagne. There should still be some dough in the fridge.'

Terri waited impatiently behind her, ready to further her admonishments, but Rachel stopped her, pushing her out the kitchen door.

'Offer everyone the aubergine tart as a free starter for the first hour. We'll call it a chef's special in honour of closing week.'

Terri was ready to bring up the whole aspect of money, time, and dangers of changing the routine this late in the game, but Rachel knew the right things to say. 'It will give us some extra time to prepare the lasagne and it'll keep everyone sweet and onside while they wait.' She winked, pushed her friend out the door, and turned back towards the kitchen.

Manning the front of house, Terri tried to forget the chaos in the kitchen as she carefully studied each and every Stromboli patron who came in to be seated.

Rachel would pull it together, though; she always did. It never ceased to amaze Terri how her friend could be so scatty in life, and yet so ultra-focused in the kitchen.

Most of the time, at least.

Tonight, the bistro was a blur of a few regular faces and walk-in tourists.

Not one stood out to her as a potential food critic. She couldn't even fathom what would give it away. Would they bring a laptop or a notebook and pen to take notes? Would they be dressed up or down in an attempt to blend in with the more casual bistro atmosphere? Maybe they would eat alone, but that seemed like it would be a dead giveaway.

In any case, if she did get a hunch of who it could be, she would seat them in one of the nicer booths at the back – the leather-backed ones with the best view of the dining area.

She'd already earmarked it as reserved, just in case one of the waiting staff gave it away to someone else.

Though the restaurant had been doing well since its inception almost three years ago – mostly due to word of mouth and a dedicated following among the locals – Terri was always eager to grow their reputation as a must-visit Dublin dining destination. A positive mention from a discerning restaurant expert with such a wide reputation could be amazing.

She worried that while they had a good thing going, something like a negative critique in a major foodie publication could really undermine what they had built. The thought had terrified Terri to her core since receiving the call from the magazine's lifestyle editor last week.

What had made it even more terrifying was that the eventual write-up would likely come right on the heels of the restaurant's re-opening in a week's time. Tonight was their last night at Stromboli together, before Terri returned in five days' time.

The short absence was to allow both co-owners time away for Rachel's long-awaited wedding to Gary Knowles. The ceremony was taking place in New York, and while Terri was honoured to act as chief bridesmaid on her friend's behalf, she wasn't so enamoured at having to take so much time away from the restaurant and travel all the way across the Atlantic to spend time in a city that for her held little appeal.

Or indeed enamoured at the groom, but that was another story.

All the more reason why tonight, the head chef's last evening before she zoomed off into the Caribbean sunset with her motorbike-mad new husband, needed to be perfect.

But as always, Rachel had little appreciation of down-to-earth business matters and was much more interested in the creative side of the enterprise – the food.

Amazing really, Terri thought, unleashing her best front-of-house smile on an arriving customer/potential food critic, that a dreamer and a pragmatist should make such a good team.

Chapter 2

Much later, Terri personally escorted the last diners out of the darkened restaurant, wishing them well as they drunkenly said their goodbyes.

She still had no idea who the critic was or even if he'd appeared at all, she thought worriedly.

She highly doubted that the lively couple throwing their arms around each other as they headed towards the Ha'Penny Bridge had anything to do with a highly regarded European culinary publication, but you never knew ...

Just their luck that the critic who could potentially make or break their little restaurant would appear when both co-owners were out of the picture.

As she watched the staggering couple make their way down the street, Rachel materialised at her side.

'So, all's well that ends well,' her friend said, referring to her second-round lasagne which had gone down a treat. 'But can we talk real business now?'

Exhausted, Terri followed her to their shared office at the back of the dining room.

Rachel had already brought back some panna cotta to share. Eating leftover dessert was a tradition the two had relished every day they worked together since the opening of the restaurant. Justin dropped off two small cups of cappuccino along with the other waiters' order books and till receipts, and Terri began punching in numbers, calculating costs and sales.

Rachel on the other hand sat back, sounding a little exasperated. 'When I said "business", this wasn't exactly what I had in mind.'

'OK. What *business* did you have in mind?' She hated to admit it, but Terri knew all too well what her friend was up to. She watched as a devilish grin popped onto Rachel's face. Her blue eyes danced and her full Sicilian lips curled.

'Less than a week to go and we still have so much to discuss!' Rachel grabbed her leather duffel bag, pulling out a large, thick binder from the depths. The binder's pages were torn and bent from use, as random pages stuck out and little pieces of fabric added to its weight. 'Should we start with a to-do list for when we arrive?'

'How about you just tell me what to do, where to go, and how to stand and I'll just follow along?'

Rachel rolled her eyes at her friend. 'Great chief bridesmaid you are. Only four more days, Terri!' Her face was a combination of amused, overwhelmed and more than a little annoyed.

'I know, I know,' Terri laughed, taunting her. 'Four more

days 'til the moment you've been dreaming of since you were a blob in your mother's womb, or whatever.' She knew her friend was passionate about love and life in general, but especially so about her wedding, while she herself didn't understand how any grown woman could invest so much time and energy in one single day. Terri had no doubt in her mind that when Rachel was growing up, she probably had a binder filled with wedding ideas just like the one she carted around now.

But that was Rachel. She lived for nostalgia, festivity, and anything romantic.

'Go ahead and laugh, but you'll miss these conversations when it's all over. Heck, maybe it'll inspire you to go through all this yourself.'

'You're so right,' Terri drawled. 'Your wedding of the century will be so fantastic and inspirational that I'll probably go out the next day and grab some random New Yorker and get him to marry me just so that I can experience what you're going through. Of course, you make it all sound so appealing – what with the poking and prodding at dress fittings, the crash diets and phone calls with the snotty wedding planner ...'

Terri had just barely touched on the gamut of drama that Rachel had brought upon her since she had begun planning her wedding to Gary a couple of years before. Although in reality it had been even longer, as they'd had that ... false start the first time round.

Either way, it felt like a lifetime. Terri had been Rachel's springboard, her face of reason and calm, and, on one particularly nasty occasion – her bodyguard against a couple of other vicious brides fighting over a designer dress that had gone on sale at a famed Dublin bridal shop.

'Anyway, you know my rule.' She looked back down at the stack of restaurant paperwork she still had to go through before she could go home and hit the pillows.

'OK, but can we just chat about *one* thing on the to-do list? We probably won't get a chance to talk at brunch tomorrow – what with the others around.'

'Brunch? What brunch? And what others?' Terri pulled out her diary planner from the bottom of the desk, pulling up the date page for tomorrow.

Circled with a red marker was Rachel's beautifully ornate handwriting: 'Bridesmaids Brunch: 11 a.m. sharp.' The word 'sharp' was underlined several times – obviously Rachel's attempt to keep Terri on point for once.

She looked up, her narrowed eyes lasering into her friend's face. '*When*, exactly, did you write this here?'

'Oh, I don't know, maybe a couple of weeks ago?' Rachel innocently waved her hand away as she estimated the date. Actually, it was more like a couple of months ago that she'd filled the planner with pre-wedding events she had mapped out.

This brunch was special, though. It was the first time her chief bridesmaid and the others, her cousins, would get together to discuss the finer details of their duties, such as the hen party, and wedding day arrangements.

'Fine, fine, of course I'll be there – how could I miss meeting the evil stepsisters?' Terri said, referring to Rachel's relatives, her distant but only remaining family. She closed the diary and returned to her actual job. 'Now, can you please go back to work, bride to be? I'm sure there's a very messy kitchen out there that needs to be sorted.'

Smiling, Rachel walked up and hugged her from behind as Terri resumed typing numbers into a calculator.

She turned to walk out of the office door but then paused.

'Oh, one more thing. Don't forget to bring good underwear. We're doing the final dress fitting afterwards.'

Groaning, Terri turned round to protest, just as Rachel nipped out quickly, shutting the door behind her.

She leant back in her desk chair, rubbing her temple with her fingers.

It had been a long week, and now she was facing an even longer week of wedding palaver.

While she normally happily listened to such important details like what cake flavours Rachel had picked, and sometimes even participated in the debate between peonies and lilies, by now the wedding had practically taken over their friendship.

But she reminded herself that this would only last another week, less than that actually, as the wedding was happening in four days' time.

One more week and this would all be behind them. Then, once Rachel was back from honeymoon, she and Terri could get back to their normal friendship. More importantly, with her friend's dream wedding finally out of the way, both she and Rachel could focus on the bigger picture, and finally direct both of their energies and attentions towards the restaurant for once and for all.

At least, that's what Terri hoped.

Chapter 3

Outside the restaurant, Dublin had fallen asleep. The city streets were dim, as nearby city-centre businesses shuttered their windows and turned off the lights. Even the late-night revellers, noisy college students and tourists who typically planted themselves outside nearby bars had dispersed.

All that remained were people like Rachel and Terri – late-night workers all striving to finish their jobs and get back to their homes and families.

Families ...

Rachel thought about the word in the back of the taxi taking her home to her and Gary's shared house a few miles away. As the driver navigated the narrow city centre streets, and passed over the bridge to the south-side of the city, she stared out over the River Liffey at the twinkling water below.

As a child, she had grown up in the country, in a tiny house with just her and her dad after her mother died when she was twelve.

Her father, Sicilian by birth, was keen to pass on his family's heritage and by sixteen, Rachel had built up an entire repertoire of dishes and desserts, all straight from her great grandmother's recipes.

When her father passed away while she was at college, Rachel felt that those recipes were the only part of the family she had left, and her interpretation of them in the restaurant day in, day out, was her way of keeping that heritage alive.

It felt weird and more than a little sad to be planning a momentous day in her life like her wedding and not have anyone at all in attendance from her side of the family. Which was why she'd reached out to a couple of cousins on her mother's side, girls around Rachel's age who she didn't know particularly well, but seemed happy to stand by her side on her big day.

Family was hugely important to Rachel, and those girls (and Terri of course) were the closest she could get on her big day.

Though, she and Gary would soon be starting a new life together and soon after that, Rachel thought – hugging herself at the very idea – starting a family of their own.

She couldn't wait to be a mum and she knew Gary would be a great father, especially to a boy. He was a real lads' man, and while he'd sold his beloved motorbike a couple of years before, he was still bike crazy.

As evidenced just then by the engine parts visible from the spare bedroom of their small terraced house, as Rachel let herself inside.

She smiled indulgently, and getting undressed just outside their own bedroom door so as not to wake him, Rachel slipped into the bed beside her beloved husband to be.

Gary murmured softly as she kissed him on the cheek, and wrapped her arms tightly around him, hardly unable to believe that this time next week they'd be man and wife.

And not long after that, maybe even parents.

Finally, she was getting her happy ever after.

The following morning, Rachel got up early in the hope of catching her fiancé to chat about last-minute wedding details before he went to work.

Gary owned a small builder's firm, and while things had been slow for a couple of years, a recent resurgence in the Irish economy meant that work was starting to pick up at a fast pace and he was constantly on the go.

What with her late-night work at the restaurant, they rarely had a chance to discuss their nuptials in any great detail. Of course Rachel had taken charge of the majority of the preparations, but she was happy to do so – it was what most brides did, after all.

'Can we just go through the itinerary for New York? I want to be sure that we're all on—'

'Ah, Rach, I'm late already. Do we really need to do this now?' Gary was impatient, not understanding why this kind of thing mattered so much to her, especially when he was on his way out the door.

'But our plane leaves *tomorrow,* hon. Once we arrive in

New York, there won't be time to do anything other than get married.'

'But isn't that the point of a wedding abroad?' he pointed out. 'We show up, the planner has everything sorted in advance, and we just go and do the deed on the day. No hassle.'

Rachel knew that he was dead serious, and truly believed that the wedding planner alone had arranged everything. The woman had done quite a lot, yes, but only in very close consultation with the bride.

'It's a bit more complicated than that. We have a meeting with Michelle when we arrive, yes – but also with the florist, the celebrant, as well as the catering manager. Oh, and while I think of it, don't forget the final fitting you have for your tux later. Did you remember?'

'Yes, Rachel. I remembered. Six o'clock. Hopefully, the boys will be there as well.'

'Hopefully?' She looked petrified.

'If they can get off work on time. In our trade, it's not as easy as just putting a closed sign on the door, you know. Only joking,' he added with a grin, seeing her face. 'I've put the skids under them, so it should be grand. But then after that, I want no more wedding blather until we arrive in New York. OK? Let's try to make our last few hours free of talk about flowers and cake and all that nonsense. You're obsessed.'

Rachel swallowed hard. At this point, *not* talking about the wedding was nearly impossible, couldn't he understand that? Outside of the restaurant, it was pretty much *all* she talked and thought about these days.

Never mind, she thought, kissing her fiancé goodbye as he set out for work, she would just save it all for that morning's brunch with her cousins and Terri.

'OK, I promise. But speaking of obsessed ...' Rachel decided now was as good a time as any to bring the subject up. 'Those oily engine parts in the spare room ...'

'I know, I know, I'm sorry. They're Sean's,' Gary said referring to his best friend and fellow petrol-head. 'I told him I'd take a look at something for him – it'll only be a little while – and anyway they're not doing any harm there for the moment, are they? We'll be away for the next couple of weeks anyway.'

'I know, but we'll want to get that room redone soon, so all that stuff will need to go.'

'Redone?' Gary looked blank.

'Well, as a nursery, of course,' Rachel laughed. 'I was thinking the crib could go by the window, and maybe a little dresser on the opposite wall ...' She could easily envision exactly where each piece of furniture would go. Thoughts of pastel blues and pinks danced into her head as she imagined herself and Gary putting their future child to bed. She couldn't wait to be a mum and planned on getting pregnant as soon as possible after their wedding.

Her fiancé did not have nearly the same enthusiasm for redecorating as Rachel though, and reacted rather like he did to talk of the wedding.

He ran his hands through his thick brown hair.

'Right. Listen, I'd better get going. It's late. See you later, OK?' He planted a quick kiss on the top of Rachel's head.

'See you later, honey.' She smiled indulgently. Gary's reaction was no surprise. She'd always been able to see right through his macho persona. While he pretended to show an aversion to talk of weddings and babies, underneath it all she knew he was on the very same page.

Why else would Gary have asked her to spend the rest of their lives together?

Chapter 4

They swarmed around her like wild birds homing in on their prey.

Trapping her in her seat at the café table, their pink-lipsticked mouths pecked at her. Heavy make-up stained her cheeks and their perfume engulfed her in an overwhelming scent cloud of roses and alcohol.

All Terri could do was sit there with a pleasant smile as she greeted Rachel's cousins for the first time.

'It is *so* lovely to finally meet you!' The first girl, aged in her late-thirties, whom Terri guessed was the older sister Linda, had an accent that was drawn out and exaggerated, as if she was much more important than someone like Terri could ever hope to meet.

She extended her delicate, lotioned hand out across the table to grab hold of Terri's, who attempted to play along, despite recoiling at Linda's slimy and totally unnecessary touch.

The younger cousin, dressed oddly similar to her older

sister in a yellow sundress with a navy cardigan buttoned to the top, took her turn in doting on Terri.

'Rachel talks about you the whole time. You'd think that *you* were the fiancé with all the things she says. It's all "Terri did this" and "Terri did that". To meet the famous Terri in person is quite the honour. Though we should really have done this much sooner, given how little time we have.'

Terri could not decide if this was a backhanded insult or just an innocent comment. As chief bridesmaid, she probably should have got the bridesmaids in the party together earlier, but with the pressure of the restaurant, she'd had little time or energy.

Besides, Rachel had painted her cousins as gossipy types who did nothing but judge and cackle at their own jokes. So, while the younger sister Cora might feel that Terri had skirted her duties and ignored the two of them completely, now having met them, she silently congratulated herself for not doing this sooner.

It was actually Rachel's reminder that had set her plans into action. After locking up for the night, she had rushed home and pulled out her laptop.

She searched her emails for a message from Rachel to all of the wedding party, and using the contact details listed, sent out a quick note to Linda and Cora asking them if they could meet her at the café a little before the appointed time.

Her intention was that the three could get together and quickly discuss the tentative plans Terri had made for Rachel's hen party in New York.

But given the way the women were prattling on about this and that – the brunch menu offerings, and the colour of Terri's hair – she started to regret ever dragging them into it.

She stopped Linda midway through a sentence about the price of freshly squeezed, organic orange juice. 'Listen, as I mentioned in my email, I want to discuss the plans for Rachel's hen party. Where I think we should start is with the—'

'Oh, Linda and I have already organised that. There's no need for you to worry about it.' Cora was blunt as she waved her hand at Terri's ideas.

'Wait? What?' She was in complete disbelief. She had never been in a wedding party, let alone be named the chief bridesmaid, yet she still knew that it was definitely *her* job to plan and supervise the hen party.

And besides the wedding itself, it was another landmark event Rachel talked about non-stop. As the two couldn't get more time off together from the restaurant to do something in Dublin, Rachel was really looking forward to a last night out in New York as a single woman.

'We went ahead and talked to the wedding planner, Michelle, and she made all the arrangements.' Linda, like her sister, was dismissive of Terri's surprise.

It was if they had expected her to fail at the task.

'OK ... well ... can you at least tell me what you have planned?' Terri's interest was well and truly piqued.

On many occasions, Rachel had told Terri that she didn't know her cousins terribly well, so for them to think that they knew her better than Terri seemed a bit absurd, at least in principle.

Linda pulled out several brochures and slid them across the table. Little sticky notes were attached to the pages with dates and times written on them. 'We thought we would start at the spa. There's a great one in the hotel already. Michelle says they give the best manicure and pedicures.'

Terri nodded. The wedding party, along with all confirmed guests were staying in the same midtown New York hotel, thanks to a group discount organised by Rachel's trusty wedding planner.

A spa day wouldn't be too bad. And with all the stress of the planning Rachel had taken upon herself, her friend might finally be able to chill out and enjoy it.

'And then, after the welcome dinner, we're all going out for drinks!' Cora became extremely animated as she described some New York bar that hosted American line dancing. 'I hear it's real authentic.' Her fake American accent was even worse than her fake posh one.

Terri couldn't help but laugh at the notion though. Line dancing?

'*And* ...' Linda eyed her with a sheepish grin on her face. She leaned in close across the table and lowering her voice to a whisper, she excitedly announced, 'We booked tickets to the "Wild Stallion Show"!'

Cora giggled like a young schoolgirl, nudging her sister to continue. Linda lowered her voice further as Terri tried to get a better grip on what she was saying, 'The men get completely naked apparently! Can you believe that? Rachel is just going to *die*.'

Oh God … Terri had no doubt that Rachel would have some kind of strong reaction, yes. In all their conversations, never once had she ever mentioned to Terri that her idea of a great night out in New York included gyrating men in cowboy hats and tiny speedos.

Terri would have stopped them, would have tried to change the cousins' minds, but with the tickets already booked and the girls so proud of themselves, she couldn't realistically say a word against it.

She would just let this ship sail on its own and hopefully make it up to Rachel in her own way.

Cora and Linda continued chatting about details of the hen night.

They went through their own potential outfits, the merits of wearing heels with all the walking they were to do, how much money to tip the strippers, and if it was worth getting a massage with the spa day package. Terri simply nodded and smiled, all the while checking her wristwatch for the time, as well as the café entrance for Rachel's arrival.

At eleven on the dot – on time as always – the bride-to-be walked through the door gracefully, looking as though she had just stepped off a runway.

Her bulky blue wedding binder was clutched tightly in one slender arm, and she held on to a pair of large, designer sunglasses with her opposite hand.

She took off her wide-brim hat as she approached, her

dark hair falling like waves down her back. She had grown out her usual shorter style for the wedding, so there was enough length for a traditional bridal up-do, and while her friend always looked sensational, there seemed an almost ethereal glow about Rachel now that work had finished, and all she had to focus on was her beloved big day.

Rachel smiled brightly when she saw that Terri had already arrived.

Not only that, she had seemed to have struck up a pleasant chit-chat with her cousins. Still, Terri returned her smile with a pleading, helpless look that screamed, 'Save me!'

Rachel greeted her cousins with the same fervour as the two women had greeted Terri. The first five minutes of the conversation alone were spent with the two sisters going on and on about Rachel's new hairstyle, and the dress she was wearing. At one point, they even forced her to stand up and do a twirl so that they could admire the garment.

Rachel next showed off her Tiffany engagement ring – a large diamond with clusters of smaller stones surrounding the oval shape – and relayed the story about Gary's proposal – the genuine one in Central Park – Terri noted, smiling.

By now, it was almost as if Rachel had forgotten about Gary's first, and much more dubious proposal, that had stemmed from a mix-up following a yellow-cab accident on Fifth Avenue.

Two years before, after a visit to Tiffany & Co, Gary was knocked down on the street outside the store, and in the ensuing melee ended up with a Tiffany's shopping bag belonging to a man who came to his aid. Inside it was a diamond ring, while the other party mistakenly walked away with Gary's recent purchase, a silver charm bracelet.

Happening across the engagement ring while her boyfriend recovered in hospital, Rachel quickly jumped to the wrong conclusion, leaving Gary in somewhat of a bind. Now, Terri felt an unbidden twinge of regret as she thought about the other party involved in that mix-up – for more reasons than one.

Rachel was explaining to the cousins that for her, there was no other place in the world for Gary and her to seal their vows. She would return to New York, under those same city skyscrapers and in that very same location, and promise her everlasting love to the man who had made her greatest dream come true.

'Gary and I have a connection to that city that will last as long as this diamond. We just *had* to go back and get married there.'

Terri had to bite her tongue at this bit, because she knew well that Gary had had very little say in the location, or indeed the wedding itself.

Despite their big day being apparently a shared desire, she knew he'd hardly lifted a finger with any of the arrangements, or barely offered a definite opinion on anything remotely involving the wedding. He was either too busy or too tired to help Rachel make decisions.

And when it came to picking the event's location, he gave

his fiancée free rein to decide, but had not defended her choice.

Instead, Terri knew he'd let his fiancée fall on her sword when his mother became upset over the distance the family would need to travel to attend the ceremony.

Rachel spent days going over the details with Mary Knowles in hopes of smoothing everything out while Gary, on the other hand, sat back and let her deal with the dramatics that ensued when the invites first went out.

For her part, Terri as always, had not been shy in communicating her annoyance over Gary's lack of interest and involvement.

There'd never been any love lost between the two of them in any case – especially after what had happened in New York before – but also, because Gary couldn't be bothered, Terri had little choice but to act as stand-in. She even went with Rachel to the tux selection in her fiancé's place because he conveniently couldn't take time away from a job.

Whenever she expressed these valid concerns, however, Rachel brushed her off. As usual, she justified Gary's behaviour with some excuse about his workload, or how he had in fact made a decision on this minor thing or that.

As always, Gary Knowles was Rachel's blind spot, and at this point, Terri really should know better than to try to change it.

All she could do in the meantime was try to get over her long-held dislike and suspicion of her friend's husband-to-be.

But more often than not, the guy made that impossible.

As the four women tucked into brunch, Rachel began discussing the agenda for the rest of the week.

'Gary and I are leaving tomorrow morning on the early service to JFK. Terri's on our flight too and we should arrive at around three or so, New York time. What time's your flight on Thursday?'

'Not getting in until all hours unfortunately. We couldn't afford the earlier flight. But we'll be there in time for your hen night, don't worry.'

Terri brightened a little as she recognised the opportunity for her and Rachel to spend some time alone in the city before the wedding, without the dreaded cousins trailing them.

'Gary and I have a million and one things to do before the big day, of course. We have to meet with the florist, the stylist, and Michelle too, of course! Oh I can't wait.'

'It all sounds so exciting.' Cora was sincere and unlike Terri, seemed totally entranced by all aspects of the wedding planning.

'Then the night before, we have the welcome dinner for all our guests. It'll be small but a nice opportunity for people to meet up beforehand, and for us to say thanks to everyone for taking the trouble to travel to be with us. It should be glam enough, so be sure to bring dresses and heels!' she told them excitedly.

'Sounds brilliant,' Cora interjected. 'Any decent men going to be there?'

'Oh yes. Single men preferably!' Linda was practically bouncing out of her seat in excitement.

'Well …' Rachel took out her binder and opened the page to the confirmed guest list for her New York wedding. She ran her finger down the page, stopping on the names of the men primarily from Gary's side. 'Gary's first cousin Aaron will be there, as well as a couple of lads from the firm, Jack and Tom. I think Tom is seeing someone, though. And of course there's Sean – the best man – but between you and me …' She made a face.

'Then on my side, of course Justin will be there with his partner …' Rachel continued down the list, then paused and glanced at Terri with dubious eyes, unsure if she wanted to continue or not. 'And Ethan,' she added quietly.

Terri's breath stopped short. She stared at Rachel, unable to believe it.

At no point had her friend ever mentioned that she had planned to invite him to the wedding.

The cousins immediately picked up on the atmosphere.

'Ethan who?' Linda asked. 'Does he work at the restaurant or something?'

Terri folded her arms across her chest, wrinkling the black button-down shirt she wore. With her gaze never wavering from Rachel, she replied curtly, 'Ethan Greene is my ex. And I did not know he was invited.'

Chapter 5

'This colour's just *horrible*. Who in their right mind decides on such a pastel shade for Irish skin tones?'

Terri rolled her eyes at Linda's complaints. First it was the dress length, then it was the straps, now she had moved on to the colour. Given the surprise Rachel had landed on her at brunch earlier, it was getting all a bit too much for her to take.

'Well, she picked the colour to go with the whole Tiffany's theme obviously.' Terri attempted to justify Rachel's choice for her, but she knew that it would be futile.

The girls had no clue about the story leading up to Rachel and Gary's engagement, and so the part Tiffany & Co had played in it would be lost on them.

Thankfully Rachel wasn't going overboard on it either: just the bridesmaids' dresses and a few other little touches here and there with the flowers and on the cake.

Terri sighed. At this stage, she just wanted the entire day to be over.

Cora sneered as she poked her head out of the dressing room.

'Terri, zip me up, will you?' She duly obliged and the two waited for the other woman to appear to show the dresses off to the waiting bride who, Terri hoped, was blissfully unaware of all the complaining her bridesmaids were doing.

Linda soon poked her head out and the two headed to the showroom where Rachel had buried her nose in her binder. A pencil in her hair and a pen in her hand, she diligently took notes. She was furiously scribbling on a piece of paper when the girls approached the small podium.

It was the fitting attendant who saw them first.

Rachel looked up as she dropped her binder on to the chair next to her. Her hands covered her heart and then her mouth.

Terri could tell she was genuinely choked up over the moment.

Her voice muttered through her hands, 'You look *so* beautiful.' She stared directly at Terri when she gave her compliments. The other girls only received a quick up and down glance of approval.

Rachel stood up and walked to Terri's podium. She circled her awkwardly, breathlessly taking in the robin's egg-blue-coloured silk and how it draped across Terri's pale shoulders.

The scooped sweetheart neckline plunged a bit lower than Terri was comfortable with, but she did agree that this particular colour was actually quite good with her hair.

The alterations attendant followed behind Rachel, as they made notes about Linda's and Cora's dresses. Linda would need to watch her eating as her zipper had already begun to struggle.

Cora, on the other hand, practically swam in the thick dress she had picked as her style choice. The attendant scolded both of them as she ushered them quickly back to the dressing rooms.

When they returned, Rachel was missing. She had slipped out to try on her wedding dress one last time.

The three bridesmaids sat side by side, waiting patiently.

As the moments ticked by, Terri worried that there was something wrong with Rachel's dress – a nightmare that her friend had confessed she'd had several times recently.

Her fears were made worse when the attendant returned, seeking Terri's assistance.

'Should we come as well?' Linda began to stand, heading towards the door.

'No. She only wanted to see her chief bridesmaid.' The attendant attempted to handle the situation gracefully, but Linda let out a frustrated and exaggerated sigh as she returned to her seat.

'Well, I suppose we'll just sit here and wait until she feels that we're important enough to be graced with her presence. It's not like we have anything better to do today besides wait around.' Linda stuck her chin out and bitterly turned her head away, as Terri and the attendant retreated to the dressing area designated for brides only.

Sounds of whimpering came from inside the dressing room as Terri picked up speed. She urgently knocked on the door as the attendant stood some feet behind her.

'Rach, it's me. Open the door, OK?'

The muffled cries stopped for a moment as she whispered, 'Just you?'

'Yes. I'm sure the attendant won't mind giving us a second alone to chat.' Terri turned towards the woman who nodded sympathetically. Crying brides were the norm for her.

She turned to walk away towards the showroom once more as Rachel cracked open the door just enough for Terri to slip in.

The bride-to-be sat on the floor in a pile of white lace and silk. Her back rested against the dressing room's lavender walls as her shoulders shook from crying.

Terri joined her friend on the floor, sitting cross-legged in front of her.

Rachel's black eyeliner ran down the sides of her olive cheeks. Her lipstick was faded and patchy. However, her tears and messy make-up had not diminished her beauty, which still radiated through her wedding dress.

Terri reached over towards a nearby side table, and grabbed a small pack of tissues.

She handed one to Rachel who blotted the tissue against the black liquid around her eyes.

'Are you ready to tell me what is going on?' Terri was not about to pry, but she worried about the bridal gown running the risk of wrinkles or tears if she couldn't get Rachel to move up off the ground.

She scooted next to her, carefully moving the skirt of her gown out of her way.

'I'm scared, Terri.' Rachel leaned her head on her friend's shoulder, her emotions overwhelming her afresh. 'What if this isn't real either? What if everything falls apart again? What if Gary doesn't really mean it?' Her voice edged on the verge of panic as she wrung her hands out in front of her.

Terri edged Rachel's head upwards so that she would face her. She was wrong before; her friend *hadn't* forgotten about what happened the first time round.

And she was now worried that her lifelong dream would be shattered once again.

'Rachel, of course it's real. OK, maybe I can understand the jitters after last time, but this time there's no confusion, no mistakes.' She picked up Rachel's hand and indicated her engagement ring. 'This is your ring – all yours, given to you in good faith by Gary, 100 per cent his decision. Forget about before, that's all in the distant past at this stage. He loves you and you love him, and that's all that matters, isn't it?'

'But *you* don't love him, do you?' Rachel shot back accusingly. 'And I know you still don't trust him either. What if you're seeing something in Gary that I'm not? I'd hoped this wedding taking place in New York was fitting, and would be a great way for us to recreate the romance of before. But all throughout the planning, he's just been so ... *distant*. I just don't know if he actually realises that I'm doing this for us, that it's not just my dream wedding fantasy.'

Terri felt like a heel.

She thought she'd tried her best to hide her ongoing distrust of Rachel's fiancé, but clearly she hadn't been trying hard enough.

In fairness to the guy, he did seem to be treating Rachel with the care and respect she deserved this time round, but Terri still couldn't forget the less-than-ideal circumstances surrounding their first engagement, and try as she might she still couldn't help but hold that against Gary.

'It's not that I dislike him or anything,' she assured Rachel. 'It's just after everything that happened last time . . .' She shrugged. 'Who knows?' she said, deciding to change the subject altogether. 'Maybe I'm just jealous that he's stealing my best friend away. After all, it's been just the two of us for so long now . . .'

Rachel interrupted her. 'That's not true. You had Ethan,' she sniffed.

'Do you really want to bring that up now?' Terri tried to hide her frustration. When Rachel had let it slip at brunch that Ethan and his ten-year-old daughter Daisy were going to the wedding, she had attempted to push the thought away.

It wasn't as though she could stop her friend from inviting him. Ethan had a huge part to play in what had happened in New York last time, and she knew that Rachel considered him a friend and they had kept in touch – the circumstances with Terri notwithstanding.

'Look, let's just stay on the subject here and now,' she continued, pursing her lips. 'Gary loves you. What happened last time will not happen again, and you shouldn't let it cloud your judgement. That's all way behind you now, and next Saturday, you two are going to be married in New York and all set for happy ever after. There is one thing you might have to worry about, though ...' She gestured to her friend's gown, the skirt still lying in a messy pile on the ground.

Rachel looked around at herself as she realised what she'd been doing. She jumped up, Terri grabbing her arm to balance her.

'Oh no, is it ruined? Did I wrinkle it?' She spun around, attempting to see the back of the dress in the mirrors.

'No, it's not ruined,' Terri reassured her. 'It's perfect.'

She stood back and took a proper look at her friend in her wedding dress.

Delicate lace straps formed a keyhole opening around the curves of her shoulder blades. The front of the gown was covered in more lace floral appliqué. Large white buttons raced down the entire length of the back. The A-line silk skirt and the chapel length train were perfect complements for her curvy frame.

She reached over to a hook and gently took down a small diamanté headpiece. It sparkled brightly in the shop's lighting.

Terri stood on her tiptoes as she gathered Rachel's dark tresses into a loose bun and sealed it in place with one of her own hair ties.

Stepping back, she took in the sight of her friend in the dress she would wear walking down the aisle.

A maternal sensation took over as she smiled brightly at her.

'Don't you start getting sentimental on me now. It's my job to be the crying bride. You're supposed to tell me to cop on.' Rachel turned to face the mirrors as she wiped the remaining bits of mascara and eyeliner from her face. She took in a deep breath as she said, 'Now, what do I say to the others?'

'Well, you certainly can't let them know you've been crying – they'd love the idea of trouble in paradise. Anyway who cares what they think? Let them wait. Indefinitely.' Terri began impersonating Linda's whiny, insipid voice and drawn out accent, 'It's not like they have anything better to do ...'

A timely knock on the door from the attendant ushered them back outside. Out front, Terri as chief bridesmaid took her place next to Cora and Linda.

The cousins had occupied themselves looking through celebrity gossip rags and chatting about some celebrity's mistress and another's lack of style.

When Rachel finally came out of the dressing room, neither could be bothered to put down their magazines and acknowledge the woman standing before them, let alone question whether or not she'd been crying.

Terri cleared her throat as finally Linda looked up at the bride.

'Wow, Rachel ... you look stunning. Normally, I find lace

to be old-hat, but on you, it looks totally inspired. What do you think, Cora?'

The younger sister remained focused on her magazine, 'Yes, yes. I agree. Lace is so outdated.' Linda elbowed her hard and gave her a piercing look. Cora took a long look at Rachel and attempted to rectify her mistake, '... But on you ... it's just ... timeless.'

With that, the girls returned to their magazines, Rachel and the attendant discussed transit options for the dresses, and Terri sat back and took in the moment. Tomorrow, she would be flying to New York to see her best friend make her long-held dream come true, with a romantic Central Park wedding to Gary Knowles.

Over the next few days, she knew that for Rachel, she could get past being away from her beloved restaurant to spend time in a brash American city she knew she wouldn't like, with this pair of insensitive head-wrecking relations in tow, and could even manage to cast aside her misgivings about Gary.

What Terri was not sure she could survive, was coming face to face once again with her ex and his adorable daughter.

It had been a good eighteen months since their break-up, and Terri knew that she should be over it by now.

Though she'd thought they might be able to overcome the issue of living in different cities, it was a hurdle that eventually proved too difficult.

Besides, Ethan and Daisy's life in London had continued

on perfectly well without her in the picture, just as she had predicted.

And Terri wasn't doing so bad for herself, either. Yes, she cared about him, had allowed herself to fall for him, but it wasn't long before the reality of their situation hit hard, and unlike Ethan, she wasn't going to kid herself that obstacles didn't exist.

But the mere reminder of him, and how their budding relationship had ended almost before it began, still had the emotional impact to knock her to the core.

Terri knew that her decision to let Ethan and Daisy go was the right one.

And she knew that when she saw them again in New York, she would just have to keep convincing herself of that.

Chapter 6

The mobile phone vibrated wildly against the large wooden desk, shaking the papers and the pencils from their place.

Ethan's concentration was broken as he struggled to pull himself away from his work to check on the alert that popped up on the phone's screen.

Four o'clock already? Oh hell, not again.

His mind raced as he struggled to go through the list of all the things he needed to collect before he left.

He turned towards his work desk and picked up the sloppy pile of paperwork in one hand and his brown leather briefcase in the other.

Hurrying out of his office, he grabbed his umbrella and coat from the hook outside. His secretary and personal assistant, Nancy, stood as she watched him open his briefcase on the edge of her desk. He ruffled through the contents in a panic, tossing papers he no longer needed back on her work area.

When he failed to notice her, she leaned across the desk and rested her hands against the leather carrying case, her bouncy brown hair falling like waves across her chest. 'Is there anything I can do for you, Professor Greene?' Her voice was honey-sweet. It oozed out of her brightly painted red lips.

'No, it's fine, Nancy. I'm just running late today.'

Nancy looked at him, puzzled, her brow furrowing as she took a glance at her computer screen. 'There's nothing in the diary for the rest of the day. Have I forgotten something?' She batted her long black eyelashes at him innocently as he tossed a large notepad into a brown organiser.

Ethan did not register her flirtatious looks. In fact, he had got so used to the majority of his secretaries being outwardly coy with him. In the last year alone, he had gone through three personal assistants. His last, Anna, had to be let go when she decided to get a little bit too close for comfort – literally.

From then on, he unintentionally became the gossip of the faculty. His colleagues teasingly deemed him the 'playboy professor'. It was a title Ethan was not fond of. And his newest personal assistant wasn't exactly doing her best to help him crush that reputation either.

She had spent most of her first two weeks' probation sporting tight outfits that unbuttoned rather too easily for his taste. He had considered asking one of the more senior administration staff to talk to her about her appearance, but was too nervous to do so. Instead, he let it go, hoping that his obvious attempts to avoid her flirtatious advances would send the right message.

For now, he knew his best course of action was just to ignore it. Instead of looking at Nancy's young, unblemished face, he kept his eyes down and focused on grabbing every bit of paperwork he would need while he was away in New York.

He faced her as he handed her a stack of papers he did not intend to bring with him. 'It's my daughter. I pick her and her friends up from school about half four on Wednesday. You should probably put that in your calendar.'

Nancy stood up straight as she used her dainty hands to brush out the creases on her tight silk blouse. She glanced at the clock on the wall. 'Of course. But, Professor Greene, it's already past four now.'

He was already walking out the door of his firm's office as he turned back round to her. 'Yes, I know. That's why you should put it in your calendar. I never remember.'

London's streets were rainy and cool for a late August day.

Ethan pulled his coat around him, buttoning it up at the top. The walk to the primary school that Daisy attended was just a few streets away, yet he could not speed any faster past the bustling crowds of tourists and commuters to make it to the metal gates of Parkridge Primary.

As he turned the corner, he let out an exasperated gasp.

The gates were closed and the school's playground was practically abandoned.

All that remained were a couple of young children running around on the playground's equipment as their parents watched from benches in the foreground. He glanced down at his wristwatch, which already read 4:30.

Damn. He had missed pick-up time yet again. His only option was to face the judgemental headteacher, Mrs Lears.

The interior of the primary school was in darkness, giving it an almost eerie glow. Children's paintings hung around the walls, and locker doors were plastered with posters and stickers. Teachers mingled in and out of their classrooms, talking animatedly to one another as they packed up their rooms.

Sitting outside the head teacher's office was a young girl of about ten years old. Her blonde hair covered her face as she hunched over a large picture book about the United States. Her blue eyes looked up momentarily as she noticed the pair of black leather shoes standing before her.

She sighed theatrically. 'Silly Dad. You're late. Again.' Daisy continued reading to herself, turning the page on a section about New York.

Ethan sat down next to her on the ground, glancing over her shoulder at her book. He whispered in her ear, 'So, how much trouble do you think I'm going to be in?'

'Lots. She's not in a very good mood. I heard that Patrick Durkin brought a frog with him to school today and it got out of his locker and into the hallway. Mrs Lears and Mr Sanderson chased it around the entire school all morning.' She smiled at him excitedly as she told her story.

'Did they find the frog?' Ethan asked, tucking a strand of fair hair behind her ear.

'I'm not sure, but by the way she's acting, I would guess not.' She used her head to motion towards the headteacher's office. Ethan could hear the woman loudly admonishing her secretary about a phone call.

He put his head in his hands dramatically as he pleaded with his daughter, 'Please don't make me go in there.'

Daisy's blue eyes sparkled, showing delight at her dad's childish reaction. 'Hey, it's not my fault you're always too late to pick me up.' She nudged his elbow as he pretended to fall over onto the cold tile floor. 'Get up, you lazy thing.'

'I'm up, I'm up.' Ethan pushed himself to stand and walked towards the office door.

Brushing off his overcoat, he took a loud deep breath and headed inside. Daisy stood, peering into the window of the office at her father as he approached the headteacher directly.

'Mrs Lears! It's so lovely to see you once again. How are you doing on this fine afternoon?' He was overly cheerful, he knew, but it was his best defence.

He understood only too well that he was not one of the headteacher's favourite parents – by a landslide. This was certainly not his first trip to this office, and it probably wouldn't be his last.

The stern-looking woman in a black knitted suit turned toward her assistant and said loudly, 'Ah. It must be Wednesday as Mr Greene is here yet again to see me. What is it today, Mr Greene? Did you lose track of time or did time lose track of you?'

'A little bit of both today, I'm afraid. I had set a reminder, but was knee-deep in a paper. I left a little late.' He knew trying to explain his way out of this would do no good.

'So, let me get this right ... your daughter comes after your research papers?' She had a point and Ethan recoiled at her harsh tone.

'No, no, not at all. It was just that I, ah ... I lost track of time.' Ethan surrendered, admitting defeat. The headteacher handed him a clipboard of papers to sign. He filled in Daisy's information and his own, having practically memorised the sheet back and front. When he was finished, he handed the paper to the secretary and quickly exited the office.

Ethan found his ten-year-old still sitting on the cold floor. She had returned her attention to her book. He walked past her, motioning with his hands for her to follow quickly. Whispering, he urgently said, 'Come on, buttercup, let's get out of here before she tries to sign me up for detention!'

Chapter 7

A little while later, they walked in through the door of their Richmond townhouse.

Daisy took a seat on the couch, with Ethan joining her. He looked down at her, with her young face once again buried in her book, and felt a rush of love that always overwhelmed him. 'You know what? You never told me what happened with the frog and that boy. Why did he bring the frog in the first place? Did he get into trouble?'

Ethan loved listening to his daughter talk. Her sing-song voice always reminded him of his deceased wife, Jane, and her love of good story-telling.

Daisy placed her book in her lap and turned toward her father. 'Can we not talk about Patrick?'

'Why? What's wrong with Patrick ... well, besides the whole bring-a-frog-to-school thing?'

'It's just that ...' She looked down, her cheeks reddening

with embarrassment. 'If I tell you, do you promise not to make fun of me?'

Ethan smiled. His daughter was one of the bravest girls he had ever met. She was bold, witty, and always ready to tell it like it was. This sudden burst of shyness was a total shift in her personality. It was another sign of her mother that he loved to spot.

He took his hand and placed it across his chest dramatically. 'Cross my heart, I will not laugh.'

Daisy sighed and said, 'Well, yesterday when we were walking home with Mrs Tulane, I picked a flower and I told Patrick that I liked him, and when I asked if he liked me back, he threw it on the ground and told everyone what I had done.'

Ethan studied her face. She was obviously upset by all of this.

'You know, your mother gave me a flower once,' he told her, and watched her face light up at the mention of her parents' history. 'It was our final year at university. Jane was in my history class, and she followed me home afterwards. It took a lot of nerve, but she rang my doorbell, handed me a flower, and asked me out.'

Daisy looked at him with wide, wondrous eyes. 'She did not!'

'She did. I swear it, and from that moment on, I knew that I would love her forever. It was the most romantic thing anyone had ever done for me.'

'Patrick told me that only boys gave girls flowers,' she sulked.

'Daisy, the right boy will love you for picking him a flower. Patrick obviously has no idea what he's missing.'

He rubbed her head gently, messing with her curly locks.

As he stood to start making dinner, Daisy looked up at him and whispered a question, 'Did Terri ever give you flowers?'

He was stunned. Daisy hadn't brought up Terri Blake in conversation for some time now. He had hoped she had got over his ex, and the fact that their relationship hadn't worked out, but she was apparently still on her mind.

He replied softly, 'No, Terri never gave me flowers. But she did bake me bread, of course.'

Daisy smiled. 'I remember that.' She asked the next obvious question. 'Will Terri be at Rachel's wedding?'

'I'm sure she will. Terri and Rachel are best friends, after all. Remember that was why Terri wanted to concentrate on the restaurant?' He had used Terri's commitment to the restaurant as an excuse for why the two had ultimately broken up, but Ethan didn't believe that for a second.

'Why don't you buy her some flowers?'

'What? Who?'

'Terri. Why don't you buy her flowers? Girls love that, don't they?' She stared at Ethan as he looked down at the ground. He wasn't sure where to go with that, or how to make Daisy understand.

She continued, this time more sure of herself, 'Dad, I know that you love Terri, and I really think she loves you too. If she's going to be in New York, why don't you try to get her back? I'll help.'

Ethan still cared about Terri. He really did. And in his heart, he was pretty sure that she cared about him and Daisy too.

But Terri was a pragmatist to the core, and her fears about committing to not only a long-distance relationship, but one with a widower and a young child, had overwhelmed her.

At the time, Ethan had tried to convince her that yes, there were obstacles to overcome, but they could get through them and everything would work out for the best.

He was a firm believer in taking things as they came, whereas Terri had let doubt cloud her judgement, and this had made her take a step back.

So many times had he wanted to go back to Dublin to see her, to check on how the restaurant was doing, and most importantly, to plead with her to reconsider.

To take a chance on him, and instead of focusing on all the things that weren't perfect, just give in to the possibilities, and see how things went.

But ultimately Terri was not the kind of woman who let her heart rule her head, and while Ethan loved that about her, it meant that their relationship was over almost before it had the chance to begin.

Now, for the first time in almost a year, the two of them would be face to face once more. In New York, Terri wouldn't avoid Ethan, or his phone calls.

He wondered if perhaps Daisy was right.

Could Rachel's wedding, amidst the magic and wonder that embodied New York City, be the perfect opportunity for Ethan to show Terri that maybe their relationship deserved another chance?

Chapter 8

Terri paced back and forth throughout the airport lounge.

The clinks of the champagne glasses and the easy-listening music only made her anxiety worse. From the massive floor-to-ceiling windows, she watched as one by one planes would slowly lurch up to the runway and then speed off into the sky.

It was unnatural. It was terrifying. It was flying.

Terri had never been a fan of flying or travelling in general.

While she had often dreamed of putting her toes into white sandy beaches or taking in the world's most beautiful sights, those dreams came crashing straight down to earth at the reality of what she'd have to do to get there.

Instead, she would go to places via train, car, bus ... whatever she could find that stayed on dry land.

Now, she was faced with the idea of flying not only to a different country, away from her home in Dublin and her beloved restaurant, but she would also have to soar thousands of miles over endless oceans.

Vast, uncharted oceans.

Her blood pressure skyrocketed as she tore little bits of cocktail napkin into confetti shards upon her lap.

Her eyes were fixed on the aircraft flying directly into the sun. Their silhouettes disappeared as they slipped further and further away out of view. Each time Terri saw them go, she would take a sip of her champagne mimosa, praying it would have some magical effect.

'You really shouldn't drink too much before flying, you know.' Gary sat down across from her in a plush leather seat. He had just returned with another beer, his second of the day.

'I could say the same about you.' Terri raised her glass in a toast as she downed the remaining few gulps.

'What's there to be nervous about anyway? It's just flying. People do it all the time.'

Gary was trying to play nice by pretending to be concerned about her, and Terri knew it. She had a hard time believing he was sincere, but she supposed she should give him credit for trying.

While their relationship had never been fantastic, it had all but degenerated after the fiasco that was his and Rachel's first so-called engagement. While her friend still insisted her fiancé had been at heart insecure back then, Terri wasn't convinced this was a good enough excuse for his behaviour.

Still, now that it was absolutely confirmed he would soon

be her best friend's husband, she supposed she should try to make more of an effort.

'Oh, I don't know ...' she replied honestly. 'There's the fact that you're essentially flying in an expensive tin can over an endless ocean ...' She flagged down a nearby member of staff in the bar, and requested another refill.

It was her third, maybe her fourth, even? She had lost count.

'Yeah, but think about where you'll be at the end of it,' Gary insisted. 'All worth it.'

'Not especially. Unlike the majority of the world, I've never had any rabid desire to visit New York. No offence,' she added quickly, given the circumstances.

Gary stared at her. 'None taken. I don't get it, though. What's not to love?'

Terri rolled her eyes inwardly. The truth was that all the fuss people made of the city had turned her right off.

At the end of the day, what was it? Only another concrete jungle congested with traffic and people, tourists running rampant ... She felt another headache coming on just thinking about it.

Or maybe it was the champagne ...

Rachel appeared with a large bottle of water in her hand. She slumped next to Gary, just catching the end of the conversation.

'Yes, yes we've heard it all before.' She smiled at her friend. 'But I'd be willing to bet by the time this trip is over, New York will have captured your heart too.'

*

Her big day – the one she'd spent so long planning, and practically her entire life dreaming about – was finally happening.

Now that everything was in motion, Rachel wanted desperately for all in New York to go exactly as planned.

No hiccups, no complaints, no worries.

Just a couple of days' relaxation time with her fiancé and bridesmaid, before finally, a real family and a brand new future waited for her at the end of a lantern-lit aisle in Central Park.

Just like she'd always envisioned.

Yet now sitting in the airport lounge, Gary's nervous, suspicious ticks and Terri's pre-flight nerves were making her worry. This wasn't the cheery jubilant pre-wedding atmosphere she'd hoped for.

Gary had been touchy and rather distant the past while, and seemed to have had lots of last minute work niggles to sort out, so much so that Rachel had finalised most of the packing and travel details by herself, instead of sharing the pre-wedding excitement with her husband-to-be.

But perhaps, unlike her, he wasn't quite in celebratory mode just yet, and everything would change when they touched down in the Big Apple, and were back in the same romantic mode as their last visit, when Gary proposed.

She'd always felt that a return to Central Park for the actual ceremony was a real brainwave, especially when the place held such romantic significance for them.

And she couldn't wait to see what magic Michelle, the

wedding planner, had worked on the venue for the ceremony, right in the heart of the Park.

Taking a deep cleansing breath to calm herself, Rachel tried to ignore Terri's jitters, Gary's distractedness and cast aside her own concerns.

Everything would work out perfectly with this wedding, the day of her dreams.

It had to.

Chapter 9

Terri put on her headphones and blasted classical music through them to try and drown out the sounds of the plane engines.

Gary texted away furiously to someone unknown, and Rachel reviewed her wedding binder once more.

Each waited anxiously for the sound of the announcement of their flight gate opening, all trying hard to forget the extra baggage they were about to depart with.

A soft, gentle voice came over the intercom a little while later, and Gary leapt to his feet, snatching his carry-on bag from the seat next to him.

Rachel, too, jolted alert as she stuffed the binder back in her own bag.

She walked to the desk where an airline attendant had been holding her most precious cargo – her wedding dress.

Terri followed behind the couple nervously. Her legs seemed like jelly as they made the long walk to Gate A4.

The plane filled up quickly with the three taking their spots in the cabin. Rachel snuggled close to Gary as she placed a blue eye mask over her head.

She watched anxiously as Terri fastened the wedding gown garment bag to the window seat alongside her. It would be her companion for the trip, apparently worthy of its own, fully paid-for seat, while her (considerably less voluminous) bridesmaid dress was stowed in the hold.

When Terri's efforts to secure the dress met with Rachel's approval, she fell back into her seat and returned her attention to the wedding magazines she had picked up in the terminal kiosk.

Terri, on the other hand, knocked back three sleeping pills as she attempted to slip into a long, deep sleep.

Her eyelids grew heavy as the plane began to take off. Her mind slowed and ebbed as she could feel the force of the plane's wheels leave the ground.

She glanced across to where Gary sat alongside Rachel. In the window beside him, she could spot the hints of clouds coming into view. Her heart raced and the blood pounded in her ears. She began commanding herself to sleep. It was her only hope at this point.

As the plane settled in at cruising height and the cabin lights turned on, Rachel reached over the aisle towards her friend. 'Are you doing OK? You're looking a bit peaky.'

'I feel like it to be honest.' Terri wasn't sure if she should blame it on fear, the sleeping pills, or the alcohol she had consumed so far.

Rachel grinned wickedly. 'Let's get your mind off it. We do need to discuss some important details after all ...'

Terri groaned inwardly as her friend ceremoniously took out her wedding binder and presented it to her bridesmaid.

'Page 34, Seating Chart. Just look it over and see if there's anything amiss? I feel like I'm forgetting someone ... but with Gary's side being so much bigger compared to mine, we can't afford to mess this up.'

Terri grabbed the pink binder tab and flipped through hand-drawn layout after layout until she found page 34.

On one side of the page was a list of the wedding guests, only twenty or so. On the other page was the layout of the Central Park Boathouse's banqueting room. Round circles were set up in place of the tables, while long tables and squares indicated where items like the cake table, serving tables, and dance floor were to go. Each circle had a table number and then eight or so letter combinations highlighted in different shades.

Terri turned towards Rachel who was studying her, waiting for her to find fault. 'You're right. There's quite a few people on Gary's side.'

Rachel looked down at her hands. 'I know. I wish there were more for me, but it's the ones there that count, isn't?'

Terri nodded and then added quietly, 'They will be there too, you know. They will be with you every step of the way.' She could tell that the absence of Rachel's parents was naturally becoming even more pronounced as her dream day approached.

'I know they will,' Rachel whispered across the aisle. 'I really hope they'd have liked Gary.'

She looked back at her future husband who was snoozing loudly with his mouth gaping open. Then she rolled her eyes and giggled, breaking the sombre mood.

Terri returned to the guest list. 'OK. So on this table for your side we have your aunt, the two wicked stepsisters of course, Justin and his plus one ...' Then she swallowed hard as she scrolled past two other names, 'and Ethan and Daisy.'

A sudden ache shot through her stomach, twisting it into knots. Her head grew heavier by the second as she struggled to remain focused.

'It's a lot of people at one small table, I know. But I couldn't decide who to move. You think it will be OK? I'd hate for everyone to be scrunched.' Rachel's worry wrinkle popped on her face as she frowned regretfully.

'I think ... I think it will be fine. Daisy's just a child. She doesn't need much space.'

Suddenly Terri didn't want to continue this conversation.

She needed a way out. 'Rach, I ... I'm not feeling too well. Do you mind if I nod off for a bit? Wake me up when lunch is served, OK?' She didn't give Rachel a chance to answer or continue on.

Instead, she reclined her seat as far as it would go and placed her headphones back in her ears.

Her green eyes closed tight, keeping out the dim lights of the cabin.

Listening to the airline radio's classical music station, Terri felt herself falling deeply asleep – the pills and the alcohol only pulling her further and further into a memory.

She was at Ethan's house in Richmond, her first visit. They had been seeing one another tentatively for about a month, and he'd invited her to London for the weekend.

Daisy was fast asleep in her room, and Ethan was pouring Terri a large glass of red wine.

He sat next to her on the couch, pulling her into his solid frame, as she looked around and tried to get comfortable.

This place was a home ... she thought. *A real home.*

A place for a real family.

Ethan kissed her forehead as he gently ran his fingers through the strands of her hair.

She could feel him inhale and exhale, each breath more perfect than the next.

But suddenly, she sat up straight and looked back at him, and took a deep breath as she began, 'I can't do this, Ethan. I'm sorry.'

He looked at her, dumbfounded. 'What are you talking about?'

'I can't do this – you two here in London, me in Dublin with the restaurant, Daisy in school ... I wasn't cut out for this – this kind of relationship.'

She'd been thinking about it for a while now, wondering why she'd ever thought something like this could work. 'I think we need to face up the reality of all this.'

'Face up? To what ...?' He stared at her, unsure if she was

truly serious. When she looked back into his eyes unblinking, he knew that she was.

'Let's be honest with ourselves – now, before things get too confusing. The last while has been fun, but your lives are here and Daisy doesn't need her dad focused on some woman back in Dublin. And I … well, I'm just not cut out for this. The distance thing, I mean. Daisy needs more than that … she needs—'

'A mum?' His words stung her as he instantly found the words for what she had wanted to say.

'Exactly. I'm not that person. I cannot help with home-work or pick her up from school, or tuck her in at night. Heck, I barely remember to go home myself after closing up most nights. I'll never, ever be the kind of woman you and Daisy need. And it's about time we recognised that before everyone gets in too deep.' Terri stood as she walked to the door, slipping on her heels and jacket.

Ethan grabbed her arm. 'That's not how it is. Daisy and I – we don't need you to be … anything. We just need you to give this a chance. Yes, there are some stumbling blocks – the distance being the biggest one, but we can get through that, I'm sure of it. Just give it a try at least. Terri, please, take a chance – on us?'

'I really can't. I'm sorry. Tell Daisy—' Terri struggled to find words. 'Tell Daisy I said goodbye.'

Chapter 10

'Miss?' A gentle tap pushed at Terri's shoulder, waking her up. 'Miss? I'm sorry to wake you, but could you please put your chair back up. We're about to land.'

Terri groggily sat up straight, bringing the back of her chair with her.

She turned to her left to check that Rachel's wedding dress bag was still in place, undisturbed by the flight.

On her other side, Rachel and Gary were talking in low, hushed voices. She could see by her friend's face that she was upset, but her mind was too woolly to think too hard about what was going on.

She cleared her throat loudly as Rachel took notice. 'Oh good, you're awake,' she said distractedly. 'Lunch service was hours ago, but I didn't want to wake you. The flight time passes easier when you're out.'

'No, no. It's fine. I'll grab something when we land. Is everything OK?'

'Of course.' Rachel attempted to brighten up, but her face still bore a worried expression. 'I got you a bottle of water, though. I thought you may need it, given all that you have been drinking since before, and you ate nothing on top of it.'

Terri hated to admit it, but she *was* feeling out of sorts. The effect of the alcohol was still coursing through her, and the pills had made her head swim as she struggled to shake herself out of it.

The water helped, but as the plane came in to land, she knew that her best bet at this stage was going straight to the hotel, and getting a good rest in a proper bed before all the wedding craziness really kicked in tomorrow.

As the threesome and the wedding gown disembarked from the aircraft, Terri grabbed Rachel's hand, hoping to lighten the mood.

'So ... this is it. We're finally here – in New York!'

She did her best to sound genuinely enthusiastic for her friend's sake, and Rachel gamely played along as she grinned back excitedly, trying to ignore her fiancé racing silently ahead up the gangway.

So ... concrete jungle where dreams are made of ... Terri thought, recalling the lyrics of a popular song about the city.

Let's hope this place lives up to its billing.

'So, how long do we give it, do you think?' Gary murmured an hour later.

'Give what?' Terri responded, testily.

'Until she realises that your dress really isn't coming down that empty conveyor belt.'

Terri looked at Rachel, still standing alongside the moving conveyor belt, arms folded in front of her chest as she tapped her foot against the tile floor of the airport.

She had not moved position for at least a good half hour, while Gary and Terri had both given up, preferring to wait it out at one of the side benches against the wall.

By the looks of it, they were the only passengers from the Dublin flight still remaining in the baggage claim area.

'I think you probably should break it to her that it's time to give up,' Gary said passively as he picked away at his fingernails. He was obviously wishing to be anywhere but here.

'How is this my job?' Terri was not going down without a fight. 'You're the husband-to-be.' At least, Terri hoped that Rachel would listen to some voice of reason.

'Well, it is *your* dress. If you'd listened to her in the first place, it would've been safely in your arms, sharing a seat with hers.'

Terri hated that he was right. If she *had* listened to Rachel's protests that the two dresses should stay together, this would not have happened.

But Terri was determined not to have to cart the heavy bridesmaid dress around the airport with her, mostly because she knew she'd need quite a lot of liquid courage to calm her nerves, and didn't trust herself to guard it with her life – as Rachel did hers.

Ripples of frustration and damaged pride raged through her as she walked over to where her friend stood rigid.

'OK. So this is not looking good.' Terri really couldn't think of much else to say.

Rachel spun to look at her. Oddly enough, she was not seething mad and looked nowhere near close to shedding a tear. Instead, Terri thought she looked ... determined.

Rachel spoke quietly as she returned to face the conveyor belt. 'It will be here. I know it will. Just give it five more minutes.'

'But—' She held up her hand to stop Terri from saying another word.

'Five. More. Minutes.' Rachel's voice remained calm. She wasn't going anywhere.

Terri stood next to her, checking her phone for any missed messages from Justin or anything concerning the restaurant.

No news had to be good news, she assured herself.

In any case, she couldn't imagine a crisis popping up today – at least not one more pressing than the current case of the missing dress.

The minutes ticked by. Still Rachel didn't move. In her head, she was saying prayers to every known higher power that the dress would appear, that it was simply lost in the shuffle, that some guardian angel working for the airline would discover it and place it on the belt.

Another half hour passed, and Gary excused himself to take a call from some unknown source.

Rachel didn't care. She had spent the last hour of the flight arguing with him over his decision to go straight to bed when they arrived in the city, instead of going out celebrating at the same restaurant they'd been to the night he proposed. She'd arranged it as a surprise, and an attempt to get the pre-wedding excitement started.

'Sure go with Terri, can't you?' he'd said, completely missing the point.

And as another long minute passed, Rachel was starting to feel her great vision for her dream New York wedding already slipping away.

With her chief bridesmaid currently yawning as she paced the tiles, waiting for a lost dress, and her fiancé showing little enthusiasm for the whole endeavour (in truth he seemed bored), things certainly weren't getting off to the best start.

Terri could no longer stand the wait. Her head ached, her feet were tired, and her body was tired. And she was getting sick to the teeth of listening to the same taped security reminder announcements playing on a loop in the baggage area.

She just wanted to get to the hotel, order some room service, and knock herself out for the rest of the day. But by now, she knew that this evening was shaking up to be completely different from what she had planned.

When at last, Rachel turned silently and trudged off toward the baggage claim office, Terri could feel the frustration and disappointment radiating off her.

She only hoped and prayed that the woman waiting behind that counter was sympathetic to a frustrated bride, an already jet-lagged tired bridesmaid, and a missing-in-action fiancé.

'Excuse me,' Rachel's voice had lost all of its usual honey sweetness and warmth. Instead, it had turned into something unusually fierce and tight. 'You seem to have misplaced my friend's garment bag. We've just arrived from Dublin on flight 4984. I would have thought it would be difficult to lose something like a garment bag containing a bridesmaid dress, but here we are. Could I ask you to please go back there and find it, as I'm getting married in two days' time and we really need that dress.'

Terri was impressed. Rachel did not shout. She did not even raise her voice. Instead, she stared down the woman in the blue uniform as if she were lecturing a bold child.

Unfortunately for Rachel, the airline worker had seen many such cases and was largely unmoved by her wedding woes.

'I'm sorry to hear that, ma'am,' she replied, impassive. 'However, there isn't anything that I can personally do at this time.'

'That you can personally do? What does that even mean?' Rachel snapped suddenly and Terri's eyes widened. Her friend rarely raised her voice like that – and to a complete stranger, no less.

'Again, I'm sorry to hear that you are frustrated with our service, but I cannot do anything more than take your information. If and when your bag arrives—'

'If – *if* the bag arrives?' Rachel's unblemished face had suddenly turned a particular shade of beet red.

The woman soldiered on, 'We will call you as soon as possible and arrange a courier to bring it to you if you are located within 20 miles of the airport. Now I need the owner of the bag to fill out this contact form ...'

Rachel took the clipboard from the woman and thrust it at Terri without her gaze leaving the airline rep. It was as if she was mentally urging the woman to be more sympathetic to their situation.

Terri rushed, scribbling down the contact information with Rachel's assistance. When she finished, she thanked the woman, grabbed her friend by the arm and escorted her out of the office. That was all they could do for the time being.

Luckily, Gary was waiting for them outside.

'So ...' he whispered, looking down at his brown leather shoes, 'what did they say? Good news?'

Terri looked on as incredibly, Rachel smacked him on the arm with her wedding binder, as the three walked quickly to the taxi stand out front.

The wait for transportation wound all the way along the terminal building.

At least a hundred other weary travellers were waiting for their chance to hop in one of those bright yellow cabs that Terri had heard so much about.

Rachel had wanted to order a town car in advance, but apparently Gary would not hear of it, insisting that they were already going to enough expense with the wedding.

Terri tried not to listen as the two argued, thinking it all very ironic considering Gary's previous experience with New York taxi cabs ...

When twenty or so minutes later their turn finally came, and Gary loaded their suitcases (minus the missing bag) into the back, Rachel returned to her binder. Quickly glancing at the driver's clock, she ran her finger down a long, detailed schedule chart she'd obviously made some time ago.

Muttering softly to herself, Terri watched as she used a pen to cross off more than a few items on the list.

Then, loudly enough for Gary to hear as he rode in the front seat, she turned to Terri.

'Gary wants to snooze at the hotel tonight instead of joining me for a celebratory dinner at this lovely little spot in Little Italy. Fancy being my date instead?'

Terri's heart sank. 'Well ... I had actually planned on just going straight to bed myself later. It's been a long day and you know, we could try to get a head start on the jet-lag ...'

'Nonsense. For one thing, you've been a night owl for as long as I've known you, so jet-lag shouldn't even be an issue for the few days you're here. And two, you slept the whole flight over.' Rachel wouldn't hear another word of protest and Terri realised that it wasn't so much an invitation but a plea.

Given the circumstances, how could she refuse? She could hardly go off and leave her friend on her own. But she cursed Gary for inadvertently landing her in a spot.

'OK,' Rachel continued. 'Next on the agenda for today,

we're supposed to check in at the hotel, and then meet Michelle. Forget the hotel, we should just go straight there. What time is it now?'

'5:30.' The cab driver spoke up. He seemed quite taken with Rachel and her brisk take-no-prisoners attitude.

Great, Terri thought. Now she had no choice but to be co-opted into the wedding administration side of things, too.

By rights, it should just be the bride and groom submitting to such a boring ordeal. She hoped it wouldn't take too long and that she might have at least some time to herself today, before heading out again to the restaurant with Rachel later.

As her friend mapped out the next leg of their journey, Terri took a moment to take in the surroundings. So far, she thought the place was all fairly generic, concrete motorways, boring old houses etc., and she didn't see what all the fuss was about, but then again they were only on the outskirts, apparently.

'Terri, did you hear me?' Rachel tapped her on her shoulder, prompting Terri to sit straight up in her seat. 'I've sent Michelle a text about the dress situation and that you'll be coming along to the meeting. She's thrilled and says she can't wait to meet you.'

Terri suppressed a long sigh, wishing the feeling could be mutual.

Chapter 11

'Welcome to New York!' Michelle Pierre gestured wildly, as a little later, Terri, Rachel and Gary walked through her white linen doors in downtown Manhattan.

It soon became very clear to Terri that this woman truly put the 'management' in 'micro'. She even dictated where each of the three should sit around her desk, with Rachel taking the middle seat and Gary and Terri surrounding her.

'I trust you got in to town OK, and hope that the Hotel Grand is exactly as you pictured it? It is one of my absolute favourites for my out-of-town clients.'

'Unfortunately we haven't had the chance to check in yet, but I'm sure it's wonderful,' Rachel enthused.

'Ah yes.' The woman sighed theatrically. 'It seems we have some not-so-little problems to work out today.' Her gaze zeroed in on Terri. 'Maid of honour—'

'Terri.' Terri couldn't stand being referred to as a role and not a person.

'OK, Ter*eee*.' Michelle nodded coldly in acknowledgement. 'A missing bridesmaid dress is something you do *not* encounter every day. If you had purchased a seat for it of course, this would not have happened ... But as we have to deal with these emergencies, we must act fast. There's no guarantee that the airline will have the dress in time, so ...' She clapped her hands together. 'I have worked my magic, and arranged for you to meet Jonathan at his salon in the Garment District.'

'Fantastic. Thank you so much, Michelle.' Rachel brightened immediately.

'Yes. He is waiting for you now, so do not delay.'

'Today?' Terri couldn't believe what she was hearing. Did this woman actually mean she had to go pick out another dress this very day, not tomorrow when they were more settled in?

'Why of course, today! Right now, in fact.' Michelle looked down at her large gold wristwatch impatiently. 'We are already running way behind schedule and the salon closes at seven. If we're gonna get you fitted and an appropriate dress selected and altered, you will need to leave immediately.'

'And just how am I supposed to get to this place?' Terri replied, trying to ignore Rachel's pleading glances.

'By subway would be best, I would say. A cab in this traffic won't get you there in time at this hour. Therefore, I have taken the time and care to write down directions for you.' She removed a white card from her suit pocket and dramatically slid it across the white desk.

Terri looked at Rachel with tired eyes, but her best friend was nodding vigorously as if agreeing that yes, there was indeed no time to waste.

Never mind that Terri had barely set foot on a New York *pavement* since they'd arrived; never mind that she'd have to navigate her way around the bloody subway!

It looked like she was about to become seriously acquainted with this city, whether she liked it or not.

Rachel watched with some sympathy as Terri shuffled out of the door of Michelle Pierre's office, directions in hand.

At one point, she turned dramatically to look back at her with pleading, terrified eyes. Rachel could not help but feel for her friend, and promised to keep in touch and make arrangements to meet up afterwards.

'It'll be fine, honestly. Manhattan is actually very easy to get around. Just take a cab back when you're finished.'

'Yes, the worst of rush hour will have cleared in a few hours,' interjected Michelle helpfully. It was a pity that Terri had to rush off like that so soon after arrival, but arranging a replacement bridesmaid dress was an absolute must, especially when the airline had been so lacklustre.

Michelle coughed lightly, bringing Rachel's attention back to the wedding plans. There was so much to do and what with their late arrival today, there was really only tomorrow to get everything finalised.

'So to today. We have flowers to discuss. They are certainly one of the most important aspects of your vision. And if not perfect or in line with that vision, it will surely detract from the majesty of your event.' Michelle emphasised the word 'majesty' as if it would make a bigger impact on them.

For Rachel, it made sense.

Alongside her, Gary yawned, took out his mobile phone and studied the screen, an annoying tick of his that really bugged her. She couldn't stand it when people messed with their phones in the middle of a conversation; it was the same thing as picking up a newspaper and hiding your face with it, effectively shutting out and insulting your companions.

As she and Michelle discussed the merits of blue gerberas versus white lilies best suited to the overriding Tiffany blue theme, she tried to ignore her fiancé's fidgeting, until suddenly he stood, rising to his feet like a shot.

'Ah, I have to go,' he mumbled. 'It's work. There's a problem on site and I need to FaceTime Jack.'

'Now? But we're in the middle of an important meeting, Gary.' Rachel couldn't believe it. What mucky building site could be more important than the final arrangements for the biggest day of their lives?

'Sure I know nothing at all about flowers. I'm happy with whatever makes you happy. And with Michelle, you're in the best of hands.' He pointed to the wedding planner as if she were sitting on a golden throne – both stroking the woman's already inflated ego, and giving him even more leverage to make it out the door without trouble.

However, Rachel wouldn't be so easily mollified. She too

stood and apologised to Michelle as she offered to walk her fiancé to the door.

As soon as they reached the doorway, Gary leaned down to kiss her cheek, but she grabbed his arm, bringing his face level with hers.

'What is going *on*?' she hissed, under her breath. 'First dinner tonight and now you cannot even be bothered to stay for a quick meeting about our *actual wedding*?'

She guessed that this would be tedious for him, painful even, but he had little excuse.

She had done most if not all of the planning up to now, with the understanding that he'd be involved in the last-minute details while here.

She'd thought he was disinterested beforehand because nothing was really tangible until they got on the ground. But clearly being here in New York, where they were about to pledge the rest of their lives to one another, made not a whit of difference ...

'Love, nothing is going on. I just have to sort out this work thing. It's a big project, and isn't it better that these things happen now instead of on our honeymoon?' He gave her a quick kiss and headed for the elevator.

Rachel took a deep breath, and raked her fingers through her dark hair.

First, Terri was reluctant about being in New York at all, and then Gary wouldn't go to dinner – couldn't even last through this meeting.

While she understood that not everyone would be as keen

about transforming her fairy-tale New York wedding vision into a reality, she had hoped for more support.

She had hoped that *someone* would be there for her at such a momentous and important time in her life. The loss of her parents, especially her mother, seemed to loom large as the loneliness grew.

But she had no time to sulk today. She had flowers to pick, lighting options to go through, and menus to finalise.

She would deal with Gary later, and she could only pray that Terri, wherever she was going, would return safe and sound and with a bigger and better replacement bridesmaid dress.

With this fruitless hope in her heart, Rachel turned back towards the wedding planner's office, determined to have her dream wedding visualised.

Chapter 12

Terri was determined too – to find Berkman's Bridal Salon on her own. Despite being, as Rachel often said, 'directionally challenged', Terri was now focused and centred.

How hard could it be? she asked herself. *It's just a glorified dress shop in the middle of a city ... one of the biggest cities in the world, mind you ... where I know no one ... have trouble telling north from south ... and this woman's handwriting is chicken scratch ...*

Panic set in as she continued to walk down one street to the next.

The directions that Michelle had so 'generously' written down for her only gave her a vague sense of a subway she had to take, and what street to wind up on. Nowhere did it say how to get to the blasted subway station, which train she needed, and where to go when she got off.

It was a bad treasure hunt that Terri had no desire to play on a day like this. Especially considering her head was still pounding from a combination of travel weariness, sleeping pills, and alcohol consumption.

She slowed as she saw a street sign come up – a glimmer of hope. But no, it was just a number. How the hell were people supposed to find their way around this place with only street numbers instead of names?

But her pace seemed only to enrage the locals, who clearly did not want to deal with lost tourists. They bumped into her one after another.

Women in heels clicked past her in frustration, while men in suits attempted to avoid her pleading glances. If Terri had the nerve to ask one of these stylishly dressed but patently disinterested passers-by how to get anywhere, she most likely would not get very far.

That whole rude New Yorker stereotype was starting to make sense to her now. Making matters worse was the noise. The honking, the yelling, the police sirens all filled her with anxiety as she took off on a near jog to find a side street to compose herself.

Terri needed a plan. There was no way she was going to figure out the mystery subway without one. She pulled out her mobile phone and attempted to look for directions, but a lack of knowledge about American network providers, and the skyscrapers towering above all of Manhattan messed with her weak internet connection.

Terri then thought of her phone's compass feature, but compass reading was never her forte – not that anyone had actually taught her how to use one to begin with.

Just as she began to panic once more, a man dressed in a white button-down shirt and a pair of jeans came running at her.

He carried a broom as he literally tried to sweep her away. Loudly, he shouted, 'No loitering! Away! Away!' Though Terri could just barely understand him with his heavy accent, she got the gist of his intentions pretty quickly.

She apologised profusely as she moved from her spot up against his building, but he continued to yell at her in a language she could not comprehend.

In a rare moment of weakness, Terri placed her head in her hands, her brain pounding with stress and her eyes beginning to well with frustrated tears.

The man, looking at her properly for the first time, stopped shaking his old wooden broom and dropped it to the ground.

He put his hands in the air as he faced her. 'Lady, I'm sorry. Please, don't be upset.' He smiled at her gingerly, attempting to show some goodwill.

'I'm sorry ... I'll ... I'm going now.' Terri spun around, unsure what direction she should head in. The man smiled at her knowingly.

'You lost, lady? I can help. I know New York like the back of my heart.' He crossed his heart like he was making a promise, completely unaware of the real idiom. His sudden change of temperament oddly made Terri trust him a bit more.

'I'm trying to find the subway? I need to get to ...' She

tried to read the writing on Michelle's card, but was failing to understand the directions with all the numbers listed. It was the weirdest address she'd ever come across.

The man took a step closer to her, peering over her shoulder as he read: '42nd and 9th? Garment District. Bryant Park. Very popular area for ladies like you. Fashion, good shopping. Lots to do there for tourists.' He was enthusiastic now as he realised he could genuinely help her.

'Do you know how to get there?' Terri was hopeful. Maybe this guy was her New York fairy godmother sent to both scare the life out of her, and get her to where she needed to be.

The man suddenly took the card out of Terri's hand and as she began to protest, ran back into his store at the front of the brick building.

She followed tentatively as she weaved through the maze of his tiny grocery and convenience shop. She found him leaning over the counter as he slowly wrote down detailed instructions on the blank side of the card.

When he finished, he handed the card back to her and returned from behind the counter. He led Terri out of the door as he said to her: 'Follow these and you get there in no time. Elton promises.' He scooted her towards the right, pushing her in the direction of the correct subway station, and telling her the number of the train she needed.

Before Terri could leave, she turned back to him, more grateful than she had been in her entire life. 'Thank you. Thank you very much!'

She skipped off in the direction he'd pointed, following the lines of people weaving through the streets on their own journey through Manhattan.

Elton's directions were very detailed, naming and identifying landmarks and local shops as she went.

As she passed each one, Terri made a check mark next to its name, helping her go from one location to the next until finally the subway station came into view. The glass exterior helped it stand out from the crowd and Terri was easily able to identify the big '6' showing her the way to her train.

Once on board, she managed to grab a seat nearest the sliding doors, just in sight of the sign telling her when it was time to transfer to the next train.

Finally having a moment to concentrate, she looked around.

So this is the famous subway ... The train was packed with locals and tourists alike. Most kept to themselves, listening to music in giant hip headphones while others kept their noses in their books and electronics. To her right, a man strummed on a guitar as he peddled for change.

The whole experience felt surreal, yet strangely authentic and kind of exhilarating. So much so that Terri actually found herself thanking Michelle for forcing on her a baptism of fire through this vast city.

Once out of the subway, she emerged from below ground to discover a totally different Manhattan. Unlike the office block central in which the wedding planner's office was located, this area seemed much more vibrant, full of quirkier and more interesting buildings. Gone were the black-suited crowd and plush mirrored glass and concrete buildings.

Instead, Terri watched in surprise as women in funky shoes and men in flamboyant suits passed her by with smiles upon their faces.

In this part of town, she stopped to stare at window dressings and people sitting at sewing machines.

Large men pushed even larger clothing racks across streets and up into buildings' small, hidden entrances. And shops opened their doors giving the crowd of passers-by glances at their colourful rolls of fabrics and accessories.

The Garment District ... she repeated, recalling Michelle Pierre's description of the area.

Berkman's Bridal Salon stood out like a sore thumb among the more colourful shops. Just like Michelle's office uptown, it was decked out in white and lace, while faceless mannequins in large, elaborate bridal gowns lounged in its windows.

Terri walked to the door, but found it locked. She looked down at her phone – it was still only 6:45, and Michelle had said the place closed at 7.

She took a few steps backwards to look into the store windows, only to be stopped by the sound of a distorted male voice on an intercom. 'Name? Appointment time?' the sound commanded.

Terri walked back to the door and searched for the call button.

She held it down and spoke. 'Hello. Michelle Pierre sent me. I'm with Rachel Conti's wedding party. A bridesmaid dress went missing in transit from Dublin.' Silence came over as she struggled to think of what else to say, 'Michelle told me that a Jonathan would be able to help me here.'

She could hear a quick laugh as the man answered back, 'Ah yes. The girl who was dumb enough to stow away her bridesmaid dress. One moment please.' A loud buzzer sounded as Terri pushed the metal and wood door forward.

The stale stench of expensive perfume hit her instantly as she looked about the room, only finding more seas of white silk and lace.

As she struggled to find the front desk, a tall thin man tapped her on the shoulder.

She spun to face him, nearly hitting him in the process.

In a cool, slick voice he said, 'Terri, sweetie. Jonathan DeMoyne. Michelle has told me nothing about you, but I have a pretty good sense already ...' He couldn't contain himself as he studied the visitor's dishevelled appearance and her messy make-up.

She was not his usual kind of customer, that was for sure.

Terri brushed his insults aside. 'It's, ah ... nice to meet you. I know we don't have much time so ...' She feared if she gave him any extra time to talk, it would do nothing but eat away at her already diminished ego.

'Begin? I already have. Michelle sent me photographs of your old dress. That particular shade is very last year, but I suppose I should tell the bride that and not you ...' His voice trailed off. 'Either way, I found some comparable designs that should work for your body shape and ... complexion. They are already laid out in the room along with some proper undergarments. I assume you will need those as well.'

Without a word in response (she suspected there was little point), Terri followed him to the changing room, whereupon she slipped into the body hugging underwear and strapless bra.

One by one, she tried on dress after dress – none really working for her or giving her the same confidence as the one she'd had. Luckily for her, Jonathan seemed to agree. Terri only needed to take one or two steps out the door before he would send her back with a wave of his dainty hand.

Finally, reaching for the last dress in the pile she allowed herself to look around at the designs on the other rows of gowns nearby. A red strapless number with an empire waist caught her attention. 'Um, does that dress come in blue?'

He flashed her a smile and grabbed the dress from the rail. As he handed her the sample, he whispered, 'Maybe you have better style than I thought. This is one of my favourite designs.'

Terri could see why. The dress was form flattering while still looking elegant. It hugged her body in all the right places, and the skirt swooshed from beneath her legs as she walked. It was clear what the winner was going to be as she actually allowed herself to twirl in the 360-degree mirrors of the fitting room.

Jonathan quickly worked his magic, taking measurements and notes as he poked and prodded at the sample piece.

When he finished, he gave her an alterations ticket and instructed her to come back the following afternoon to pick up her replacement dress.

As she left the salon, Terri surprised herself by sending a short prayer to the heavens asking that her previous dress remained lost somewhere in the ether.

The one she'd just tried on was simply perfect to give her the confidence she needed to face the world – and Ethan – on Rachel's big day.

Chapter 13

The Terrace was exactly as Rachel remembered from her first visit with Gary two years before.

With its white linen tablecloths and the waiters dressed in black tuxedos and white gloves, the restaurant embodied the pure, classic New York that Rachel adored.

However, she couldn't quite allow herself to enjoy the surroundings until she was certain her bridesmaid would in fact be joining her.

Concern struck Rachel again as she texted her friend once more, hoping to hear some good news at the end of this rather disastrous day.

As she was about to hit Send, a woman totally underdressed for the occasion and venue, strolled into the restaurant. She looked frazzled, like a wild thing.

Her fiery red hair frayed at the edges and her shirt was untucked and unkempt. But at least Terri had made it.

Rachel stood and waved at her friend, motioning her to come and join her at the table.

'How did it go? Did you at least find something you liked? Something that will go well with the rest of the girls' dresses?' Rachel knew she could trust her, but her mind raced at the worry of someone in the wedding party standing out like a sore thumb on the day.

'Don't you worry, your highness. I managed to find a dress in the correct shade of blue that will coordinate to Michelle's satisfaction.'

Terri pulled out her phone and showed her a picture of the dress she had selected. Before she left, Jonathan insisted that she take a picture so the bride could see it.

The thought had never even occurred to Terri but he was right, of course.

Rachel grabbed the phone and she was glad to see, for the first time that day, a genuine smile appear on her friend's face. 'Oh this is perfect. Absolutely perfect. And it will go beautifully with the flowers ...'

She handed Terri her own phone so her bridesmaid could look through photo after photo of the flower choices she had made – along with those she'd discarded.

Terri nodded and smiled, all the while desperate to eat, and indeed drink. After the day she had, she needed a very large glass of wine.

Once they'd ordered their food, and Terri had downed her first delicious mouthful, she turned to Rachel. 'So, what happened with Gary on the plane? When I woke up, you two were fighting. Do you want to talk about it?'

Rachel sighed as the waiter put down a tiny piece of duck confit on a gold and white china plate. 'He's just not ... here, Terri. He doesn't want to be here, I think. When I told him I'd made reservations for tonight, he said that I was too controlling, that I was taking away from the fun.'

'Can I be honest?' Terri hated that for once, she may have to agree with Gary of all people. 'Maybe you have been a little highly strung about all this lately – understandable of course, but Gary doesn't really get that. Maybe it was his way of asking you to tone it down, a little, now that the worst of the mania is over?'

'The worst is over ... but, Terri, it's only just beginning! I wanted this time before the wedding to be about us, to bring back the lovelier memories we shared here before. That's why I picked this place for tonight. Gary brought me here the night he proposed, and I thought he would really enjoy coming back here and reliving the experience. But I was wrong.' She looked down at her plate, crestfallen.

'It's not that he's right or that you're wrong. He's obviously not that excited about wedding planning because really, it's just not what men are into, is it? It's the day itself that's important surely.'

Rachel still looked glum. 'Let's just hope he still feels that way.'

Terri reached out and touched her friend's shoulder. 'Don't think like that. It's been a long day, for the both of us.' She pushed her starter away.

89

While she'd thought she was ravenous, she realised that she was by now almost too tired to eat. As a night owl, as Rachel pointed out, she'd assumed jet-leg would be a piece of cake for her, but she guessed it was the travel and the drama that was wearing her out.

It was clear her friend was flagging too, though for very different reasons. Rachel had put so much effort into the preparations for this wedding, yet things had started to go wrong almost as soon as they'd landed in the city.

Terri couldn't blame her for feeling less than optimistic.

As chief bridesmaid, she owed it to Rachel to keep her spirits up. 'Let's head back to the hotel, get a good night's sleep and then start afresh tomorrow. What's on the agenda anyway?'

Rachel grabbed her binder from her handbag underneath the table, and began to read from what was obviously a carefully planned schedule.

'Early breakfast at the hotel and then a meeting with the caterers to taste-test and finalise food and drink options. *If* Gary can drag himself out of bed in time, that is.'

'Well, if he doesn't, count me in for that.' Some good old fashioned taste-testing sounded good.

'Then afterwards, we have to meet with the celebrant to discuss the wording of the vows.'

Great, Terri thought, brightening. Discussions about wedding vows would have absolutely nothing to do with her, so she'd have a little bit of time to herself to chill out or take in some of the sights.

'But afterwards, I need someone to come with me to the airport to pick up Gary's mother.'

'What? Can Mary not figure out how to get to the hotel on her own?'

'I promised I'd come and collect her, because she's nervous about being in a cab on her own. That Liam Neeson movie about those girls getting taken turned her off apparently.'

Terri giggled, but Rachel shook her head. 'Seriously, we're lucky she agreed to come at all, so I don't mind going out of my way if it keeps her happy. It's a surprise for Gary too, as he thinks she's flying in on Friday morning, but I thought it would be nice for her to be here a little earlier, so the two of them can spend a bit of time together before the wedding. And it means she can come on the hen night with us too – help her feel more included in the celebrations.'

'O – K.' Terri wasn't convinced that fifty-something Mary Knowles would be all that enamoured of the cousins' line-dancing and male strip-club arrangements for the hen night, but you never knew …

But it was typical of Rachel to be so thoughtful when it came to her future mother-in-law. Clearly she felt it was important that Mary was involved right from the outset, and knowing Rachel would continue to go out of her way to include Gary's mum in their new life together as man and wife.

Family, as always, was most important to her and Terri idly wondered if Gary understood the significance of that, and what it would mean for their future.

'OK then. What's on the tasting menu tomorrow ...' The two drifted into a conversation about the sample menus that Michelle had selected in coordination with the caterers. Despite herself, Terri got into the spirit of things, as Rachel ran through her own activities that afternoon, and her experience with lighting selections and a florist who would not stop talking. She listened patiently as her friend described in great detail all the choices to be made, and items to be finalised.

By the time the two departed for their hotel at close to midnight New York time, Terri was convinced of at least one thing that day.

She was never, *ever* getting married.

Chapter 14

The following day, Terri just about managed to survive another morning of wedding planning madness, and for his part, even Gary managed to play nice.

He did not even bring up Rachel's late return to the hotel the previous night, or try to get out of his obligations with the minister.

After a long afternoon of tasting plate after plate of hors d'oeuvres and entrée selections (sometimes multiple times just for fun) and debating over the merits of each, Rachel and Gary's wedding feast was fully finalised, and having dispatched her fiancé on an unexplained errand, Rachel and Terri set off once again for JFK to pick up Mary Knowles, this time in a plush town car.

Terri wondered privately if she'd ever get a chance to get to know the city, what with all the shuttling here and there, but then told herself that ultimately helping Rachel was the reason she was here.

And it wasn't as if she had any great desire to see the place in any case.

The hotel they were staying in seemed pretty generic, a chain establishment much the same as any in Ireland or London, and from what little she'd seen of the surrounding area, it was full of the same uninspiring brand-name shops as back home.

Still, her little sojourn around the Garment District the day before had her intrigued, and she did at least want to visit Central Park, Times Square and some of the other tourist hotspots during her time here.

But for now, it was back to the airport and another round of waiting there, this time not at the carousel, but in the arrivals area for Gary's mum.

She and Rachel stood front and centre in the loitering crowd, scanning the newly disembarked passengers' faces for any sign of a fifty-something Irish woman travelling alone.

After a few minutes had passed, Rachel gasped. 'Oh my goodness. Look who it is!' she exclaimed, pointing at a couple of passengers heading their way.

One was a young blonde girl in a purple dress. Her hair was pulled into a bun atop her head and she skipped along happily.

Realising immediately who it was, Terri's heart skipped a beat as she looked to the left and spied her companion. Almost at the same time, the young girl spotted Rachel and Terri, and a huge smile broke out on her face.

Terri stood rooted to the spot, her heart racing a mile a

minute as a delighted Daisy and a clearly surprised Ethan came towards them.

Oh God ...

'Hello there!' Rachel gushed, engulfing Daisy in a hug. 'Fancy meeting you here!'

She wondered suddenly if Rachel had somehow planned this, but no, her friend wouldn't do that, surely? It had to be coincidence, and in any case Ethan looked just as uncomfortable as she felt.

'Hello there, bride-to-be,' he greeted enthusiastically. 'I must say, you two are looking very fresh after a seven hour flight. And where's the happy groom?'

'Oh no ... we arrived yesterday,' Rachel explained to him. 'We're just here to pick up Gary's ... oh there she is! Mary, over here!' She waved at her mother-in-law-to-be, who was shuffling nervously through the arrivals doors, and then took off on a sprint towards Mrs Knowles, leaving Terri and the others alone.

'So ... great to see you,' she began awkwardly.

'You too,' Ethan replied, his blue eyes boring into hers. 'How have you been?'

'Great, great. The restaurant is doing well, though hopefully it won't all fall apart while we're away ...' She was babbling but she couldn't help it. She turned her attentions to Daisy, in the hope of regaining her composure and escaping Ethan's penetrating gaze. 'Wow, look at you – you've got so tall!'

Rachel and Mary joined them in the meantime, and

together the small group went outside into the daylight, making small talk about the wedding as they did so. The taxi queue was achingly busy once again, and Terri was relieved that this time they didn't have to wait in line, and their driver from the city was waiting elsewhere in the terminal for a phone call from Rachel to come and collect them.

It also meant that this unexpected encounter would be brief and she wouldn't have to see Ethan again until the wedding.

But she hadn't counted on Rachel's determination. 'This is crazy – Ethan and Daisy, you should come with us in the town car, there's plenty of room,' she said, making a call to the driver.

'Honestly, we're fine. We don't want to impose ...' Ethan began, but Terri caught his dubious glance at the length of the queue.

'Nonsense,' Rachel insisted. 'You're our guests; I wouldn't dream of leaving you in the lurch like this. Honestly, you've hardly any luggage either. It's no problem.'

Great.

Terri wasn't relishing the thought of sitting in a confined space with her ex and his daughter all the way back into Manhattan, but at least Mary Knowles would be there too to break the awkwardness.

When all the bags were stowed, Mary, Rachel and Daisy piled into the back together, while somehow Terri ended up on the next row beside Ethan.

There was a strained silence for a little while the others

chatted animatedly together, until eventually Ethan spoke. 'So, how long are you staying? Just for the wedding or are you making a real holiday out of it?'

'Nope, a short stay is more than enough for me.'

'Oh yes, how could I forget your dislike of travel. How did you survive the six-hour plane ride over? It must have been a nightmare for everyone concerned.'

It was actually a nightmare, and you were involved, Terri thought, recalling the restless dream she'd had the day before on the flight about their break-up.

After a few minutes' more small talk, they ran out of things to say and she stared out of window, willing the journey to end.

'So, Rachel, looking forward to married life?' Ethan turned back to the others and the group chatted easily about the wedding plans and nothing else in particular for the remainder of the drive.

Terri listened as Rachel and Daisy chatted as if they were old friends, leaning in close to one another, whispering secretly and giggling every other sentence or so.

Her friend was so easy, so carefree with this kind of thing. Rachel was born into the role of mother, and seeing her bond so quickly and naturally with Ethan's daughter was truly endearing. Terri knew that it could never be like that for her, at least not so easily.

She was right to have recognised those shortcomings too, she reassured herself as the car swept them into the bowels of Manhattan once more.

Ethan looked relaxed and happy, and Daisy was positively thriving.

There was no question that they were miles better off without her.

Back at the hotel, Ethan went to check in, Rachel took charge of getting Mary settled in her room, while Terri managed to let out a deep breath she'd been holding since first seeing Ethan at the airport.

'Come on, Terri!' Daisy's small voice called out to her then, as she made her way towards the elevator. 'Let's go and get a hot dog; Dad promised we could as soon as we arrived.'

Terri winced, caught. She was sure the new arrivals would want to rest in their hotel room, not go out exploring the city right away.

'Well, I had planned on helping Rachel with some more of her wedding … plans …' Terri tried her best to think of an excuse, something that would get her out of having to be with Ethan and his dazzling smile one second longer.

Just then, Rachel reappeared behind them. 'It's fine. Everything's under control,' she said, with a hint of a smile playing about her lips. 'I'm just going to show Mary around a little, and then meet up for dinner with Gary later. No more wedding stuff today, bridesmaid. You're free as a bird.'

Terri wanted to murder her. What was she playing at?

'Pleeease,' Daisy implored, Ethan coming up behind her.

'Please what?' he enquired.

'I'm trying to get Terri to come out and get a hot dog with us. She said in the car that she hadn't tried one yet.'

That was true but only because she had no interest, not when she'd read somewhere that they were the most unhygienic ...

'Ah, you must come then. A foodie like you can't come here without trying an honest to goodness New York hot dog.' He winked. 'And I know just the place ...'

Rachel was smiling. 'Yes, Ethan certainly knows his way around this city.'

He chuckled at their shared joke. 'I'll just go up and check on the bags and we'll head out. It's not far, just a couple of blocks away. OK?'

Terri relented despite herself. She didn't seem to have much choice. 'OK then, why not.'

A few minutes later, Ethan rejoined them in the lobby, looking as fresh as if he'd just travelled across the road, rather than the Atlantic.

He clapped his hands and excitedly proclaimed. 'OK ladies, let's go find ourselves some hot dogs.'

With a giggle and a nod of approval from her father, Daisy ran off ahead down the street, falling in alongside a random group of joggers.

Her blonde hair bounced as she weaved between people, pointing out landmarks and buildings.

Terri followed along, with no idea where they were going.

She and Ethan were silent, both unsure of exactly what to say.

Neither was willing to risk making waves.

For Ethan's part, he was simply happy to be with Terri again, just the three of them. He wanted to remember what it was like to have her at his side like this as he watched his daughter play and explore.

As for Terri, she wanted nothing more than to forget.

With each step, she could not help but remember just how good it felt to know that Ethan was right alongside her, especially as she walked into a great unknown.

Chapter 15

Ethan, taking the reins, broke the silence first, offering up the most bland and passive thing he could think to ask, 'I hear the restaurant's still thriving. I've been keeping an eye and it seems like everyone in Dublin is still raving about it.'

Terri looked down at her shoes.

Talking about her successes had never come easy to her. Yet she almost had to hold herself back from launching into all of the great and amazing things that had happened in her professional life over the last year or so.

With some restraint, she looked at him and said, 'Yeah, it is. It's amazing, the place is packed to the gills almost every night, and the bakery turnover has doubled.' She continued, her heart melting a bit with each of his glances, 'But at the moment, we're waiting for a review from this major critic to come out. It could destroy us.'

He stopped on the street, turning to face her. 'Why would you say that? Did something happen?' His hand rested on

Terri's arm, keeping her in place. The sudden, caring touch registered something inside her, but she allowed herself to ignore it.

'No, nothing happened and I've no reason to believe it will be terrible. I just get … I don't know, nervous. It's scary to think that it could all be gone because some random person didn't like the wine or thought the fish was too salty.' She found herself saying way too much to him. Ethan wasn't there to comfort her like he once was. He was here to make nice company. She had to keep that in mind and reel it in.

Ethan didn't seem to mind though as he pressed her for more. 'Then why worry?'

She began walking again, heading in Daisy's direction, breaking the connection between them. 'I forgot. You were always the optimist.'

They both spotted Daisy then, standing at a bright yellow food vendor cart.

The owner, a burly man with stains all over his white t-shirt was leaning down to chat with her. She was excitedly asking questions about everything listed on the menu. She pointed out pictures and ingredient lists. And as Daisy noticed Ethan and Terri coming to join her, she could hear her loudly proclaim, 'My friend Terri owns a restaurant in Dublin.'

The man looked up with a big grin at the two adults as they approached. Daisy introduced them. 'Dad, Terri, this is Calvin. He's owned this stand since …' She looked up at the man for assistance.

'Since I was eighteen.' He beamed.

'That's a long time. And he says *he* has the best hot dogs in New York. Can we get one, Dad? Please?'

'Well, I had somewhere else in mind, but ...'

He ordered the group three hot dogs and Daisy watched curiously as Calvin carefully prepared hers. Terri couldn't help but smile at her innocence and how amazed she was at something so simple.

Calvin handed the young girl the wrapped-up treat first, and she peeled back the layers of the tin foil carefully, watching the steam rise.

Daisy took a large bite, smearing ketchup over her face. She looked at her dad and then back at Calvin. A look of sheer pleasure crossed her face as she proclaimed, 'This is amazing!' Calvin handed her a napkin as she wiped the red stain from her lip and nose.

The group continued on, walking along what looked to Terri like the outskirts of some kind of park area.

'Where to next, Dad?'

'I suppose we should go into the park. How about the zoo? It's a beautiful day for a stroll.' He didn't bother to look at Daisy as he said it, instead, his eyes were fixed upon Terri's as he tried to read her blank expression.

She looked around in amazement. 'This is the park, Central Park?' Finally, a New York landmark she'd heard of.

Daisy giggled. 'Yep. This is *the* park. And I think you'll love it.'

All Terri could give was a simple nod of her head as she

tentatively agreed to continue exploring with these two people whom she'd tried her utmost to cut out of her life.

The walk towards the Central Park zoo was the perfect length for Ethan and Terri to attempt to catch up on each other's lives.

He told her all about his new position at the university, including the dearth of suitable assistants. He joked as he talked of Nancy, 'I think it's a curse or something. Next time, I'm asking for someone over the age of ninety.'

Terri laughed. 'Knowing your luck, that ninety-year-old would still have a crush on you.'

'What about you? No handsome waiters making a play? Any freezer romances?'

He knew he was stepping over a line, but he felt it was worth the risk.

She took it in her stride, using her own joke to combat his, 'No, not at all. You know I'm not one to get too hot and bothered in the kitchen.'

In truth, there had been a few others. All just casual things Rachel had attempted to set her up with. Some were Justin's friends, others were guys she had met at the restaurant. But really, none of them were truly worth it.

None of them was Ethan.

Once inside the zoo, the two walked a bit closer together, a bit more in step with one another.

Daisy ran ahead, as if completely unaware. She was enraptured with the old zoo, as she stopped and stared at each exhibit, from the red pandas moping around in their habitat, to the snakes slithering around in their cavernous homes. Each exhibit held something new, something exciting.

Occasionally though, Daisy would hide behind an exhibit or duck into a dark corner to get a peek at her father.

She could see it in the way that he leaned into Terri as he talked, his hands tucked into his pockets and his smile growing wider than she had seen in months, that he was back to the dad she knew when he and Terri were last together.

But Terri needed work. While she too smiled, it was not like her dad did. Even Daisy could sense that she was holding on to something, refusing to let go and truly relax. She shrugged her shoulders too much while she talked, and looked down at the ground for far too long.

Daisy had to spring into action. She'd been thinking a lot about seeing Terri again throughout this visit, and had jumped at the chance to get her to come out with them today.

Now it was time to put the next part of her plan into action.

'Dad, I want some popcorn. Can we get some popcorn?' Daisy tugged at his arm, pulling him away. She knew he hated that.

'No, buttercup. You just had a hot dog, and we don't want to ruin dinner later.'

'But, *Dad*!' she cried out, as other mothers and fathers turned to look at them with sympathetic eyes.

Terri could not help but feel for Ethan. It was never easy

or natural for her to step in, especially considering her mother's memory, but she felt compelled.

She kneeled down before Daisy and tried to change the subject. 'So where are you two going for dinner later, or is your dad making it a surprise?'

Inside, Daisy was secretly happy that Terri was taking notice, but she couldn't stop now. She had just begun. She looked back at her sulkily as she wiped her eyes with her knuckles. 'I don't know! He won't tell me! He just tells me when I can and cannot eat!'

'Daisy, come on now, this isn't like you. We were having such a nice afternoon. It's only an hour or so till dinnertime. Can this wait? Let's go and find those monkeys.'

'I don't care about the stupid monkeys in the stupid zoo. I'm *hungry*!' She stamped her foot just as she did when she was five, and not the mature ten-year-old she was now.

Terri stood back, letting Ethan step up and play dad to the obviously tired girl. He looked at his daughter, unsure what was going on.

Daisy never behaved like this. Was she really as tired and hungry as she looked? He decided to play it safe. 'I think we should go back to the hotel now, and you can rest for a while. It's been a long day.'

He reached out his hand, and Daisy took it wearily.

The three silently walked out of the park and into an idling taxi.

Once they reached the hotel, Daisy realised she had to figure out what to do next.

If she played this right, she could get both a nice night in, and her dad on the right track.

An idea struck her.

'Dad, can we go and see Rachel? I want to show her my dress for the wedding.' She was insistent as she led him by hand to the elevator, Terri trailing behind.

Ethan looked at her for help, but instead she replied with, 'I think that is a great idea. I'm sure she would love to see what you plan on wearing. I'll send her a message to let her know you're on your way up to see her.'

This was the perfect escape for Terri. She could go back to her bedroom and hide, and sleep off the old feelings that were developing in Central Park's leafy canopies.

With nothing left on her agenda for the rest of the day, she would finally be free to enjoy her stay without interruptions.

Chapter 16

That was, until a knock came at her door an hour later.

She had already changed into a comfy plush robe, the one that came with her room and had drawn a bath in the whirlpool tub. She had also found an innocent, decidedly non-romantic comedy to wash her day away.

The only thing that was missing was a clean glass for her drink from the mini-bar, but room service was on the way.

When she heard the knock, she rushed to open it, not thinking to check who it was. She let out a little gasp as she realised the person before her was not a hotel worker but Ethan himself, leaning one of his long arms against the door frame.

'Wh–what are you doing here? Where's Daisy?' Terri looked about the hallway, trying to spot where the young girl might be hiding.

Ethan smiled at her, his eyes twinkling a bit. Inside, his heart raced at the sight of her as it did each and every time he looked at her.

Pushing all of his nervous energy aside, he began. 'She's staying with Rachel this evening. Gary is out with his mother, so the two of them are having a slumber party in her suite.'

'I see.'

'The thing is, I have a couple of tickets to the Met gallery – the opening of a new exhibition. Would you like to join me?'

Her long pause prompted Ethan to pull out the big guns, 'It's a gala of sorts, I believe – featuring food by Chef Marco L'Adorna.' He purposefully butchered the last name to give it more authenticity.

Rachel had talked him through this in detail earlier. With Daisy's inventiveness and Rachel's resourcefulness, he hoped he might be able to woo Terri back.

For Terri, the chef's name, although totally mispronounced, was almost irresistible. She and Rachel had followed the chef's rise closely over the last couple of years. He was a revered genius of reinvented classic American and Italian fusion.

And Ethan was offering her an opportunity to sample his genius …

Terri had no idea how this had happened or where this was coming from but she figured she could get through one night of being with Ethan, for this.

At least, that's what she promised herself.

'I'll have to change. Can you give me a half an hour or so?'

'Yes, I was hoping you weren't planning on wearing the hotel's robe,' he joked. 'While it's a great colour on you, I don't think it would work for the Met. But whenever you're ready, I'm just down the hall.'

Terri watched him stroll just twenty feet from her door, look back at her leaning up against her room's door, and then smile as he walked into his own room.

As he disappeared from view, she ran back inside and called Rachel's suite.

Her voice could not even hide the nervousness as she narrowed her eyes at her friend through the receiver. 'You planned this, didn't you? Today at the airport and everything else ... What on *earth* are you playing at?'

Rachel hung up her cell phone and turned to the girl bouncing on her giant hotel bed. 'I think it's going to work.'

Daisy bounced even higher, excited that her plans were falling into place.

Of course, it took a little intervention from Rachel, but she felt she was one step closer to pulling it off.

As Rachel sat down on the corner of the bed, she reached over and hugged her as thanks. As the two chatted about their plans, Gary peeked his head out of the bathroom door.

He watched as Rachel bonded so easily with the little girl, how she instantly knew that she would want to order pizza and watch a movie on the Children's Channel, while he went out with his mother.

If it were him sitting where Rachel was, he would be utterly lost, completely unsure of how to talk, let alone act, around a child.

He coughed, getting his fiancée's attention as he beckoned her to have a side talk with him in the suite's dressing room. She asked Daisy to pick out the movie they should watch while she hurried off to speak with him.

'Are you sure you don't want to come out with me and Mam tonight?' Gary thought he should ask again, just in case. It was very good of Rachel to arrange to fly his mother in a little earlier; she'd been a bit off with him about this whole New York wedding thing, and it was nice to have her back on side.

He couldn't remember the last time he and his mam had gone out for dinner together – if ever – and he wasn't sure where to take her. Nowhere too fancy anyway. Somewhere in Times Square maybe? He thought she'd enjoy the lights and the buzz.

In truth, it was probably a good thing Rachel wasn't coming along as he knew his mam felt a bit intimidated by her, especially when it came to food.

Hell, Gary was intimidated himself sometimes.

'No, no. I'm delighted to have you two spend some time together. And I'm just as happy staying here with Daisy.' She looked over at the girl scrolling through the TV channels. 'Plus, it'll be good practice,' she winked at him teasingly.

Gary gulped. 'Jaysus, we're not even married yet. Can we save the kids talk till after the honeymoon at least?' He ran his hands through his hair, ruffling the slick backed look he had created earlier.

Rachel's face fell. 'What do you mean? I didn't think we had anything to talk about ... we both want kids – don't we?'

Gary sighed. 'Right, yeah I suppose. Anyway, I'd better go, Mam is waiting.' He grabbed his coat that was draped over a chair.

Rachel was frowning, but she reined herself back, not wanting Daisy to hear her private conversation. 'What's the rush, Gary? Why are you running away like this in the middle of a conversation?'

'Jesus Christ why does everything have to be so ... *intense* with you? Why can't you just let things happen? Not everything needs to be organised in a binder, you know.' He knew he was taking it a bit too far, but Gary was annoyed.

'Fine for you to talk about being intense when you haven't had to lift a finger for anything to do with this wedding at all,' she shot back, stung. 'I'm just trying to create the best possible day, the best future for us. I'm going to be your wife, and we are going to be a family. It's what I want, what I've always wanted. Why can't you understand that?'

She tried to keep her voice down, so Daisy wouldn't overhear them. Talk about timing.

'Well, maybe there's more to it than what *you* want ...' Gary instantly knew what he'd said was wrong. Rachel stared at him, wide-eyed and wounded.

With nothing more to say to him, at least nothing more

that she could put into words, she turned back towards the bedroom where she could hear Daisy's movie choice begin to play.

Gary listened as she called out to her with forced joviality, 'What did you pick, sweetheart?'

It was too late for him to go after her and have it out, though. It wasn't exactly the time or the place, and anyway, his mother was waiting.

With that, he put on his leather dress-shoes and headed down to the lobby where Mary Knowles waited for him.

Hopefully his mam was well rested and in good form, and wouldn't end up spending the entire night filling his ear with complaints about New York and the wedding being so far from home.

Women, Gary groaned, sometimes you just couldn't win with them.

Chapter 17

Terri flexed her fingers, shook her hair out, and took two deep breaths before knocking on Ethan's hotel room door.

She stood back, trying her best to look cool and relaxed, as if she was 100 per cent at ease with this situation.

But the truth was that her heart was racing, her stomach was filled with butterflies and bricks all at the same time, and her fingers and toes wiggled nervously as she struggled to gain some composure.

This was exactly what *not* to do with your ex, especially when it was pretty obvious you still had feelings for him. She knew she was risking her heart, yet again, in playing along with this fantasy.

And if she were to get hurt or worse, hurt him, she would be to blame.

After a few moments, the door to Ethan's room flew open. He was dressed in a black, slim-fitting suit with a simple white button-down shirt. His tie, a skinny grey pinstripe, was draped over his shoulders, as if it were meant to be worn that way. He leaned nonchalantly against the hotel's papered walls, his blue eyes smiling in greeting.

The sight of him made Terri's knees buckle a bit.

He looked her up and down briefly, studying the way the purple dress hugged her curves and how she crossed her legs, even though she was standing fully upright. It was a little quirk about her that he had forgotten but certainly missed. Finding his own breath, Ethan admitted, 'I know that this is stupid and terribly clichéd, but I cannot tie this tie. Will you help me?'

Terri nodded as she entered his room, a mirror image of her own except with two beds. Daisy's purple suitcase was laid out on one, while his black suit carrier was folded neatly on a lounge seat.

He walked back towards the sleeping quarters, and led her to a giant, gold ornate full-length mirror on the wall.

Inhaling deeply, Terri took a couple of steps towards him and stretched out her arms across his broad shoulders from behind.

Her fingers just barely touched the spot where some dark facial hair was beginning to grow in. She was so close, she could spot little bits of stubble on areas of his face where he had forgotten to shave. His aftershave, just gentle enough to be noticed, filled her senses with memories and sensations.

Her eyes closed as she reminded herself where she was, whom she was with, and what needed to be done. Ethan could see her in the mirror struggling with it all.

Even her hands shook a bit as she made a quick, Windsor knot.

When she finished, she stepped back, immediately admiring her handiwork. He smiled at her as he faced the mirror to check on the job. With a cheesy thumbs-up and a lopsided grin, he pronounced it good to go.

The two left the hotel room silently and downstairs in the lobby, they ran into Gary and his mother.

Terri noticed that Gary looked a bit down in the dumps, almost crestfallen as he introduced Ethan quickly to Mary as an old friend of Rachel's, saying nothing at all, she noted amused, about the collision outside Tiffany's of two years before. Clearly the doting son still hadn't owned up to what had actually happened back then, and while Ethan was friendly and mannerly as always, it was interesting that he had been described as 'Rachel's friend' only.

Perhaps the two hadn't quite buried the hatchet?

A little later, she stood frozen in place outside the impossibly grand Metropolitan Museum, as sophisticated New York men and women dressed to the nines passed her by, each chatting away as if it were nothing.

This was a crowd that someone effortlessly stylish and sociable like Rachel could easily blend into.

But Terri felt out of place, completely unprepared for such a decadent affair.

She turned uneasily to face Ethan as she whispered into his ear, 'I'm not sure about this. I'm really not dressed for such a posh do. Everyone seems so … wealthy and sophisticated. I don't belong here.'

As she spoke, a stunningly beautiful and very thin woman in a black gown with a long train passed her. She clutched on to her escort's arm as she practically glided over the carpeted entranceway.

Terri's anxiety rose even higher.

Ethan laughed heartily and offered her his own arm, just the same as the passing couple, as he whispered back, 'Don't be silly, you belong everywhere. And there isn't a woman in this whole building that could hold a candle to you.'

Terri blushed as she took his arm, entwining it.

They walked side by side into the building and towards the gallery section roped off for the event.

The affair was being held in a room displaying modern American art from the 1920s and 1930s.

As cocktail hour began, Terri insisted on taking a turn about the room to study the displays. She and Ethan seemed to be the only ones interested in the exhibits though, everyone else was too busy mingling and networking to admire the beautiful work of some of the country's most talented artists.

A man in a black tuxedo and white gloves came round with a tray of drinks, lowering it to offer the selection to Ethan and Terri.

She wanted to resist out of fear of drinking too much and losing her composure, but at the same time she was not going to let a good night out and some obviously expensive champagne go to waste.

She sipped hers gently, holding the dainty flute in her fingers. Ethan, on the other hand washed his back and returned the empty glass to another waiter as soon as he had finished.

'I never thought you were a great one for champagne,' Terri teased him, knowing it was not his favourite and he was more of a red wine man.

'I'm more of a great one for food, actually. I'm starving and that's what we came here for, isn't it?' He took her hand, leading her off in the direction of another server holding a tray above his head.

They followed the man to the entrance of the catering area.

'Oh my goodness. Chef Marco ...' Terri whispered excitedly, pointing to a man hunched over a tray of purple, white, and yellow food creations.

The chef shooed the servers out one by one and then turned his back to continue his work.

Terri stood in complete awe, unsure what to do or say. This guy was famous the world over, and his work had had a huge influence on her and Rachel when in college. She couldn't quite believe that just then, he was standing only a few feet away from her.

Ethan, on the other hand, took a more proactive approach. As a waiter exited the kitchen area, he grabbed his tray, thanked the man and returned to Terri quickly before the guy had any time to protest.

As he placed the silver platter before her, he proudly said, 'Compliments of the chef.'

'I cannot believe you just did that,' she laughed, eyes widening. 'You're very bold.'

Terri picked an item off the tray, a vegetable medley of sorts, and smiled widely at her partner in crime.

'I wanted to taste this so-called magician's work myself, and I wasn't about to wait around and be served.' He took a bite and Terri followed, each chewing in silence for a moment.

After a single bite, Terri placed the half-eaten canapé back on the tray and used a napkin to spit out the contents of her first taste.

Laughing, Ethan followed suit. 'What in the world was *that*?' he gasped, coughing slightly. He flagged down a drink server and downed another glass of champagne, allowing the taste to disappear in the alcohol's acidity.

'I have no idea, but that was one of the most vile things I have ever tasted. I can't believe it. Maybe it was a fluke, some accident or something?' She was still chuckling, tears of laughter springing from her eyes as she tried to salvage her make-up.

The couple moved away from the catering area, and found their seats at a table near the back of the gallery.

Ethan casually draped his arm around the back of her chair, his hand not daring to touch her flawless skin. Both sat back and relaxed a little as the curator of the new exhibition presented his short lecture to the completely uninterested audience. When he finished, everyone in the room politely clapped, while Ethan let out a jaunty English cheer just to shake things up. Terri nudged him in the side as a room of glaring eyes turned to face them.

He laughed, not caring.

Dinner came shortly after. And with each bite, both Ethan and Terri continued their back and forth looks, knowing smiles, and random bursts of laughter.

As the rest of the table politely sipped their potato and lobster soup and tasted their trout, Terri pushed plate after plate away.

Chef L'Adorna, it seemed to Terri's expert palate, was certainly not up to par.

And while she guessed she should be disappointed or at least a bit heartbroken after such hero-worship, she found herself not caring at *all* about the food.

Feeling emboldened by the champagne, she turned to face her companion. 'Come on, let's go.' She stood and this time offered him her hand.

Ethan looked up at her, surprised. His hand clasped hers as they hurried out of the room and then broke into a run through the gallery and back out onto the carpeted walkway.

Terri rounded the corner with him following behind, and waved her arm to hail a cab.

'Back to the hotel already?' he said, looking a little crestfallen. 'It's not yet midnight, Cinderella. Only ten, and actually, only 5 p.m. in real life,' he joked, eyes twinkling as he checked his watch.

'OK, then, where should we go before the clock strikes

midnight?' Terri felt exhilarated. Suddenly the entire city was laid out before her and she wanted to experience it. 'You're the expert.'

But from what little she knew of the place, she guessed that New York was the kind of town best shared, preferably with someone special – like Ethan.

Why not? she reassured herself. She was here for a reason and so was he and on Sunday morning they'd once again go their separate ways.

They enjoyed each other's company but both of them knew well that they had no future together.

So what was the harm in having a little fun?

Chapter 18

When the cab driver gruffly asked where to, Ethan answered with yet another one of those confusing street number combinations that all New Yorkers seemed to understand.

She couldn't fathom why they didn't just use street names like everywhere else.

The cab pulled up alongside a stone building soon after, and as Ethan opened the door for Terri and took her hand, hurrying her inside, she didn't even get a moment to see where she was.

Instead, he shuffled her up a moving elevator to a ticket booth. At this time of night, the place which Terri suspected was some kind of office building (why had Ethan brought her to an office building that had a ticket booth?) looked deserted, with only a few people who seemed like staff peppered here and there.

Oddly, they needed to go through a security check, and she raised an eyebrow at Ethan as he removed his watch and urged her to ready her clutch bag for the X-ray machine. Then finally, he ushered her into an elevator, whereupon an attendant, pushed a button to the 86th floor.

Then suddenly, as the sound of a recorded-voice filled the elevator, it finally dawned on Terri where he had taken her.

As the golden doors flew open, they moved outside onto an observation deck, high above the city, and her breath hitched. The calm beauty of the pitch black sky over a twinkling Manhattan that seemed to go on forever beneath them overwhelmed Terri, and she held on tighter to Ethan's arm as they stood atop a now deserted Empire State Building.

'Wow. This is … this is something else.'

He walked her to the outer edge where she could make out some of the landmarks below.

'I'm glad you like it. I always think it's at its best at this time of night, so peaceful. Most people tend to visit during the day.'

She could only nod in agreement. There was something magical and slightly dream-like about it. If Rachel were here she would say that it was like a scene out of a movie, but ever practical, Terri thought it was merely the reality of how high they were, and how monumental the city seemed as they looked down upon it.

Ethan watched her face as she circled the observation deck.

She searched and scanned almost every bit of the landscape as he pointed out buildings and sights. He stood close behind her, and could feel her quiver a bit. Guessing it was from the cold air, he removed his suit jacket and put it around her arms.

She turned to face him, his arms still resting lightly on her shoulders.

'Thank you,' she whispered. 'This was a great idea … I love it.'

As he stared into her emerald eyes, Ethan wanted nothing more than to remain in this spot, frozen in time, with Terri in his arms against the ever-romantic backdrop of the New York skyline.

This place had always been special for him and he loved sharing it with her.

The words unleashed before he could stop them. 'I've missed you, Terri. I've missed this.' He watched her for a reaction, waited her for to stop him, but she didn't, so he continued, 'I think I know why you left, why you couldn't be with me any longer, I really do. But tonight, let's not worry about reality – just live in the moment, OK?'

He made one more move, closer to her and she did not resist, she could not. Her feet were cemented to the ground, her body anticipating, wanting what she knew would come next.

Ethan scooped his arm around Terri's waist, pulling her close as he lowered his head to meet hers. His lips dived into hers, stealing her breath away. Her body sank against his, while he used his other hand to stroke her fiery curls and caress her face.

Then she pulled away a little, using her hand to gently

push against his chest. The air escaped her as she heaved from both surprise and excitement. She pressed her head into his chest and let it rest there.

'Please, please say something.' Ethan was desperate to hear from her.

No matter what she had to say, he just wanted to hear her voice. He knew what he'd just done was probably too sudden, too rash, but he couldn't help himself. Seeing her again had brought back all the emotions he'd tried to rid himself of every day since she left him.

'Ethan I-I-I'm sorry.' Terri suddenly broke free from his arms and rushed inside, not wanting to look back. 'I have to go.'

She put her hands on her lips, feeling a warmth that still resided on her own skin after his touch.

And as she entered the elevator with his jacket still round her shoulders, feeling very much like Cinderella before the clocks struck midnight, just before the doors closed, Terri stole a backward glance at Ethan staring out into the night sky, and sent him a silent apology.

I'm so sorry ...

Chapter 19

'Terri? I know you're in there. Please open the door.'

She rolled over in bed, placing the white blanket over her head, hoping the world would just disappear.

'Please. I just need someone to talk to,' Rachel's voice broke a little, as she lowered it to a whisper. 'Something happened with Gary last night. I don't know what to do. I need to talk to someone.'

Terri turned over again, this time allowing her body to drape over the side of the bed. She reached towards her phone, and glanced quickly at the time, noticing a few missed messages and calls (all from Rachel). It was 8 a.m. and the memory of the night before still burned in her brain.

Getting up, she trudged to the door, slowly opening it just a crack.

'Thank you.' Rachel moved towards the bed, sitting on the mess of overturned blankets while Terri went directly to the in-room cafetière to prepare them a pot of coffee.

She had a feeling it would be badly needed by both of them.

Rachel launched into a hurried retelling of her exchange of words with Gary the night before, about his annoyance with her approach to planning the wedding, the worrying things he'd said about them having children, to him returning late last night and slipping into bed alongside her without a word. This morning, she opened her eyes to find him already gone before she woke, obviously still miffed about their argument.

She fought back tears as she let it all out. Terri handed her a coffee and listened as she sipped the hot liquid from the paper cup.

'What am I going to do? The welcome dinner is tonight, and our wedding is tomorrow – barely twenty-four hours away! How am I supposed to fix this in time?' Rachel sniffled, as she reached for the tissue box sitting on Terri's nightstand.

'You can't fix it, hon.'

'What?' The bluntness of Terri's answer shocked her.

'You can't fix it. I hate to say it, but maybe Gary has a point, you have been somewhat ... obsessive about the wedding.'

'But ... but why wouldn't I be? It's supposed to be the most important—'

'Yes, yes, the most important day of everyone's life, I know. But, Rachel, despite what you think, the day itself, while important, shouldn't be the be-all and end-all. What's more important is that you and Gary are on the same page. And from what you've been saying, that doesn't sound like it's the case – about one thing in particular, I mean.'

Terri didn't really have the energy, or the inclination to go through all this just now, but she knew better than anyone how Rachel could be about something she'd set her heart on. And she suspected she knew what was going on with Gary. Rachel's detailed account of last night's fight had given her an inkling.

'I don't know what you mean ...'

'Rachel, I know you. The wedding's tomorrow and all that can be arranged has already been arranged. Everything's in place – you're ready to go. Which means that you have no doubt already turned your attentions to the next part of your ideal happily ever after ... am I right?'

'You mean, having a family? Well, yes of course. It's only natural that this comes next, isn't it? It's just ... I've waited so long for all this, to start a new life and new family with someone. It's important to me, you know that.'

'Exactly. It's important to you. But maybe it's not so important to Gary just yet. Maybe he just wants time to enjoy married life with his new wife, before throwing yourselves into all the baby stuff and the mania that comes with it.'

She looked shocked at the very idea. 'But he's never said anything like that. I just assumed that we'd ...'

'Exactly. You just assumed. Rachel, I love you, but we both know you do tend to get carried away by your own ideals of what the perfect reality should be. You've been dreaming of this wedding all your life and have done everything you can possibly do to make it a reality. So why not just relax a little and enjoy the moment, rather than looking too far into the future and concentrating on your next ideal, the whole happy family thing.'

With a jolt, Terri realised that she too was guilty of such a thing, though in a completely different way. She recalled Ethan's words from the night before.

Just live in the moment ...

But that was different. She was more than able and indeed perfectly willing to face up to reality; Rachel was the one who'd always had trouble letting go of the dream.

'But what if Gary doesn't want kids?' Rachel sobbed. 'It would break my heart. I can't wait to get started. Only last week, I was talking about painting the spare room.'

Terri now knew for sure that this was likely the root cause of Gary's distant behaviour recently. If his fiancée was already talking about turning bedrooms into nurseries with less than a week to go before their wedding ... perhaps she couldn't blame him for getting cold feet.

She knew better than most how Rachel's ability to get swept up in one of her dreams could be overwhelming, and for her friend's sake, and the sake of her happily-ever-after vision, she needed to bring her back down to earth.

'Rachel, try to take things one step at a time, OK? This time should be about you and Gary, and the commitment you're making to one another. Stop running ahead of yourself. Just enjoy the ride.'

Again, Terri couldn't help but think that she was some-what of a hypocrite in advising Rachel to do that, when she couldn't do the same thing herself.

But speaking of enjoying the ride … 'By the way. What was all that last night with Ethan? Those tickets didn't just materialise out of nowhere – nor did that so-called errand to the airport. Don't think I didn't see what was going on.'

'Oh come on. I thought last night was the perfect oppor-tunity for you two to have some time alone together – some time to figure out what is truly going on with you. The tick-ets … well they were always going to be my gift to my bridesmaid. I was planning on going with you, but then I fig-ured Ethan would make a much better date.'

'Well, thanks for the gift, but I don't appreciate the meddling.'

'Ah come on, Terri, admit it. Ethan makes you happy and you make him happy. Of course you should be together, but you can't see that, or worse you refuse to see it. Talk about me being blinded by dreams, you're the one who's blind, if you can't see how you two are meant to be together.'

Terri sat back down, her head resting deep in the palms of her hands.

An overwhelming exhaustion overcame her. She did not want to have this discussion. 'Rachel, we've already been through this; it could never work. Ethan and I don't even live in the same country, never mind that I'm not the maternal type, like you. I'm sure even Gary can see how good you are with Daisy, and you would be an amazing mum to any child you might bring into this world. But that's not me. I was never one for dreams of big weddings and perfect families.'

'What were your dreams about then, Terri?' Rachel asked, genuinely curious. 'The restaurant? Because from where I'm standing, that's very much a reality. So what else? World domination on the sourdough front perhaps?'

Terri could not respond. Her mind raced with Rachel's words.

What *was* her dream? Did she even have one? Was she supposed to have one? Surely that kind of thing was just for kids growing up, not adult women in their late thirties with jobs and mortgages and restaurants to run?

She didn't know. All Terri did know was that this conversation was supposed to be about Rachel's aspirations, not hers.

She tried to direct her friend back on topic.

'Give poor Gary a break,' she said then, still unable to believe that she of all people was now feeling sorry for Gary Knowles. 'He loves you and you two are getting married tomorrow in this fantastic city …'

'Fantastic city?' Rachel raised an eyebrow. 'So you're a New York convert then?'

Terri thought again of the Manhattan lights shimmering beneath her the night before as she and Ethan stood atop the Empire State Building, the lively atmosphere of Central Park the day before, and the regal beauty of the Metropolitan Museum of Art.

She was certainly getting there.

Chapter 20

Ethan and Daisy were heading out for lunch in Times Square.

'Dad, did you ask Terri if she wanted to come with us?'

'No, buttercup. She wouldn't be interested.' Ethan knew that it wouldn't be long before his daughter asked about Terri.

He hated to have to disappoint her young heart yet again.

Her eyes narrowed. 'What did you do last night? Didn't you follow the rules? Please tell me you weren't stupid, Dad. Girls hate stupid men – especially girls like Terri.'

'Oy. We do not say "stupid", and no, I was not, as it happens. We had a nice time, but just as friends.'

He tried to be diplomatic, as if he was fine with the situation. But in his head, Ethan was unsure what had happened – how one moment of pure joy turned into Terri running away from him again.

'I don't believe you, you know.'

'Daisy, we've been here before. Life isn't like fairy tales.

You can't just *make* people fall in love because you want them to.' Ethan's wounded heart and indeed pride was catching up with him, making it harder to give her Daisy-friendly answers.

'I don't believe you. You love her, Dad. She loves you. It *is* supposed to work out.' Daisy walked off to change into her outfit. She slammed the bedroom door behind her, leaving her father alone in the living area.

He lay flat on his back on the bed, attempting to replay each moment as it had occurred last night. But nothing registered amiss. Nothing rang alarm bells or told him it was wrong. They'd had a great time, had been enjoying each other's company, just like before.

Yet he had lost her again.

He felt Terri's absence everywhere as the day lingered on.

He wanted to laugh with her about how awful the tourist restaurant's food in Times Square was, or how he and Daisy had got lost in the subway on the way there, much to his daughter's delight.

He wanted to point out the trumped-up billboards for Chef L'Adorna's restaurant, and reminisce about just how awful the man's cooking was in reality.

But Terri was somewhere else in Manhattan, off on her own mission to pick up her bridesmaid dress, help Rachel with the final touches in preparation for that evening's welcome dinner party, and to set her plans in motion for Rachel's final night as a single woman. Or so she hoped.

Now, as wedding guests filed into the hotel dining room, she kept her mind occupied on the night ahead, trying to focus on ways to get Rachel out of the cousins' outrageous hen party plans for later.

She tried to drown out the voices of Linda and Cora as they went on and on about how their time at the spa that afternoon with Rachel had been 'sheer bliss'.

Instead, her eyes were fixed on the doorway as she waited for Ethan and Daisy to arrive at the party. She wanted to be aware of them well in advance so as to compose herself for the inevitable, embarrassing face to face.

Looking away briefly, she then studied Rachel and Gary. Though they were hosting the party with cheerful aplomb, the happy couple stood quite some distance away from one another, each conversing with other guests.

Rachel had the same, forced smile she'd worn all day. She and Gary evidently hadn't cleared the air, and the bride was obviously not enjoying herself.

Terri sprang into action. She went to her friend's side, saving her from another moment with Cora and Linda's mum, a distant relative with whom Terri knew she had little in common. Whispering in Rachel's ear, she said, 'At eight, after the meal is finished, you and me are getting out of here, OK?'

'What's happening at eight?' Rachel's interest was piqued.

'It's a surprise. But I'm going to ask you to play along with whatever I ask OK?'

'Just you and me ... but what about the others? I thought we were all going out for the hen night.'

'Let's just say that your cousins' version of tonight involved cowboys and strippers. Mine involves something you might actually enjoy.'

Rachel giggled, sounding much more like her old self.

She certainly needed an escape from this glum atmosphere in which Gary still wasn't speaking to her, his mother sat in judgement of her, and her cousins' shrieking voices were giving her a headache.

Thank goodness for her best friend.

Ethan and Daisy arrived just in time for dinner to begin.

His seat and Terri's were directly across from one another as she'd arranged. She wasn't going to shirk anything; she and Ethan were adults and she knew they needed to have this out sooner rather than later. She didn't want any unnecessary awkwardness or embarrassment lingering for the wedding tomorrow, so there was no pussy-footing around.

Daisy sat alongside her father, and turned to chat with Justin, Stromboli's chef, who had just arrived in the city a couple of hours before.

Seeing the opportunity, Terri caught Ethan's attention. 'Can we talk?' she said forthrightly. 'I'm sorry about last night. I shouldn't have left before you.'

Despite himself, Ethan was annoyed. She was always so damned mature, so adult about things. He was fully prepared for an uncomfortable situation tonight. He'd thought it would be awkward, certainly hadn't expected it to be this ... civilised.

He tried not to be angry, but when he'd come in earlier and had seen her giggling with Rachel, he'd become annoyed. He wanted to see her conflicted as he was about what had happened last night. Terri acting like nothing at all was amiss felt like simply another slap in the face, and an affront to his feelings.

Didn't she care about him at all?

'I take it you got back to the hotel OK ...'

'Yes. I found a taxi out on the street. I was going to wait, but I wasn't sure you'd want me to ...' Her voice trailed off and she took a deep breath. Ethan knew exactly what was coming.

'Last night ...'

'Was fun,' he finished, before she got the words out. He didn't want to hear it, didn't want to draw things out any longer than was needed. Clearly nothing had changed; Terri might care about him but still wasn't prepared to take a chance that they could be more, that they might have a real future together.

He didn't understand it, but he had no choice but to respect it.

'Yes, it was fun.' She laughed a little, obviously relieved.

'How's Rachel?' Ethan went on, intent on changing the subject. 'She seems a little strained. Pre-wedding jitters? I remember those well. I had a serious attack just on the morning Jane and I were to walk down the aisle.'

'Seriously?' Terri was surprised at this sudden confidence, and also a little stung by the mention of Jane. She followed his gaze towards her friend, who did indeed look glum.

'Absolutely. Horrible feeling; completely overwhelming as if everything is spinning out of control. Rather like how I felt when I first found out we were having Daisy.'

Then Terri glanced at Gary and suddenly she had a brainwave.

'Ethan, could you do me a really big favour?' she asked.

'Of course. What do you need?'

'I need you to talk to Gary, actually. It's what you said about pre-wedding jitters. He and Rachel had an argument last night, and I get the feeling he too is a little ... overwhelmed by all this marriage and baby stuff. Maybe he needs to talk to someone who's been there.'

'I'm not sure Mr Knowles and I are the best of buddies, considering ...'

'I know, but you got him to see sense very effectively, last time, didn't you?'

'OK, I'll give it a try,' Ethan nodded, still content to do anything she asked of him.

After dinner, he got up, whispered in Daisy's ear, and then walked over to where Gary and Rachel sat at the head of the table.

He said hello to Rachel, then reached out to shake Gary's hand.

Then in a time-honoured wedding custom he had learned years ago from his father, Ethan pulled out two cigars from his suit pocket.

Chapter 21

Ethan leaned against the railing of the terrace outside the dining room.

The two men were alone, and even though over dinner Ethan had run through in his mind what he was going to say to the groom, he felt a little lost for words.

Though he had kept in close contact with Rachel, he and Gary were hardly friends; the opposite if anything, considering how they first met.

Launching straight into talk of pre-wedding jitters seemed too sudden. Easing into it seemed even more haphazard.

So Ethan waited for Gary to speak first, hoping that some kind of transition would come from that.

'Great cigar, man. You just don't get these things around much any more.' Gary didn't smoke, hated the taste of cigar, but it seemed like some kind of manly challenge from Greene, and he wasn't going to shirk it.

In truth, he'd been dubious about inviting this guy to the

wedding, but Rachel was insistent that Greene had been such a major part of their 'New York love story', as she called it.

'Truth be told, I honestly don't smoke them much myself, but my father taught me long ago that when you're invited to a celebration, you should always carry one or two around. As a toast of sorts.'

'Rightio. Let's make a toast then.' Gary raised his cigar high in the air, giving him the opportunity to cough out the thick smoke filling his lungs.

Ethan saw an opening, 'To you and Rachel on the eve of your wedding. While life may not go as planned, or maybe even better than planned, may you share an overwhelming happiness to last a lifetime.'

Gary laughed. 'Hear, hear. Short and sweet. That's how I prefer my toasts too. And as for the planning part, I think Rachel would love that.'

Ethan chuckled. 'Yes, I'd noticed. She's a wonderful girl, but I'm sure that aspect can be a little frustrating to live with ...' He had found his conversation starter, and was venturing in even further.

Gary rolled his eyes. 'You can say that again, bud. We were arguing about it only yesterday. Big knock-down dragged out argument over nothing. Well, to me, nothing. To her – *everything*.' He looked down at the ground and kicked a little pebble over the ledge.

'Let me guess.' Ethan pretended to pause for believability. 'Is it money? Work? How about children?'

'Ha! Right on all counts. Did you and the missus talk about children before, you know, having yours?' Gary was unsure if he was crossing a boundary.

Ethan sighed. It was always hard to talk about his beloved wife, Jane. 'We didn't actually, and looking back, I'm not sure why. It's such a momentous decision. But I wanted one and she wanted one, so why not? But I was scared too. I think some women just know they're destined to be mothers, while some men need time to be fathers. Me, I needed time.'

Gary gave him a long look, then nodded. 'Now that all the wedding stuff is ready to go, Rachel's moved on to talking about baby rooms and kids' stuff. And when I see her with kids – even just yesterday with Daisy, I know she'll be a great mother. But it's like you said yourself, it's not her. It's me.'

Gary was coming to terms out loud with something he hadn't really thought about before.

Ethan was nodding. 'Fatherhood turns you into a different person, make no mistake. You have this entire life so dependent upon you to be there, to need you to be more than just yourself. Some men shrink to that task. Others rise.'

Ethan was speaking from the heart now. The last few years of being a single dad had completely changed him in terms of his priorities. Daisy would come first for the rest of his life.

Nothing would ever change that.

'I want to be that man too, I think. I'm just not sure if . . .'

140

Gary trailed off, thinking about the argument they had last night and the days before, how unfair he had been to Rachel. 'But I don't know if I can live up to what she wants. I'd like to give it a bit of time, wait until we're a bit more used to married life before diving into such a big responsibility.'

'Well, then tell her that. You only get one life, and I think Rachel is definitely the kind of woman who'll make it worth it. But you have to let her know how you feel, if you're not ready. Don't just go along with it for her sake, or you'll all regret it.'

'You're right, Greene. You're bloody well right.' Gary snuffed out his cigar and clapped Ethan on the back. 'Thanks for the cigar.' He hurried back inside, while Ethan remained on the terrace looking down at the busy New York streets.

His mind moved automatically to Jane, the woman he had planned to spend a lifetime with. He thought about what he'd just said to Gary.

You get one life.

He had lost that chance with Jane.

And it was pretty clear, he realised sadly, that he had also lost it with Terri.

Chapter 22

Terri looked at her wristwatch and then back at Rachel who was looking particularly bored, chatting with Gary's best man, Sean. Her eyes were wandering as she slumped slightly forward. Everything about her said uninterested to Terri.

It was time for her escape plan to go into motion.

She snuck off to the kitchen area and tucking herself between the swinging doors, she counted to one minute in her head, and then burst out dramatically with a concerned and upset look on her face.

Rushing to Rachel's side, Terri kneeled before her friend and took her hands in her own. 'Rachel, please tell me that you did not eat the appetiser.'

'What? But of course I ...' Rachel looked at her friend, absolutely baffled. But as she saw Terri's head bob a quick yes, she realised this was her cue to play along. 'Yes – yes I did. Why, what's wrong?'

'Oh no, I just found out that the mushrooms were porcini,

and you're allergic, of course.' She eyed her friend meaning-fully. 'Look at your hands – they're already swelling. And your face is getting puffy.' Rachel gave her a disapproving look on the last bit. 'We'd better get you back to your room to lie down for a bit. Gary can keep things going here.'

Rachel's cousin Linda stood frowning. 'She looks fine to me. And, we have a big night planned for the bride after all.'

Rachel pretended her mouth was filling with cotton balls as she tried to talk. She feigned swelling fingers and strug-gled to pull at her engagement ring as Terri led her out of the doors and to the hotel elevators, as Gary returned, just in time to miss them.

'That was brilliant,' Rachel laughed once they were safely out of earshot.

'Come on. It's your last night as a single woman, and I plan on giving you a night to remember.'

They hurried to Terri's hotel room where she and Rachel were greeted with a large bottle of champagne and two toasting flutes. The room was lined with various truffles and desserts – all of Rachel's guilty pleasures.

Terri immediately headed for the champagne. 'Now, let's drink and be merry, for tomorrow you will be married!' She handed a glass to Rachel, and poured one for herself as well. The two friends clinked their glasses together, and quickly afterwards began to devour the exotic treats that Terri had selected especially for her friend.

A sound of an incoming message interrupted the background music and Terri went to the bedside phone to see who it was. Turning back, she proclaimed, 'Second stop time. Grab your bag. We're sneaking out.'

A black, stretch limo waited for them downstairs and they quickly got in and closed the door behind them. A perfect getaway. The driver retracted the overhead roof window as they sped away. Terri stood up and put her head through the opening, and Rachel joined her.

With a cool exhilarating breeze in their faces, they watched raptured as the streets of Manhattan passed them by. As per Terri's instructions, the limo toured down some of the city's most iconic landmarks, starting with Times Square. The almost endless neon lights and advertisements made Terri gasp.

Tourists and locals alike waved and shouted congratulatory wishes to them as they passed by and Rachel shouted, 'I'm getting married tomorrow!' Sounds of laughter filled the air, much of it coming from themselves.

Their next stop was at a famed restaurant on the Upper West Side, one that Rachel had been raving about for years, but had not been able to secure a reservation during their stay.

But she hadn't counted on Terri's persuasiveness or persistence. She had struck up an impromptu friendship with Jonathan the flamboyant designer, and using his Manhattan connections, and overblowing her and Rachel's status as renowned chefs back home, had arranged for the kitchen to set up a little private dessert tutorial, much to Rachel's delight.

The resident chef had set up a workspace just for them, as between courses he walked them through the steps of how to make the perfect macaroon, one of Rachel's favourites.

The two laughed at Terri when she as predicted, continually messed up the recipe. Rachel, however was focused and determined, just as she always was in the kitchen.

The American chef doled out great advice as they went: 'The trick to making a macaroon or indeed a man happy, is to be gentle, but firm. Both thrive under a light touch.'

Rachel giggled meaningfully at Terri and as the two finished and thanked the chef for their boxes of homemade macaroons, Terri checked her watch.

'Now, bride-to-be, we must get you home before you turn into a pumpkin. In the meantime, just sit back and enjoy the ride.'

Rachel was smiling as they sat back in the car and the nighttime streets flew by. 'For someone who was so dubious about New York, you seem pretty happy here.'

'Do you know what?' Terri replied teasingly. 'I *do* think this city is starting to grow on me.'

Chapter 23

The following morning, Rachel rolled over and checked the time on her phone. Nine a.m. She had already been awake for hours, laying in bed motionless, so as not to disturb Gary.

But more so she could dejectedly listen to the rain that was falling steadily from the sky, immediately turning her perfect, sunshine-filled Central Park wedding vision into a huge puddle of mush.

She grabbed her robe, bag, and wedding dress, and tip-toed out and over to Terri's room, as planned.

Once again, Gary had been out cold by the time she got back, and despite their differences, Rachel wanted to stick to the age-old custom that bride and groom should not see each other until the wedding. If she wanted to make that happen, she had to leave now before her fiancé woke up.

She knocked on her friend's door. 'Terri,' she whispered. 'It's me. Let me in.'

Before she could knock again, Terri threw open the door and thrust a freshly made mimosa at her. 'Well, good morning, lazybones. I thought you'd slept it out.'

Rachel was taken aback. Never in her life had she seen Terri rise from bed before at least ten. But her trusty bridesmaid was already fully dressed and ready to head off to the beauty salon, her own dress wrapped and ready to go.

She had even taken the liberty of ordering a light room-service breakfast for them both.

To Rachel's even greater surprise, she began listing off the day's agenda as if by heart. 'OK, so we have about an hour before Michelle meets us in the lobby. A car will be waiting to take us to the hair salon for twelve, and then a break for lunch before make-up. Then you get dressed.

And after that, the limo will arrive to take us to the venue, where the cousins-in-waiting will be … waiting for us. Then pre-ceremony photos of the bridal party. Then shortly after that, Gary arrives with his crew for their pictures …'

Rachel struggled for enthusiasm as she listened to Terri finish reeling off the agenda of a day she had spent so much of the last few years planning. She leaned against the window and stared out at the rain, which seemed to fall as heavily as her spirits.

She and Gary still hadn't had the chance to make up and talk over whatever was going on with him. He'd been fast asleep when she'd arrived in from her jaunt with Terri the night before, and while she worried now that perhaps she should have waited back this morning, it was too late now.

She just hoped that he would actually turn up today, given his recent withdrawal. What if the same thing was about to happen all over again? What if Gary wasn't truly serious about this wedding, like he hadn't initially been truly serious about their engagement?

He'd been railroaded into that through circumstance, but perhaps he felt railroaded into this too? With all her planning and organising and trying to make everything perfect over the last year, had she intentionally overlooked the fact that her husband-to-be wasn't quite as enthusiastic?

Rachel suddenly broke out in a cold sweat at the thought of being left alone at the altar. It was bad enough to be made a fool of over the engagement ring, but if Gary was about to do a last-minute runner before their perfect New York wedding, she didn't think she would be capable of bouncing back from that.

Terri tried to distract her as she laughed again over how they'd had to sneak into their rooms last night after running into Rachel's cousins escorting two guys wearing cowboy hats back to their rooms. Rachel had hidden behind a plant while Terri crouched below a room-service cart.

'Can you believe those two? You'd better be thanking me for years for getting you out of that mess—' Suddenly, Terri noticed just how preoccupied Rachel was.

She walked to the couch where her friend was perched and sat down beside her.

'What if he really doesn't want to marry me, Terri? What if it's happening again, but this time it's my own fault? This wedding ... you said yourself he hasn't been involved much, but I was enjoying myself too much in the planning of it all to really notice.'

Terri took her hands in her own and repeated a mantra to Rachel once again, 'Sweetheart, you're an amazing friend, a terrific person, and you will be a wonderful wife. Gary loves you and I have absolutely no doubt that he will be there today in Central Park, waiting for you with pride. What man wouldn't be?'

'I truly hope so. Because this – not just the location or the dress or all the other wedding-related palaver, but the second the man I love puts that ring on my finger – is my dream. *That's* the moment I always envisioned.'

'I know that, hon.'

'And I don't know ... I don't know if my heart can deal with being shattered all over again.'

'Rachel, trust me. That's not going to happen.'

But as Terri pulled her friend close for a reassuring embrace, she sorely hoped that what she was saying was true.

Was Gary truly onboard with the wedding?

She gulped, hoping and praying for her friend's sake, that lightning wasn't about to strike twice.

Chapter 24

A little later, the two friends headed downstairs to the lobby where the wedding planner was waiting for them.

Smiling widely and dressed in a pink Chanel two-piece, Michelle kissed them on both cheeks, took the garment bags from them and passed them to the driver with stern instructions on how to keep the dresses wrinkle-free.

She then turned back to the ladies with a determined look on her face. 'Before we go, I just wanted to warn you, Rachel, that there is a slight ... issue with the food.'

Rachel stopped short, her eyes widening. 'WHAT?'

'What kind of issue?' Terri asked.

'It's nothing. Nothing really. Just that some of our catering crew is out sick –some kind of ... summer flu apparently. My catering manager is calling in everyone they have, but I wanted to give you the heads-up in case you noticed the venue was looking a bit, well, understaffed.'

'Is that all?' Terri couldn't imagine it to be too hard to find a waiting staff at last-minute notice in a huge city like this.

'Also, because of the rain, we will have to shuttle your guests to the Boathouse in cars instead of through the park via horse-drawn carriage as arranged, which obviously presents a challenge in that they will need to walk the rest of the way in the rain from the closest park entrance. We will use umbrellas, of course.'

Rachel sighed but nodded. It couldn't be helped.

'And finally ...'

She hardly dared to ask, but Michelle's face gave it away, 'What else?'

'It seems the flowers are running late. They may not be on site in time. There's flooding in Jersey.'

'By late, you mean a little bit behind?' Terri asked. 'Surely they'll be there in plenty of time for the bride's arrival?'

A deeper sense of dread was very quickly creeping in.

Michelle patted Rachel's hand. 'I really can't say for sure, sweetie. But rest assured, I'm working on alternatives ...'

Before Michelle could say another word, Rachel opened the car door herself and slumped down on the back seat. What else could go wrong today?

First the rain, then the food and now the flowers?

And very possibly the groom ... her subconscious added, but Rachel didn't dare go there again.

As Rachel and Terri drove towards the salon, neither said a word about the rain, the flooding in New Jersey, or the catering 'bug'.

151

Instead, they tried to keep their minds off these mounting problems by chatting about random issues with the restaurant to pass the time while the hair stylist worked her magic on Rachel's dark locks.

'Any word on the review?' Rachel asked. 'Did Justin notice the critic come in while we were away?'

Terri bit her lip. With everything that was going on over the last couple of days, she'd all but forgotten about the dreaded restaurant critic.

'He didn't mention anything, but good to know that all is in hand while we were away.' In truth she couldn't wait to get back to Dublin, and return to Stromboli and the kitchen, the place where she felt most at home.

The hairdresser managed to recreate Rachel's inspiration pictures perfectly and without any struggle. Terri's errant curls presented much more of a challenge for her up-do, but a good two hours later, both women were coiffed to perfection.

And when after a short light lunch on site, the make-up artist spent a further hour or so on the bride's face, and placed the silver tiara on Rachel's head for the final touch, she swung the chair around so that she could face Terri.

'Absolutely perfect! This day is getting better by the minute. You look beautiful, Rachel. Stunning.'

It was true. Her friend looked sensational, like some kind of Mediterranean goddess, with her olive skin, huge almond-shaped eyes enhanced even further by the make-up artist's talent, and her full lips highlighted with the perfect shade of red. Rachel looked like she belonged in a bridal magazine herself, with her luscious locks twisted in a perfect knot upon her head.

All that was left now was for Rachel to get ready, Terri to put her on her dress, meet up again with Michelle and be on the way.

A stylist led Rachel to the back room to help her with the dress, while Terri quickly slipped into her own with minimum fuss.

'I think I'm ready,' she called out finally, and she stepped into the room as she watched the bride assess herself in the mirror.

Her dress was only partially zipped up, but she still looked so ... complete.

The image of her friend in her silk and lace gown – exactly as Rachel had so long envisioned – made Terri feel unusually overcome with emotion, and tears of joy began to fill the corners of her eyes.

'Don't you dare cry, Terri. You will ruin your make-up, and then I'll start and definitely ruin mine. You don't want to have to sit through another couple of hours in front of that mirror, do you?'

Terri carefully blinked and sniffled, 'I won't. I won't. I'm sorry. I promise. It's just ... wow.' She went to work zipping up the rest of the dress and then tying the delicate lace bodice together.

When she finished, she placed her arm on Rachel's shoulder and looked at her through the mirror's reflection. 'I think you're ready, sweetheart. Are you ready?'

An almost eerie calm settled over Rachel as the realisation of where she was and what she was doing came over her like waves. Whatever happened, she would face it. With her best friend beside her, it was always easier to feel like she could take on the world.

'Yes, I'm ready.' She moved regally out of the room as the various stylists all stared at her in awe. The make up artist handed Terri a kit of touch-up lipstick and blush and embraced the bride for luck.

The car waited closely by the kerb, and the driver retrieved his largest umbrella to cover Rachel as she walked to the open door. Terri remained clutching Rachel's train, preventing it from touching the wet pavement. Waste of time sitting there for two hours, she grimaced, wincing at the inevitable damage to her hair-do.

Damn you, rain.

Chapter 25

Once they had arrived at the Boathouse, and met up with the rest of the bridal party (Rachel's cousins looking decidedly green) in a quiet room set apart from the wedding venue, the photographer began work on the bride's pre-ceremony photographs.

Michelle had confessed that the flowers were still absent and Terri could make out the planner on the phone with her contacts as she screamed about 'solutions' and 'professionalism'.

Despite it all, Rachel still remained calm. She posed for each photograph with a winning smile, just as instructed. She didn't try to micromanage anything or wasn't overly concerned when each of her cousins periodically rushed off to the bathroom.

She simply smiled her beautiful, picture-perfect Rachel smile and played the model bride she had always dreamed she would be.

Yet behind it all, Terri could see the worry on her face. She wished she'd had the presence of mind to pop down to Ethan's room earlier and ask him how the conversation with Gary had gone last night.

Or that she'd chosen to keep his mobile phone number in her contacts, instead of deleting it the year before, when she'd so determinedly deleted him and Daisy from her life.

But it wasn't until other guests started to arrive that Terri noticed Rachel's composure truly begin to crumble.

She began pacing back and forth while waiting to hear news of the groom's arrival. Her hands twisted her white bridal gloves till they became almost too wrinkled to wear.

Every knock on the door made her jump out of her seat, as she hoped to hear confirmation from Sean, the best man, that it was time to start.

Following one particularly sharp knock though, Terri rushed to answer it.

Her stomach dropped when she saw Gary waiting nervously behind it.

His hands were clasped firmly behind his back as he rocked back and forth on his heels. Without raising his eyes, he asked quietly. 'Can I talk to her?'

Oh no ...

Terri's stomach filled with dread. This didn't sound good. Not good at all. Was Gary seriously thinking of chickening out? He couldn't do that, surely? But she had always known that Gary was a funny fish and there was no question that she herself had always wondered ...

'You do know it's bad luck to see the bride before the wedding, don't you?' she challenged, her eyes flashing.

'Leave it, Terri. Just let me talk to her.'

Rachel appeared behind her, as if out of nowhere. She could see from the ashen look on her friend's face that she too expected the worst.

'I ... I'll go check on the flowers.'

With that, Terri stole out of the room to give the bride and groom a moment alone.

Her heart was in her mouth as she did so, barely noticing her surroundings as she sent a prayer to the wedding gods or who-ever it was that decided such things as happily ever after ...

Please, please let everything be OK.

But suddenly Terri looked around, and seeing the wedding venue for the first time, and the incredible love and care Rachel must have put into creating her vision, she wanted to cry.

It was perfect.

Gary joined Rachel in the room, his hands still firmly placed behind his back.

He finally had a moment to see her, truly see her in the wedding dress, and the breath was instantly knocked out of him as he slowly walked to her side.

He could hardly take his eyes off her in her white, delicate gown. She looked like some kind of Italian princess, way too good for the likes of him.

'Wow. You look amazing.'

She looked confused, and he realised, a little terrified. 'I

157

needed to tell you something, something I realised after our ... chat the other night.'

'Gary ...' Rachel breathed, refusing to meet his eyes. 'Just say it. Don't drag it out please. This is hard enough as it is.'

He sighed. 'I'm sorry, but this is hard for me.' He paused again, noticing that even though she looked perfectly immobile, her hands were shaking. 'When you started to talk about having children over the last while, it took me by surprise a bit to be honest. I want kids, yes, but first and foremost I want to be your husband.'

'I know that, and I shouldn't have ... I couldn't help ...'

'Look, you and I have come a long way these past few years, and there's been a few ups and downs along the way.' He reached for her hand, and softly caressed the Tiffany diamond on her finger.

Rachel stared down at it as if her heart would break.

'The problem is, I'm still a bit of a kid myself – I'm sure you know that better than anyone. And I'm not ... when the time comes, I want us both to be ready, so that you don't end up shouldering all of the burden.'

Rachel studied his face. He seemed completely sincere, and she couldn't believe that the root of his anxiety was ultimately that he was afraid of becoming a father because he himself was still immature. It was a big admission for a macho Irish guy like Gary, and she couldn't believe he was actually saying this.

But oh, how wonderful that it didn't seem to have sent him running for the hills!

Rachel would wait, she would wait until Gary felt he was ready, until he gave the signal, and in the meantime she would just enjoy being his wife and sharing his life – being a family, just the two of them.

Just then, a knock came at the door and Gary pulled away to answer it.

'Guess what? Michelle pulled it out of the fire!' Terri stood outside, two bouquets of blue and white flowers in her arms. She glanced quickly at Rachel to try to gauge the reaction and smiled, giving her a brief nod. Her friend's relief was palpable and she visibly exhaled. So she hadn't been overreacting; Terri had been worried too.

'Get your ass out of here, Gary Knowles,' her friend joked, hustling him out the door. 'Everyone's arrived.'

Standing up, Gary kissed Rachel's forehead. 'See you out there,' he whispered, slipping out front.

'What was all that about?' Terri studied Rachel for any signs of distress, but instead, she saw a woman bursting with joy.

She giggled to herself as she took the bouquet out of Terri's hands and stood in front of the doorway, readying herself for her big moment.

'They got it wrong. Turns out it *is* good luck to see the groom before the wedding. The guests are in, the flowers are here, and look,' she added, pointing to the window, 'the rain has stopped.' Rachel hooked her arm in her bridesmaid's. 'Showtime.'

Chapter 26

The Central Park Boathouse had been transformed into a fantasy wonderland.

Inside, hanging fairy lights trailed across the old wooden beams, and white wildflowers seemed to spring naturally from carefully concealed window boxes by the lake.

Tiny candles lit the aisle where Rachel and Terri, followed by the cousins, walked slowly up to where Gary waited proudly, Sean by his side, in front of the huge floor-to-ceiling windows overlooking the water.

Outside, on the lake, hundreds more floating lanterns illuminated the slowly darkening park surrounds, and gave the trees a magical ethereal quality, the lights of Manhattan twinkling in the distance all around.

The ceremony went off without a (further) hitch as Rachel Conti and Gary Knowles pledged their everlasting love for one another, acknowledging in their wedding vows the happy couple's rocky beginnings, much to the amusement of their guests, especially Ethan.

Afterwards, as the happy guests posed for photos, Terri watched Rachel and Gary, married at last. She was so happy for her friend – Rachel was beaming, her smile was practically another light in itself as all her dreams had finally come true. Gary seemed transfixed by his wife too, she noted happily. He couldn't bear to let go of her hand or let her out of his sight.

Whatever the hell Ethan had said to him last night had obviously worked.

Speaking of Ethan, he and Daisy had greeted Terri briefly after the ceremony, but had deftly avoided her ever since.

She supposed she couldn't blame him. Though she'd tried to rationalise what had happened between them the other night as merely down to the champagne or the romantic location, she knew that she should not have let her guard down and risked disappointing him once again.

And he was disappointed, Terri knew that. She could sense the annoyance and hurt in his eyes when she'd brushed him off so easily last night, pretending that the kiss had meant nothing, when of course it had meant everything.

But what was the point? They were going around in circles. As far as she was concerned, nothing had changed. Circumstances dictated that any relationship they might even consider was doomed.

In so many different ways.

So they might as well be adults about it and just move on.

Feeling somewhat empty despite her oh-so-mature decision-making, Terri stood up and slipped silently away from the celebrations and onto the darkened wooden promenade outside.

She would not be missed. The bridesmaid was surplus to requirements now, at least until dinner toast time.

Alone, with only the city skyscrapers towering above her in this remarkably peaceful spot right in the heart of the city, Terri had the perfect opportunity to enjoy the peace and reflect on her few days here.

She leaned across the wooden arm rail, out towards the black lake, careful not to get her dress wet or to catch the hem in one of the still-lit lanterns.

A burning bridesmaid would not be quite the best ending to Rachel's dream day.

She caught herself remembering her own stroll through the park and the zoo with Ethan and Daisy a couple of days before. How on her first sight of the lake earlier, she'd been convinced that the park was some kind of magical, transformative forest where perhaps fairy tales did happen.

At least, they happened for women like Rachel.

She, on the other hand, was back at square one.

A door closed quietly behind her as she saw some of Gary's motorbike mates stroll outside for a smoke, completely unaware of her presence. They held on to little white plates of canapés, the ones she had hand-picked with Rachel a few days before. The caterer had managed to pull it off despite the flu and the rain.

Behind them was none other than Ethan. She acknowledged him as he caught her eye and then turned her attention back to the cool, clear waters lapping at the side of the building.

He spoke first, clearing his throat awkwardly, 'That was beautiful.'

'It really was, wasn't it?' Terri could do small talk. And she was glad that he sounded back to normal and not so annoyed with her as he'd seemed last night.

'*You* look beautiful.'

He had spent the entire wedding staring at Terri in her blue, strapless gown, his gaze not on the bride but completely transfixed by the chief bridesmaid and how her hair seemed to glow like fire under the twinkling lights.

She turned to him, her lips forming a small grin, despite herself. 'Thank you. It's this ridiculously expensive replacement dress.'

She wasn't quite sure how to handle this. She thought she'd already made it clear that the other night was a mistake and that they should just be friends, yet here he was again talking in this undecidedly non-friendly way.

'Ethan ... I ...'

He knew he had to do something, so as not to scare her away. 'I'm sorry, I know I shouldn't say things like that. Daisy would kill me.'

Terri laughed. 'Daisy? Why?'

'Oh, she thinks I'm too obvious, desperate even. She's trying to teach me how to play it cool.'

She smiled. This sounded just like an older ten-year-old Daisy, and not the little girl desperately chasing fairy tales of a few years before.

'But speaking of Daisy, our flight's due to leave at lunchtime tomorrow and she wanted me to ask you if you'd like to meet for breakfast in the morning. There's this special place she likes that she wants to show you.' He laughed lightly. 'Apparently no visit to New York is complete without it. You know how she is. So what do you think? Say ten? Which is actually two in the afternoon in real life, so not too early.'

She had to laugh at the way he always referred everything back to UK time. It certainly made the idea of getting up tomorrow morning and going out somewhere for breakfast more palatable.

Terri thought about it. Why not? She hadn't had much of a chance to spend time with Daisy actually, and she didn't think a goodbye breakfast with her and her father would hurt anyone.

If anything it might help persuade Ethan that being grown up and rational about this whole thing was for the best.

A knock from Gary at the window interrupted them then, and Terri and Ethan went back inside to take their seats for dinner.

Smiling, Rachel handed Terri a glass of champagne and whispered into her ear. 'We'll talk about *that* later. Now, we're waiting on you for the first toast.'

Terri took her place at the top table and waited for the

microphone to be passed to her. She looked at the little speech she had written down a few weeks earlier, but today, the words didn't seem right.

As the spotlight turned on her, she stood up, looking down at Gary and then at a beaming Rachel. And the words came to her:

'Friends and family, on behalf of the bride and groom I want to first thank you for coming all this way to celebrate the wedding of Rachel and Gary. I have known Rachel for so many years. First as classmates, then as best friends, and also now business partners. I have seen every side of her, from the good to the ... not so good, as no one could ever describe Rachel as having a bad side.' Everyone laughed as she continued, and she felt herself relax a little.

'When I first heard that Gary had proposed in New York with an amazing Tiffany's diamond ring ...' she winked first at Gary, who looked sheepish and then at Ethan, who smiled knowingly, 'I thought – well, he had to have stolen it.' Rachel burst out laughing and Gary reddened.

Terri moved over and patted him on the shoulder. 'But of course, what I'd overlooked was that it wasn't the ring that mattered, it was the sentiment, the promise he was making, of happy ever after.

'And today I'd like to thank Gary for making good on that promise, and making my best friend the happiest I've seen her in a very long time.' Her voice softened a little as her gaze rested on her friend. 'And no one deserves – or values, happiness more than Rachel. It's a longstanding joke between us that she's the daydreamer and I'm the practical one, and that's so true. And while it's useful to have a pragmatist like me to help bring a dreamer back down to earth sometimes, it is so much more rewarding to have someone whose head is constantly in the clouds, take you by the hand once in a while and show you that view.'

A lump came to her throat and tears shone in her eyes, as it came to her then that this is what Rachel, her wonderful sweet-natured friend had been doing for her all these years. The world was so much more interesting, so much happier seen through her eyes.

'Rachel, it is wonderful seeing you here with Gary – on your most perfect day exactly how you visualised it, and I am very proud to have been a part of it. And while I was, as always, a bit dubious ...' she added to raised laughter from her audience, 'about having to come all the way to New York to do so, I'm also beginning to understand why you love this city so much. Looking around here tonight, there is no question that this place has a certain magic.

'And it seems fitting that as it was a visit to New York that ultimately set you two on the path to happy-ever-after, that it should all come full circle right back where it all started. So tonight, I'd like to raise a glass to Gary, Rachel and their perfect New York wedding.'

Chapter 27

The following morning, having celebrated well into the evening with the newly-weds, a bleary-eyed Terri looked again at the address Ethan had given her last night, a little frustrated that he hadn't thought to include the name of the café at which he and Daisy were supposed to meet for breakfast.

Still, surely the taxi driver would know it, she decided, hailing a yellow cab with surprising ease. Huh, maybe she was a natural at this whole New York thing after all.

The guy smiled at Terri in his rear-view mirror when she asked if he recognised the address.

'Who doesn't?' he said cryptically, and she figured this place was obviously a well-trodden tourist hotspot.

Well, as long as the coffee was decent ...

She guessed she'd need a good dose of caffeine to get over the after-effects of too much champagne the night before.

Still it had been a wonderful night, and she was so happy

Rachel's dream wedding had, in the end, gone off without a hitch.

Apart from a couple of strange cowboys turning up at the Boathouse during the post-dinner party, that was. Terri couldn't believe her eyes when she saw Linda and Cora make a bee-line for two Stetson-wearing hunks who'd suddenly materialised at the entrance, and she and Rachel could only laugh as they realised the kind of hen-party antics they must have missed.

Today, the bride and groom were heading to the Caribbean for their honeymoon, and their guests were travelling home. Gary's mum was on the same flight back to Dublin later that day, and Terri didn't relish the thought of the older woman bending her ear for six straight hours.

The truth was, she didn't relish the idea of going home at all. She was eager to go back to the restaurant and get stuck back into the normal day-to-day, but for some reason the prospect wasn't filling her with as much enthusiasm as usual, though she couldn't deny that being in this big cosmopolitan city had been stimulating, and had re-energised her passion for what should happen next with Stromboli.

There was still no word from the critic, but whatever effect his assessment – good or bad – had on the business, Terri knew they would just have to live with it. And what if the review turned out to be great? She smiled, shaking her head. Again, she needed to take a leaf out of Rachel's book by trying always to look on the bright side.

Maybe at this point they needed to think about branching

out? Opening another venue, and creating a more recognisable brand? After all, if Chef Marco could get away with it ...

She laughed as she thought again about that night out with Ethan. She still wasn't quite sure how to feel about the last few days they'd spent in such close proximity. It had been wonderful spending time alone with him and there was no question they both still had feelings for one another, but ultimately what was the point?

They'd already been down that road and it still had the very same tricky bends and difficult crossroads. Besides, Ethan and Daisy were a unit – a family – and despite their best intentions, Terri could only ever be the third wheel.

Not to mention the difficulties that being in two different countries presented.

She was so lost in thought about the last few days that she hardly noticed the city streets fly by until eventually, the driver turned down a side street and pulled up in the midst of a busy shopping area that she hadn't come across before.

Looked pretty upscale too, Terri thought, taking in some high-end retail brand names, all of which were off the scale in terms of her price range.

Must be a pretty swanky café ...

'Here ya go – 727 Fifth Avenue,' the taxi driver said, turning back to her and Terri blinked in confusion.

She looked out the window. 'Where? I don't see any ...' And suddenly, looking up at the sign on the building immediately outside, she spotted something.

Tiffany & Co.

What on earth … ?

Distractedly paying the driver, Terri got out of the car and looked up and down the street. After a moment, she understood that this must be a side entrance to the store, just off Fifth Avenue.

Maybe there was a café inside – where they served the famed breakfast? As Terri struggled to figure out where she should go, a glittering display window caught her eye.

Those gems were beautiful, make no mistake.

She smiled as she remembered her speech from last night, thinking how strange it was to finally be at the place that had started everything for Gary and Rachel a couple of years before.

And ultimately for her and Ethan.

She shook her head, realising she'd had enough drama with diamonds from Tiffany's to last a lifetime, yet this was the first time she'd ever been anywhere near the store.

What was it, she wondered, drawn irresistibly towards the display, that made this place so special? The so-called 'magic' that Rachel had always so passionately espoused?

Back then, Daisy too was convinced that it was Tiffany's magic that had brought Terri and her father together, though it had to be said that this had happened in a rather roundabout way.

Just then, Daisy herself materialised suddenly alongside Terri's elbow, as if somehow thinking about the little girl had summoned her.

Closely followed by her father.

Both were holding disposable coffee cups and Daisy handed one to Terri.

'I didn't know Tiffany's did coffee,' she said.

'They don't,' Ethan replied, grinning.

'But imagine what it would be like if they did ...' Daisy piped up dreamily.

Terri was confused. Ethan had said they should meet for breakfast, so what were they doing here – of all places?

'So this is where it all began ...' she joked, a little nervously, immediately sensing that something was off kilter. 'Scene of the crime, and all that.'

'It certainly felt like that at the time,' Ethan agreed. 'A crime, I mean. But perhaps ultimately it was a blessing in disguise.'

'That's how it's supposed to work, Dad,' Daisy said, nodding. 'Fate. Things happen for a reason, but they always turn out OK in the end.'

Terri didn't know what to say, so she just sipped her coffee.

Good old Daisy. So she hadn't lost that wonderful little girl innocence after all.

She pointed to the jewellery in the window display. 'Look at those, Terri, aren't they beautiful? See how they sparkle.'

'Yes, lovely.' Terri glanced towards the display but quickly averted her gaze. She didn't want to be admiring diamond rings she would never have, from Tiffany's or otherwise.

'Daisy is fascinated by diamonds, especially about how

they come to be, aren't you, buttercup?' Ethan said fondly. 'The idea that something so simple could end up so dazzling and perfect is a source of wonderment to most of us, I suppose.'

'I suppose.' Terri was feeling decidedly uncomfortable now. She truly didn't know what was going on. Why this sudden lesson in gemstones? And what had happened to breakfast?

'Right.'

'At first it seems like a sort of alchemy,' Ethan continued, 'but then you realise that a diamond's perfection is not accidental, but the result of hard work, determination and absolute commitment to the craft. Not too unlike baking, actually.'

'I suppose.'

Now Ethan was looking directly at her. 'So how is it,' he said, 'that someone who is so dedicated to one kind of commitment can be so utterly terrified of another?'

'I don't understand ...'

'I think you do. You have more in common with the diamond-makers in this place than you realise, Terri. You're also acutely aware of flaws, and seek them out, placing a value judgement accordingly. But as much as I respect that pragmatism, and commitment to perfection, personally I'd take flaws every time. It's what makes something truly unique, after all. And for me at least, worth more than the most perfect diamonds in the world.' He moved closer to Terri, the intensity of his blue eyes mesmerising her even more than the sparkling diamonds nearby. 'You've pointed out more than once that our relationship was doomed – flawed – from the very beginning; by the distance, my past, the ghost of Jane. But why expect relationships – life even – to be perfect? That's not how it works, it's not even how it's supposed to work, isn't that right, Daisy?'

'Yep.' The little girl moved alongside Ethan and he put his arm around her.

Terri thought father and daughter looked so perfect together, so right ... and yet incomplete.

And taken with his words, it struck her right then that perhaps she had let Ethan and Daisy down, had been so focused on this notion of a perfect family situation that she had failed to see the beauty in what they actually had.

Terri looked again at the flawless Tiffany diamonds twinkling under the lights, a beauty that promised perfect romance and happy ever after, and suddenly she understood what he was trying to say.

The real magic of Tiffany's was not in the products, but in the sentiment, the *promise* behind the gesture. This was what repeatedly cast a spell on everyone who encountered that little blue box. It wasn't about the diamonds, it was about the promise of a dream. Something she herself had pointed out only the night before in her wedding toast to Gary and Rachel.

'We weren't perfect, Terri, I know that,' Ethan was saying. 'But we were good together before and I know we can be again – if you just give us a chance.'

'I don't ...'

'Please, Terri,' Daisy put in. 'We both love you, and we never expected you to be perfect. Dad certainly isn't; he put his socks in the white wash last week and turned all his work shirts pink.' She giggled. 'I think that colour suits him, though.'

A lump came to Terri's throat then, and she had to smile at the idea of Ethan wearing pink at his lectures.

But was he right? Was she guilty of perfectionism? She knew she could be like that with the restaurant, and was often frustrated that Rachel couldn't apply the same exacting standards to her work as she had to the wedding preparations.

Yet for all her friend's dreaminess and distractedness, she remained the far better chef.

Had she let such expectations cloud her vision in all aspects of her life? Had Terri's pragmatism ensured that, unlike her best friend, she never allowed herself to dream, allowed herself to take a chance on nothing more than a possibility?

Now as she stood in the middle of New York outside one of the most famous romantic locations in the world, and across from the only man she had ever truly loved, Terri realised how wrong she'd been.

True, happy ever after wasn't about expecting perfection – it was about overcoming obstacles and accepting flaws. It was, as Ethan had pointed out all along, just taking each day as it came.

She smiled as she moved towards Ethan and Daisy, allowing the two to encircle her in their arms, and as she did so, she allowed herself to give herself up to how good that felt.

Daisy was the first one to break the spell. She looked from Terri to her dad and then over towards the entrance to the Tiffany's store.

'So are we going inside now – or what?'

Ethan's eyes widened and Terri laughed. 'Hold your horses, honey. Like your dad said, one step at a time.'

There was one important thing those diamonds and her feelings for Ethan *did* have in common though, Terri realised, as finally she gave herself up to 'what if'.

Both were well and truly ... forever.

Fairy Tale on Fifth Avenue

Each day, at precisely 1 p.m. during her lunch break, Charlotte Thatcher goes to Tiffany & Co. on Fifth Avenue, New York and asks to see the same item: a pearl bracelet with a simple silver toggle that's just her style.

Though she hears the sigh the tall, vibrant young salesman releases each time she requests to hold it, she simply can't allow herself to buy it. The main reason for her hesitation is she knows that had her husband Eric still been alive, he would have bought it as a Christmas present for her. He'd promised her as much only weeks before he died.

That was two long years ago and the very thought keeps her from following through with the transaction, because in some way, she knows that purchasing the bracelet herself will mean Eric is truly gone.

Today, Charlotte wakes up to prepare a full breakfast for herself before grabbing a pumpkin-flavoured coffee and heading into a stressful but fulfilling day of work, full of dis-satisfied clients and long morning meetings.

At 12:55 p.m., she leaves as she does every day to walk across to Fifth Avenue. She notices the Christmas wreaths, sparkling lights and pretty snowflakes decorating the shops and streets more than usual today, and she suspects this is due to the fact that Christmas is edging closer.

As Charlotte examines the bracelet again today, something is different. With a slight shift of her gaze, she notices that someone else seems interested in the piece too. She can feel the man's eyes on the pearls, though he seems to be keeping a respectful distance. Either way, she knows she must relin-quish her hold on the bracelet so that the potential buyer can get a look at it. She places the pearls on the counter carefully, shifting her anxious gaze downwards. She trudges out of the store with a glimpse back at the customer – a tall, attractive, dark-haired man with a somewhat pointy nose and rather toothy grin. He notices her looking so she hurries out.

The rest of the day at the office goes by at a snail's pace, with Charlotte fearful about the bracelet's fate. She tries to take her mind off it by concentrating on what holiday treats she should prepare when she gets home. Usually she doesn't indulge, but Christmas is a special time of the year. And she needs something to occupy her thoughts other than the bracelet and whether or not it is now lost to her forever.

The next day again at precisely 12:55 p.m., Charlotte heads out of the door for her lunch break, grabbing a pret-zel from a street vendor on the way to Tiffany's. Today she feels even more tense and nervous, and just before she reaches the door to the store, it begins to rain. She hastily reaches into her brown handbag for her umbrella and as she begins to unfold it, she catches a glimpse of someone out of the corner of her eye. It's the man from yesterday.

Charlotte gets a closer look at him this time as he enters the store, and he's certainly intriguing. She might even consider him to be her type, if she even had a 'type' any more.

She holds back once she goes inside, contemplating if she should skip looking at the bracelet today. The stranger is already at the display case and examining it, a haunted look in his eyes. She hesitates behind him and turns to walk away, thinking that she'll just come back later, but as soon as she's walked back out, releasing a long sigh, the man is by her side. He gives her a complicit smile and says: 'I'm done now if you'd like to look.'

'That's OK. I can see it another day,' Charlotte says, gazing down and shuffling her feet. When she finally glances up, the stranger is looking at her intently.

'I'm sorry for prying, and you certainly don't have to answer,' he says, 'but what makes you come back here so often? Because I know I've seen you here a few times before.'

Charlotte is taken aback. 'I'm not sure ... I guess it's just a way to remember,' she replies truthfully.

'I know what you mean; it's the same with me,' the man says, glancing at her. 'Look, I know this is forward,' he begins, his voice hesitant, 'but are you doing anything now? Maybe you'd like to grab a coffee or ...'

'I'd love to,' Charlotte replies, the words out of her mouth before she realises it. *Coffee with a stranger? This is so unlike me!* 'Where would you like to go?'

'There's a great place right up the street. They have amazing cakes and pastries, if you're interested. It is lunchtime, after all. My name is Vincent by the way.'

'Charlotte,' she says returning the introduction. 'Sounds good.' Her pretzel seems ages ago.

They walk slowly to the coffee shop/bakery, a place called The Cookie Jar, sneaking glimpses at each other from time to time while making small talk. On the way, Charlotte discovers that Vincent owns a small business, which he is rather vague about. The cashiers at the bakery seem very friendly, and Charlotte notices one giving Vincent somewhat coy glances. They indulge in chocolate chip cookies and drinks comprised of half coffee/half hot chocolate to keep warm. Charlotte has stopped in here a few times before to grab a quick mocha to go, but finds she is much more content spending time in the warm, squashy armchairs.

Charlotte and Vincent begin to chat about their situations and discover that the bracelet from Tiffany's actually has deep meaning for both of them. Charlotte can't help but feel an overwhelming sense of empathy when he tells her that he lost his wife three years ago to cervical cancer. His wife Ruth had wanted a classic bracelet like this one more than anything, but her illness had been sudden and short and Vincent hadn't been able to buy it for her before it was too late. Charlotte tells him about Eric, and they exchange mutual stories about how it feels to be so very alone so quickly.

Soon after, the conversation turns to more pleasant topics, such as hobbies and interests, movie preferences and favourite authors. All of a sudden, her lunchtime is over before she knows it. Usually a stickler for punctuality, Charlotte can't help but call into the office and ask for her afternoon meetings to be rescheduled for tomorrow. She asks Vincent what time he needs to be back, at which point he looks over at the cashier and calls out, 'I dunno, Elise; what time do you think I should be back at work?'

The woman grins and shrugs. 'You're the boss.'

Which is how Charlotte discovers that the modest, handsome stranger she's been talking to is the owner of the cutest Manhattan bakery she's ever had the joy of visiting.

'Hey,' Vincent says winking, 'You wanna get out of here? I think I've been on the clock long enough today.'

'And just where are you taking me?'

'You'll have to see,' he grins. 'You like Christmas, right?'

'I certainly used to,' she replies, completely taken by this man she barely knows, yet with whom she feels an immediate kinship.

They end up walking about ten minutes or so, and though Charlotte's high-heeled feet are aching even in that short period of time, and her business suit certainly isn't protecting her from the biting winter chill, she knows she hasn't felt this comfortable in years. When they finally stop outside Rockefeller Center, her heart nearly melts when Vincent asks if she'd be interested in seeing a 2:30 showing of the Radio City Christmas Spectacular, one of her favourite Christmas traditions. Or used to be, at least.

She feels positively giddy as they wait for the curtains to open. Vincent looks excited as well, his eyes twinkling like a child who's about to receive a present. When the show finally starts, it seems to swirl by in bursts of colour, music, and movement, and Charlotte reminds herself to remember this moment for years to come.

By the time the show is nearing its end, Charlotte and Vincent are holding hands. He throws her a coy, questioning glance before brushing her fingertips, to which she gladly assents. Tonight, Charlotte doesn't take a cab home. She lets Vincent walk her all the way to her studio apartment in the West Village. She even lets him kiss her goodnight, and she goes to bed feeling happier than she has in years.

Charlotte and Vincent continue spending time together every other night or so for the next three weeks. They do all the traditional 'date' things, like going to the movies and out to dinner, but Vincent also invites her to go rock climbing at the indoor sports centre he is a member of. Truthfully, Charlotte isn't very good at it, but she enjoys watching Vincent climb to the ceiling on the indoor walls. He's also an excellent chef, which she doesn't find all that surprising since he owns a bakery, until she finds out that it was his departed wife's love of all things sugar that led to the bakery owner-ship. He can whip up an amazing pasta dish, though.

Four days before Christmas, Charlotte is doing some last-minute packing before hitting the road to her parents' house in Albany the next morning when she receives a text message from Vincent that simply says: *Go to the place where you shouldn't get your hand caught.*

Easy enough, Charlotte thinks with a smile. The Cookie Jar. Why does he want her to meet him there? To say goodbye perhaps.

She leaves a few items left to pack on her bed and heads out of the door to catch a cab. Instead of searching for a taxi, however, she finds a horse-drawn carriage outside her building, with a curious sign on the side door. It simply says: 'For Charlotte. Merry Christmas, Vincent.'

Wondering why he thinks she would ever want to take a carriage ride alone when she could be with him, Charlotte clambers aboard all the same. The driver seems to know where to go, so it seems her earlier clue-solving skills are in vain. When she reaches The Cookie Jar, she sees Vincent approach the carriage door with an umbrella. 'It may not be raining,' he said, 'but snow can be a bother as well.'

'Thanks,' Charlotte laughs, 'but what am I doing here?'

'That's for me to know and you to figure out,' he says coyly, his eyes twinkling. 'What's colourful yet evergreen?' he asks then. 'Go to a place where it's closest to the sky.'

Delighted by the prospect of an impromptu scavenger hunt, Charlotte thinks for a moment. 'The tree at Rockefeller Center?'

They arrive in time to see a large group of small children carolling beneath the towering Christmas tree. Vincent wraps his arms around Charlotte from behind, giving her quick kisses on the neck. In absolute bliss she asks 'So is there another clue?'

'Of course. Now we go to a place where you are likely to fall, yet most likely to fly.'

She thinks again for a moment. 'Hmm ... this one's a little trickier, but I think I got it.' She smiles and looks down at the ice rink. 'I'm thinking we'll need some skates?'

'Wow, you're good! Come on then.'

Vincent pulls her gently out onto the rink, and looks at her intently with his deep hazel eyes. Then he takes a small rectangular box out of his pocket, which Charlotte immediately recognises. She gasps, not because of the blue Tiffany box or what's inside, but because of what it represents.

'Merry Christmas,' Vincent says, gently opening the box and Charlotte's eyes fill with bittersweet tears.

The pearl bracelet is finally hers. Their spouses might be lost, yet somehow this special bracelet has given her and this lovely man another chance at love.

Winter Wonderland

Dakota absentmindedly turned her taxicab down Sixth Avenue.

The Avenue of the Americas as it was officially named was bustling as always, even more so now that it was noon and many of the business executives who inhabited the sparkling glass buildings were spilling out into the street in search of lunch.

Dakota turned to her co-pilot, sprawled out on the passenger seat. Scratching behind his long, fuzzy ears, she said with a sigh, 'Here we go again, Thor, *another day, another dime.*'

Thor looked up at the petite blonde with his eternally sad eyes and wagged his tail.

'Here, let's adjust those silly reindeer antlers,' she said in the soothing voice she reserved for her favourite Basset hound. 'I know that goofy head gear is slightly emasculating but I do think that the big red bow tied around your collar really brings out the highlights in your fur.'

Thor yawned.

'The important thing is that the tourists love you. We are the epitome of all that is good and right about New York City, my friend. Where else can shoppers wind down after a long day at Macy's with a ride in a festive, holiday taxicab complete with a musically talented Basset?'

She offered him a piece of the string cheese she was nibbling on.

'Honestly, singing carols along with our passengers was one of the best ideas I've ever had. Can you believe the tips we're getting? People are actually disappointed when we get them to their destinations quickly,' she said, smiling down at the dog.

Her cell phone began playing the opening notes of Beethoven's 5th Symphony. She groaned and said, 'And that would be my mother calling, no doubt to remind me that I am far from home and without marital prospects as yet another Christmas season shifts into high gear.'

She paused mid-rant as she angled the taxi toward a man standing on the kerb, hailing her cab with a raised hand.

'I've told her a hundred times that you are the only boy for me, Thor. Who else would put up with a broke, guitar-wielding, organically grown flower child?' she went on as she allowed voicemail to answer her mother's call.

The dog thumped his tail on the seat in agreement as their latest fare opened the cab door. Dakota glanced at the pre-occupied man through the steel grate that separated the front and back seats. He was good looking with a muscular build that filled out his Armani suit nicely.

This job definitely has its perks, she thought to herself.

'Where to?' she asked, aloud.

'Katz's Deli on East Houston,' he answered as he placed his briefcase on the seat beside him. He looked up and found himself face-to-face with the hound that had hoisted his antlered head onto the back of the seat and let it rest, smashed against the grate.

The man's sudden start and subsequent burst of laughter frightened Thor who bayed loudly and jumped back down into the front seat.

'Hey, quit harassing my ferocious guard dog,' Dakota said in mock sternness. 'Now that you've frightened him, he probably won't sing Christmas songs with you.'

For the first time, the man looked about the festively decorated cab, heard the holiday soundtrack and looked into the rear-view mirror at the smiling, violet-blue eyes of the cab driver.

He smiled, 'I regret to inform your dog that I don't sing.'

'It's required of everyone who rides in this cab, mister,' she chided. 'Now pick a song or Thor will do it for you.'

'You didn't let me finish,' he responded. 'I was going to say that I don't sing with *strangers*.'

He then bowed slightly and said, 'Allow me to introduce myself. My name is Nick Marshall.'

Dakota caught his eye in the mirror, grinned and replied, 'Pleased to meet you, Mr Marshall. I am Dakota Raine. And yes, that is my legal name,' she said before he could ask. 'It's a slightly awkward reference to the location and weather conditions at the time of my conception. If you guessed that my parents were into protests, pot and free love, you would be correct.'

She turned up the volume on the all-Christmas-music-all-the-time radio station.

'OK, now that we are properly acquainted, let's hear it,' Dakota said encouragingly.

'I have to warn you that I possess a limited vocal range,' he hedged. 'In fact, some people might even say my voice is uncommonly flat.'

'I'll be the judge of that,' she told him as she further cranked up the volume.

Together the cab's occupants joined Andy Williams who was crooning, *Sleigh bells ring, are you listening?*

Dakota pulled the cab to the kerb in front of Katz's as the trio howled and sang their way through the song's final notes, '... walkin' in a winter wonderland!'

Dakota was laughing as she told him, 'Whoever suggested that you lack musical talent obviously knew what he was talking about.'

'You can't say I didn't warn you,' he declared as he opened the door and stepped out. He held out his fare and a generous tip through her open window. Fat, heavy snowflakes had started to fall from the grey December sky.

'Thanks for the lift. You and your dog are definitely two in a million,' said a grinning Nick Marshall. Although he couldn't sing, his voice gave her goosebumps just the same.

Trying not to blush, Dakota responded, 'You'd better hurry inside, your hair is turning white.'

He brushed the snow off of his head and said, 'Hey, if you're looking for a fare around seven-thirty tonight, I could use a lift home.'

'I'm sorry,' she told him. 'Honestly, I'd love to but I have a date ...'

He smiled in an effort to hide his disappointment. 'I should have known that a lady as lovely as yourself would have a full social calendar.'

She shook her head and smiled back. 'Not that kind of date. I'll be playing my own crazy mix of indie-soul music over at Think Coffee in the West Village,' she told him, just as a car horn started blaring behind her. 'Oops, gotta go! I'm double parked. It was great carolling with you,' she hollered out of the window as she reluctantly pulled away.

Later, near midnight, Dakota was saying goodnight to an appreciative coffee house audience. As she turned to grab her guitar case stashed behind the stage, a deep voice from behind her asked, 'What? No back-up singer tonight?'

Dakota looked up into Nick Marshall's smiling face. She feigned indignation and responded, 'No dogs allowed. Something about "health code violations". Can you believe it?'

'Most distressing,' he agreed and continued, 'I'd offer to buy you a cup of coffee but this place appears to be closing. Care to join me for a sandwich at the bar down the street?'

'Perfect timing,' she answered, grabbing her guitar case. 'I'm starving.'

They walked unhurriedly down the street. The late-night date continued on into the early morning as they sat across from each other at a window booth, enjoying wine and conversation.

'So, you still haven't told me, Ms Raine, what brought you all the way from Iowa to the Big Apple?' Nick asked.

Dakota shrugged and looked at snow falling outside the window, glittering in the dim bar light.

'This probably sounds corny,' she said, turning her violet-blue eyes to meet his gaze. 'I came here to make a difference with my music. I've been writing and singing ever since I can remember and there's nothing that can describe the feeling I get when I make a connection with another person through a song. The right lyrics at the right time can strip people down to their bare souls, you know?'

She looked at him earnestly, wondering if she had bared too much of her own soul to this man she had met only hours ago.

He reached for her hand. 'Dakota Raine, you *do* have a gift for moving people with your music,' he told her. 'Look, I am not a spontaneous man. I start each day with a plan of action which I always execute fully before I allow myself to sleep at night. I have a phone stuck to my ear 24/7 because I like to think I am important and in demand.' He continued, still holding her gaze, 'I do not sing of snowmen and Parson Brown with cabbies and their hounds. And I most definitely do not hang out in coffee houses hoping to get a date with the girl with the guitar even if she does happen to be gorgeous.'

She held her breath as he stopped to catch his.

'But here I am just the same, shirking responsibilities to sit in a semi-seedy joint in the wee hours of the morning, hoping a little of your magic will rub off on me.'

Dakota stood as she reached across the table to take his face in her hands. She closed her eyes and gave him a long, sweet kiss. He smelled of Vintage Black cologne and tasted of the fruity Merlot they had been sharing.

She pulled away reluctantly and sat back down.

'So now what, Mr Marshall?' she asked.

He took a deep breath and answered, 'Now I drive you home so *I* can go and contrive a means to sweep you off your feet tomorrow night,' he replied firmly.

'I can't wait to see what tomorrow brings,' she smiled.

Less than twenty-four hours later, during the final notes of her last set, Dakota once again anxiously scanned the faces in the crowded coffee shop. But the one person she hoped to see remained disappointingly absent.

Suddenly, she knew the whole thing had been too much like one of those silly chick flicks that she loved to watch but would never admit to enjoying. She looked down at her cream-coloured peasant blouse and her embroidered, flowing skirt as she flushed with anger and embarrassment. Had she really believed that a high society, Armani suit-wearing

191

businessman would leave behind the skyscraper world for a carolling cab driver?

'You're working in a *coffee* house, Dakota,' she reminded herself between clenched teeth. 'Time to wake up and smell it. The sophisticated Nick Marshalls of this world are but briefly amused by the earthy Dakota Raines.'

She shut her guitar case. 'What were you thinking?' she said aloud as she picked up the case. Then she quickly grabbed her coat and stuffed it under her free arm, unconcerned about protecting herself from the snowy wind that had been gusting all day between the tall buildings.

Dakota hurried past the small crowd of fans who had gathered to thank her for the night's music. She pushed open the coffee shop door and slammed directly into a broad chest.

'I'll spare you the, "we've got to stop running into each other like this" line,' Nick said, steadying her gently with his hands on her shoulders. 'I'm so disappointed that I couldn't be here earlier to listen to your beautiful voice, but I was delayed while attempting to persuade a white stallion to work past his quitting time.'

Dakota's mind was swirling. Two minutes ago she had been dismissing him and now here he was, as promised, taking her breath away with his good looks, his Vintage Black smell and his warm, strong hands holding her.

Nick flourished his arm grandly as he stepped aside. She saw behind him now, the white horse tethered to a white carriage. A small, elderly woman dressed in a tuxedo, tipped her black top hat to Dakota as she held open the door.

Dakota, who felt as if her mouth had been hanging open for too long, started laughing in disbelief. 'You did *not* just show up in a horse-drawn carriage!'

'Ladies first,' he responded, as he helped her in.

They sat close to one another, legs tucked under a thick blanket as the carriage rolled slowly through Central Park. The city lights reflected off the buildings and snow-covered landscape.

'I feel as if we're riding through a postcard,' Dakota said dreamily, as she gazed out of the window. She had her head on Nick's shoulder.

'It's a real winter wonderland, isn't it?' he asked her.

She smiled at his reference to the song that had drawn them together yesterday. 'There's certainly no lack of sleigh bells or glistening snow,' she agreed. 'Thanks so much for the grand tour. I'd say you earned an A+ in "Sweeping Her Off Her Feet 101".'

He shifted to face her as she lifted her head. 'Look, Dakota, as long as we are speaking in Christmas carol-ese, let me just take it to the next level of corniness, and tell you I've been conspiring with people in my line of work today.'

She looked at him, feeling curious. 'All you've really told me about your "line of work" is that you're a glorified paper-pusher. So tell me, what was the buzz around the water cooler today?'

He hesitated before answering, 'I may have understated

my position. The truth is, I've pretty much clawed my way to the top of the paper-pushing food chain. The water cooler sits in my huge corner office which boasts a million-dollar view of America's most vibrant city.' He paused as he tried to read her face. 'I'm telling you this, not to impress you with my resumé, but as a means of illustrating that I know my industry.'

'OK, I get it,' she told him, 'but what exactly *is* your industry?'

'Let me put it this way – last night when I heard you sing, I knew immediately that your voice is special. That's not a sappy sentimentality from a boy who is falling in love with a pretty girl. It's a professional assessment from a man who enjoys the view from his 28th floor glass office at Atlantic Records,' he finished and waited for her reaction.

Dakota couldn't help herself as she blurted, 'So, is that what this is all about? You're courting me like royalty because you think I can make you more money? This is how you built your career?' She felt as if the last twenty-four hours had been an emotional roller-coaster ride.

He responded calmly, 'I have no intention of making a dime from your singing. What I am trying to tell you is that I have spoken with a producer friend over at Virgin Records. I gave him the heads-up that you were playing tonight and suggested that he might want to listen in. Long story short, he visited the coffee shop this evening. What happens next is entirely between you and him,' he said as he reached for her hand.

'I don't think you are the type of girl who can be bought, Dakota. It's like I told you last night – when I'm with you, I feel something that I used to think was silly sentimentality. I wouldn't trade that for any number of additional zeros on my income statement.'

Dakota returned his soul-searching gaze for nearly a minute before she grinned and said simply, 'I'll bet you say that to all the girls.'

The carriage had slowed to a stop and the driver turned in her seat to ask loudly, 'What's next on the agenda, Prince Charming?'

Nick looked at Dakota and winked before answering the grandmotherly driver, 'Home.'

He took Dakota's hands and said, 'I'm pretty handy at flipping the switch that stokes a roaring blaze in my apartment's gas fireplace. Care to join me on the hearth for a nice chardonnay?'

Her kiss was all the answer he needed.

Lovelorn in Manhattan

As Alice walked through Central Park she could feel the snow on the end of her tongue, and for the first time in weeks she felt that things were beginning to get easier.

It was about time.

Harry had died in October. It had been six weeks from the diagnosis to the funeral. The apartment that they had spent two years setting up on the Upper East Side had not even been lived in. She had stayed there last night for the first time in the master bedroom, the one that Harry had painted a pretty tortoiseshell. She could remember each and every one of the items in the bedroom and the discussions and arguments they had had about them all. She felt closer to him there but the pain lay in her chest like a physical lump. It hurt so, so bad.

The snow in Central Park was now getting heavier but instead of heading home, she sat on a bench near the tree – their tree: the one against which he'd spontaneously kissed her that time during a walk here in the fall.

'I love you, Alice,' was all he had said, but it had been enough. The park was empty at this time of day, and apart from a few kids building a snowman, no one had passed by.

Last night in the bedroom, she had found the tickets for the concert in his best coat pocket. It was to have been a surprise for her this Christmas. The Beatles were to play at Carnegie Hall the following spring and Harry had been involved in setting up their tour.

'You've got to hear this group, they are the tops,' he'd told her and he was right, the up and coming English band were wonderful.

Just then a squirrel jumped through the snow and bounded up the tree to her left. She looked up at it and realised she'd never really appreciated how beautiful the tree was. From the top, a squirrel might be able to see all the way to Staten Island. Assuming the squirrel was interested in looking.

She smiled to herself as she walked over to it. The snow was falling harder and clinging to the bark. Alice pressed both hands into the snow, just like she and Harry had done up in the Catskill Mountains last winter.

She hugged the tree. It was nice to hug something. As she did so she noticed a small hole in the bark, one that was just large enough to fit a hand into. Alice had no idea why she did it, but she placed her hand in the hole, almost expecting to get bitten.

But instead she felt something else entirely. She pulled out a crumpled piece of paper which she quickly realised was not just a random piece of trash, but a letter. Alice went back to the bench, cleared some snow and sat down to read it.

H,

I waited for you, but once again you didn't turn up. I know I said some hurtful things for which I am sorry. I was just so scared of losing you. I don't understand why you won't leave him. If you tell him about us, we could be in London soon. This was why I wanted to see you, to tell you that the company has agreed that I should spend two years in the UK office. I said yes, because it would mean that we could be together and he would be out of our lives for good.

My heart is your heart. S xxx

Alice was pleased to see that there was still some love out there in the world. She sometimes felt that all love and hope had died with Harry. The world went on, life moved on. She decided to put the letter back where she had found it. There was some lucky, (if unhappily attached) person out there waiting on it.

Alice didn't return to the park for a few days. This was going to be her first Christmas without Harry and she didn't want to spend it with her family. So early Christmas week, she took the train to Poughkeepsie to visit her sister and then after a couple of days of trying not to argue, continued on to Albany to see her mother.

By the time she got back to the city and the park, just two days before Christmas, the snow was still lying on the ground. Alice embraced the solitude. She loved her mother but a few days had been more than enough.

She dared to visit the tree again and after looking around to make sure she wasn't being watched, she placed her hand in the hole. This time she pulled out two pieces of paper, one was the original letter and the other was something new.

You are beginning to worry me. It has now been three weeks since we last spoke and I don't think I can go on without a word from you. I think about you all day, I even dream about you. Please, please, get in touch.
S. x

That night when Alice got back to her apartment some of Harry's work friends came round for a visit. It was good to have company and it was even better to be able to talk about Harry properly, not the skating around the subject that her mother and sister seemed to indulge in.

However, as the night wore on, her mind began to drift back to the letters. She wondered who the couple were, how old they might be and why were they leaving notes for each other in a tree in Central Park. Perhaps this was just a quick distraction for one of them but it seemed the other had invested significantly more in the relationship.

'More coffee?' asked Jim, Harry's oldest friend.

Alice shook her head.

'You seem to be somewhere else tonight, though I guess that's understandable,' he added gently.

'I'm sorry,' apologised Alice. 'I've been to see my mother and the travelling has taken a toll ...'

'No need to say anything. I'll round up the rest of the guys and we'll let you be.'

Jim was always her favourite of all Harry's pals. He understood, and was sensitive.

When the apartment was hers once more, she went to the study, the one that Harry had intended to use at weekends.

Then, not entirely sure what she was doing or why, Alice started to write a note.

I am so sorry that I have taken so long to reply. He has started to get suspicious and he follows me around. I know I must tell him but please give me a few more days.

She had no idea why she was doing this. Perhaps she didn't want to let 'S' down? Or maybe she had done it for herself.

She could only hazard a guess as to when that second letter had been placed in the tree. It might have been early morning or late at night – perhaps on the way to or from work.

So Alice took the safe option and went to the park in the early afternoon. As always there was no one around, so she removed the two letters from before and replaced them with her note.

She had to be honest and admit she was getting a thrill from all of this. She felt excited as she crossed Columbus Circle, and as she passed several men entering the park, she wondered if any of them were 'S' on his way to the tree.

The following afternoon, Alice thought she would check to see if there had been a response. She pulled out the note but she was disappointed to find it was just the one she had left.

She sat on the bench for a while, scolding herself for being so stupid, for being so childish. Then out of the corner of her eye, a figure stopped at the tree then moved on.

Alice didn't get to see the person properly but she was sure it was a man. And sure enough, when she went back to the tree her note was gone.

The following morning the snow was beginning to melt a little so she thought she might take an early morning walk around the park. If 'S' wasn't going to come until the afternoon, her journey would probably be fruitless.

Except to her delight, there was another letter already there.

You have made me the happiest man in the world! To know you care about me and are still thinking of us being together has suddenly made me look forward to Christmas. Please tell him soon, so that we can put all of this behind us.

I love you more than I have, or will, anyone in the world. S xxxxxxx

Alice knew the letter was meant for someone else but it had been written to the author of the last letter and that was her. She sat on the bench and tears began to flow. Someone had told her that they loved her. This girl 'H' was far luckier and richer than she possibly realised.

She decided to head back to the apartment and write a reply.

Of course I care about you.

That was all the words she felt were necessary.

Alice grew worried after her note had been collected as there was no response the next day or the day after that. In fact, there was nothing for a whole week.

Then on a bright snowy afternoon when she had decided to stop being so stupid and give up this silly charade altogether, she found another message.

I put your note in my wallet and took it with me to London. I have found an apartment or a flat as they call it over there, one that would be ideal for the two of us. I have to start work on January 7 but it means we could have Christmas and New Year together. Would you like that?

S. xxxxxxxxx

Alice's heart sank. Was this all wrong? She was leading this poor man into believing that the love of his life was going to elope across the Atlantic with him.

What if the real 'H' decided she had made a mistake?

What if the real 'H' placed another letter in the tree? What then?

Alice told herself that she should just stop this whole charade now and come clean. But first, just one more note, one final message so that she could arrange to meet S and try to explain the truth about her actions.

I would love to talk with you soon so we can discuss everything. They say it is going to snow tonight so could we meet here in the park tomorrow, Christmas Eve, by this tree? There is so much I want to say to you, to explain.

Alice went down at the crack of dawn to place the letter in the tree to make sure S had time to reply. When she passed by later in the day, there was another note.

What a romantic idea! Of course I'll meet you by the tree. Say 1 p.m. and then we can go for a walk. There is so much I want to tell you as well. I will be working in London for a PR company; the same company who represent that new British group, The Beatles? There is talk that I may be working with the group directly. How exciting is that? I can't wait to see you. Until tomorrow.

Alice sat most of the night looking out of her apartment window at the most exciting city in the world, her mind turning over the options. The Manhattan skyline had never looked brighter and so full of promise.

What should she do? Go to the tree? Sit on the bench and wait for the man to arrive as arranged?

S was sure to be disappointed and indeed annoyed that Alice had taken it upon herself to intercept the notes, but she'd been so taken by the romance and adventure of it all that she hadn't thought this through. She just hoped that when she explained all this to him that he'd understand.

And perhaps the universe had meant for her to find the letter, and bring two lovelorn people together? Clearly H, whoever she was, had no interest in being with S, given that she hadn't responded to any of his notes.

Although on second thoughts what if he became really angry and told Alice where to go? Then she'd end up feeling even worse and on Christmas Eve too. Suddenly she wondered whether going to this meeting was a good idea after all.

She sighed. Once again she wished Harry was here; he'd give her advice on the best course of action, would know whether or not she should just let this lie or follow her instincts.

But Harry wasn't here, was he?

Alice was just getting ready to go to bed when she noticed something sitting on the bedside locker. It was the tickets to The Beatles concert that Harry had bought.

She smiled, realising the significance and the odd

coincidence that the man she planned to meet was also connected to the group in some way.

And there and then, Alice knew that her beloved was indeed pointing her in the right direction, and that one way or the other, whatever happened at the park tomorrow was meant to be.

A New York Christmas

Christmas in New York. A lifelong dream come true.

I had always wanted to visit the famed city, especially around Christmas time, so when the opportunity came up to visit my cousin Sarah, an estate agent who lived in Manhattan, I jumped at it immediately. It would be the perfect opportunity to get out of Dublin for a while and nurse my broken heart.

Don, my boyfriend of two years, had cheated on me a few weeks before, and the fact that it happened so close to Christmas made it harder.

For the first couple of weeks after the split I felt numb and broken, so a trip to New York seemed like the ideal distraction and a perfect getaway.

It would be a reset button of sorts, and while the festive atmosphere might well underscore my pain, I longed to see the legendary twinkling Christmas décor. I wanted to feel snow crunch under my feet while I walked down the streets of the world-famous city. My imagination was alive with scenes of mesmerising department store windows and sparkling Christmas trees, Central Park, ice rinks and softly falling snow, reflecting some of my favourite Christmas movies.

To put it simply, I wanted to experience a classic New York Christmas.

I sat on the sofa of Sarah's thirty fourth-floor apartment waiting for her to come home. She had a tall, fat Christmas tree, a real spruce. It made the entire apartment smell of fresh pine needles and it was intoxicating. It was simply decorated in silver and gold, and all the ornaments were replicas of antiques. Tiny red, white, and black nutcracker soldiers hung from the branches with red ribbon. Silver tinsel dangled, giving it a wild look. I loved it. It was perfectly placed next to an enormous window overlooking the city streets below.

Sarah burst through the front door with piles of paperwork and two laptop cases. She was definitely one of those typical New Yorkers you hear about, the ones who always seemed to be in a hurry, even when they have all the time in the world. They rushed around like they were in some sort of imaginary race. It was a complete contrast to my comparatively slower-paced Dublin lifestyle.

She piled her stuff on the table then turned to me with an apologetic expression.

'Let me guess, you have to work?' I asked.

I had only just arrived last night. I went straight to Sarah's where we had dinner – Chinese take-out – and did some catching up. That had been the extent of my New York adventures so far, but today Sarah had promised to show me round the city, and have dinner at the Russian Tea Rooms.

'Maddie, I'm so sorry. If I don't get to this property right now I could lose it. It has the potential of being a million-dollar deal and with Christmas only a week away I'm on a deadline. Do you hate me?' she asked.

I feigned an annoyed narrowing of my eyes, but then laughed. 'Of course not. Obviously I don't expect you to stop your life just because I'm here. Do what you would normally do. Just give me a little guidance so that I can get out and explore on my own. I'm a big girl and I can handle the Big Apple on my own. Can't I?' I said this with such confidence that I even convinced myself.

Half an hour later I looked at myself in the mirror.

I took the hot rollers out of my hair and brushed out the soft shoulder-length curls. Now it was thick and bouncy. My hair was a dark auburn-brown, and my skin was pale, typically Irish. I put on a nice matte shade of red lipstick, not something I would normally wear but it was Christmas after all, and I was in a festive mood. It really stood out against my dark hair and dark lashes. I was petite at only five foot three inches tall, so I tried always to wear one thing that made me stand out.

It added a nice touch to my otherwise basic outfit of blue jeans and red woollen sweater. I tugged on my black calf-length boots, added a grey cashmere hat, and saying goodbye to Sarah I headed out of the door.

My first stop, of course, had to be Central Park. I walked down Central Park West taking it all in. The big city buzz was there, but a lot was still missing from my classic New York Christmas fantasy. It was daytime, so none of the twinkling lights were on, and the city had not yet been hit by its first snowfall of the season. It all seemed disappointingly non-Christmassy.

Then I came upon a massive building right across from the park.

The steps were full of people eating and talking. There were two large Christmas trees on either side of the entrance decorated in red velvet bows, red and gold Christmas balls, and a large gold star on top of both. The large classical columns of the building were wrapped with green ribbon that spiralled down the entire length of them. I looked at the sign that read *American Museum of Natural History*.

Of course! I thought to myself. This place was a New York staple. I was so glad I came across it on my walk. I went to a nearby street vendor and bought a piping hot cup of hot chocolate and a pretzel and then joined everyone else sitting on the steps.

I was thoroughly enjoying my buttery salty pretzel when I got the feeling that someone was staring at me. I froze before I took another bite and looked around. There, only a few feet away sitting on the same step was the most gorgeous guy I had ever seen. Our eyes locked and instantly I was hypnotised. I couldn't look away. He was wearing a dark wool pea coat, like a sailor's coat, and a well-fitted suit underneath. His eyes were a piercing grey colour that changed to blue in the light. His dark hair was a bit messy, almost like the way a student would keep it, and he had a layer of rugged stubble on his chin. It was a contrast to his suit. He finally smiled a little at me and lifted his coffee cup in a 'cheers' sort of motion. It was then that I realised I was still in a frozen state with my pretzel in the air, half-way to my mouth. I snapped out of it, and raised my cup of hot chocolate back to him in the same manner. I suddenly felt like a messy child with butter and salt all over my mouth. Still he must have seen my greeting as an invite because he stood up.

He was tall and lean, but with a nice solid build. He walked over to me and my heart immediately began to pound loudly. Surely he would be able to hear it if he got closer. What would I say to him? He was so handsome I knew I would choke. Finally he was right next to me, towering over me. I looked up at him through my dark lashes, with a pretzel in my hand.

'Is that good?' he asked, pointing to the pretzel.

'Yes, it is,' I said uncomfortably.

'May I?' He gestured at the empty space next to me on the steps.

'OK.' I was feeling completely confused. I thought New Yorkers were supposed to be impolite and unapproachable.

'It seems like it must be good. The way you were eating

it; it looked like you were really enjoying it,' he said.

'You were watching me eat?' I asked.

'Well, yes,' he said with a grin that was childlike and made me feel like I was playing some coy game. And I liked it. It felt good, fun, and easy.

We stayed that way with our eyes locked and smiling at each other until he said:

'So how long are you visiting New York?'

'What? How do you know I'm visiting?' I asked with my mouth wide open.

'The way you stood in front of the building staring at it. Only people that are not from around here can look at it and still be in awe. The locals are so used to it they take it for granted,' he said.

'Oh, I see. Well, it is beautiful. Yes, I am visiting. To be honest I came here to have an old-fashioned Christmas with snow and festive decorations. But so far this is the only building I've seen that is decorated. I haven't been here long, though,' I stopped, suddenly feeling like I was rambling on. Why was I telling this handsome stranger my every thought?

'Well, maybe you just need someone to show you around. A New York Christmas is out there; you just have to know where to go. I would be happy to be that person. If you would let me,' he added gently.

There was a long pause. I stared at him. Looking into his sparkling grey eyes and then at his soft lips. I already wanted to lean in and kiss him. I steadied myself.

'I would love that,' I said.

'I'm Blake,' he said as he reached his hand out to shake mine.

'Madeleine.'

'That's a beautiful name. I like it,' he said, holding my hand longer than he should.

'Shall we get started then? There's something inside I want to show you,' he said as he stood up.

'Oh, now? OK,' I said, following his lead.

I followed him up the steps to the museum and threw away the last of my pretzel and empty cup into a nearby bin. He led me inside the lobby and there right in the middle was the most amazing Christmas tree I had ever seen. It was full of paper ornaments. Origami ornaments, to be exact.

'This is how we kick off our annual Christmas season here. It's been going on for almost thirty years now.'

'It's beautiful,' I said as I went in for a closer look. There were all sorts of animal decorations, from turtles to zebras. They were made of the most delicate paper. Some were shiny and others were a matte paper, but they were all expertly done.

'There must be hundreds of them,' I said in awe.

'About five hundred in all,' he said, and then added, 'So you like it?'

'Like? I love it. It's absolutely fascinating. Thank you,' I said, staring deeply into his grey, but now in this light, more blue-coloured eyes.

'Good. Then I am off to a good start,' he grinned.

'It's the best Christmas tree I've ever seen. Does that make you happy?' I flirtatiously said.

'Yes, it does. Next up to my office,' he said as he walked off further into the museum.

'Office?'

'Yes, I work here.'

I was pleasantly surprised. Now the messy mad scientist hair and wool pea coat made sense. He definitely looked the part. I scurried after him to catch up. As I placed myself alongside of him at his pace of walking he made a cute side glance at me and smiled. My heart melted.

We arrived at a door that was labelled 'museum staff only'. He used a key card to unlock the door and we stepped into a quiet long hallway.

'This way.'

'Where are you taking me?' I asked, sounding a little unnerved and wondering if I really should be trusting this random New York stranger.

He laughed and said, 'I swear, it's just my office. I know it's a bit creepy in this part of the building, but trust me.'

I laughed too. Somehow I did trust him. I can't explain it, but for some reason, it felt like we had known each other for a long time even though we had only just met.

We came to a vast staircase and climbed two or three flights before finally reaching a hallway with people moving in and out of offices. Blake showed me into his, and as soon as I stepped in I immediately fell in love with it. The wood was dark and heavy and a massive bookcase full of old books covered an entire wall. There was a heavy oak desk in the middle that was covered in piles of papers and specimens in glass jars. It was a true scientist's office. He went over to the large windows and said, 'Come and have a look.'

What other surprise could this gorgeous stranger have in store for me? I slowly walked over. When I got to the window I looked down. From this point you could see almost all of Central Park. I gasped at the sight.

'This is your view? It's amazing. You are so lucky.'

'I know. It's good, right? Especially when it's snowing.'

I looked at him. Who was this man? Why was he doing so much to please me or make me happy? It was more than I expected from anyone, let alone a stranger. He must have seen the questioning look in my eyes, because he caught my gaze and held it.

The chemistry between us was so thick it filled the room. I wanted to kiss him right then and there, but that was absurd. I barely knew this man, and had only been in his company for thirty minutes at the most. What was happening to me?

We stood at the window of his office. The surroundings were exactly what I imagined. I was in the office of a historic New York building with the vastness of Central Park below us. Blake leaned in closer to me. His scent was intoxicating. His voice came down to a whisper and then he said, 'Want to see it up close?'

'See what?' I stepped backwards a little.

'The park, of course,' he said as he motioned toward the door.

'Oh, yes of course. I would love to.'

'OK. But first we need to make a stop,' he said as he led the way out the door and back down into the main building.

A stop? I was intrigued by what this meant, but this man was full of surprises. I liked being surprised so I didn't ask. Outside, he walked down the museum front steps and I followed closely behind. It had grown a bit dimmer outside. 'How about we grab some food and have a picnic in the park?' he asked.

I smiled a big brilliant smile. Was this man made specifically for me?

'That sounds like a perfect idea,' I said.

'Great.' He led the way to a row of street vendors. He got one of everything and made us a sort of street food buffet – pizza slices, a gyro, hot dogs, a couple of bottled waters, and two coffees. When he was all finished piling a bag of goodies onto his arm, he handed me a cup of coffee and said, 'Shall we?'

His grin was spectacular. He was so proud of himself for being so clever, and I loved it. He wanted to please me and I wanted to be pleased.

We entered the park and the beauty of it took my breath away. Most of the trees had lost their leaves and their spiralling bare branches reached high into the sky. I understood how people could stroll the entire length of this massive park on a daily basis.

We sat down on a grassy area right near a long row of trees. Blake laid out our buffet in front of us.

'That's a lot of food,' I said.

He laughed 'Yes, well I couldn't decide what your first New York street food should be so I got them all.'

'That's very sweet.' I looked up from the food and smiled at him.

'Try the pizza first. You have to fold it like this,' he said as he picked up a slice and folded it before handing it to me.

I laughed a little and took a bite from the cheesy gooey-ness. He did the same with the other slice.

'Delicious!' I said after I swallowed my first bite.

'Good, and that's not even the best pizza in town. OK for a street vendor, but by far not the best. I'm glad you are pleased, though.'

We continued sampling from our street food buffet and talking away long into the afternoon.

Before long I was stuffed. I lay down on the grass looking up at the tree to give my full stomach some room to digest. He did the same.

'I am so full,' I said.

'Yes, me too,' he said.

'We're both full of New York,' he joked. I laughed and then he joined in.

Then while we were both laughing and in good spirits, the loveliest thing happened.

While we'd sat chatting on the grass, it had gradually grown into early evening. Dusk, to be exact. The sky was still a light pink from the setting sun, but also a dark blue from the oncoming night. Just then, out of nowhere and without ceremony, some of the nearby trees lit up. I sat up immediately and gasped.

'That's incredible ...' I said in barely a whisper.

I looked around as it seemed like the entire park came to life with twinkling lights. The bare trees all around us had been decorated with delicate hanging bulb strands. It was so beautiful it almost brought me to tears. I took it all in, absorbing the magic of it all.

The air was crisp and it truly felt like Christmas.

I looked at Blake, but he wasn't looking at the lights; he was looking at me. His face was lit from the glow of the nearby trees. I sensed he had been watching my reaction the entire time.

'I can't believe this is real,' I said.

'Me neither,' he replied gently, and I got the feeling he wasn't talking about the lights. Then he looked at me directly in the eye and leaned in a little closer.

'Madeleine, I don't normally do this. Meet a stranger on the steps at lunch and then take off and spend the afternoon with them. It's been really special, and unusual for me. I just thought I should say something to give you a little insight into who I am. It's as if I can't separate myself from you ...'

My eyes grew wide. I had never had a man be so forthright with me. To just put his cards on the table like that romantically. This couldn't be real. Things like this don't happen. At least, not outside of the movies.

Was this guy playing games with me? Did he have something else in mind? Was that statement about not wanting to separate from me just a way to get me back to his place? My warmed heart was beginning to turn a little cold and I felt very naïve.

'I said too much, I can tell I've made you uncomfortable,' he said.

Yet, this kind gorgeous man had done nothing to make me not trust him, I realised. I was the one planting these negative thoughts in my head. I had only just met him and I was already assuming the worst. The break-up had really done a number on me. The experience of being cheated on had scared me more than I had known. I willed myself to stop all the chatter in my head and stay in the moment.

'No, I'm fine. I'm sorry, I'm just not used to such honesty,' I admitted.

'Right, it was a bit too much. I'm sorry I don't really know where that came from.' I laughed a little and he laughed with me. The awkwardness was broken and everything was well again.

'Let's take a closer look,' I said as I stood up. I made my way to the trees and the closer I got the more I realised just how many tiny lights there were. They twinkled and glowed in the fading light. Now, it was beginning to look and feel a lot more like a New York Christmas. This was that festive magic I had expected from the city. It was all so lovely. My feelings of paranoia and lack of trust began to melt away. The season had that effect on people, I supposed. It made them kinder, made them more trusting, and more open. It was affecting me in that way now. The lights from the trees made Blake's eyes a crystal watery grey colour. They reminded me of the sea during a storm.

'I want to show you more; more of the city's festivity, if you'll let me,' he said.

'I would love that.' I replied.

He arched his elbow out, and I wrapped my arm under his. He then led me away down the path.

'Where are we going now?'

'It's a surprise. But I think you will like it,' he said evasively.

I grinned. This guy seemed to like surprising me, and I loved being surprised. I wondered what he had in store.

We strolled through the park arm in arm and talked more about our lives. Blake told me about his work and what he did at the museum.

'I was actually just taking a break from finishing a paper when I was sitting on the steps earlier. I had fully planned to go back in and finish. Then I saw you,' he said.

'Oh, no I'm so sorry. Had I known, I would not have let you stop working for this,' I said, feeling guilty.

'It was worth it. I had to take that chance when I saw it. I would forever regret it if I didn't,' he said.

My heart fluttered into my throat. His honesty was so disconcerting, yet was refreshing. He never hesitated; he just blurted out what he was thinking, and I admired that.

Finally we emerged from the park onto Fifth Avenue, the world-famous shopping mecca. I immediately felt excitement when I saw the huge giant snowflake hanging above the centre of the avenue and recognised where we were.

'Come on, this way,' he said, leading me further down the street.

We came to a huge building across from the entrance to the park, and slowed our pace when arriving at the front of it. Then, I figured out where he was taking me, the Bergdorf Goodman department store. I looked in the windows and squealed with delight. The displays were beyond words.

It was an outdoor White Christmas scene. The setting was a winter forest, and the mannequins wore long sequinned designer gowns in Victorian style. They were draped in white fur capes that trailed several feet behind them. The background was full of Christmas trees and various branches and shrubs all decorated with artificial snow and glitter, which also covered the ground.

Everything was white and the light reflecting off the scene in the city darkness made the entire window glow. Even the accessories were white, including the glittering diamond bracelets and necklaces worn by the mannequins. It was a vivid, magical wintry scene and I was completely absorbed in it, trying to take it all in. So much so, that I forgot I wasn't alone.

'Do you like it?' Blake asked.

'I love it! It's everything I could have hoped for. This is the kind of thing I longed to see,' I rambled on.

Melissa Hill

Blake laughed at my enthusiasm and said, 'I'm so glad. I rush by here every year and never really stop to take a closer look. I guess because in the back of my mind I knew I wanted to share it with someone.'

I looked up at him. Every second longer I spent in his company I was falling for this man, and it was scaring me. I watched him look at the window, smiling. I could stare at him forever.

'There's another great one further down the street at Saks, if you want to keep going?' he asked.

My eyes widened. 'Saks?' I repeated in barely a whisper.

Blake laughed so loud the other onlookers all turned to look. He was obviously delighted by my enthusiasm. 'You are too cute,' he said. Then he looped my arm in his and led me further along the busy street.

We stopped at another street vendor along the way.

'We can't go see the Saks windows without hot chocolate,' he insisted.

'But I've already had one today.'

'Oh, do you have a chocolate limit or something?' he joked. 'It's the holidays. Enjoy yourself. And at Christmas, hot chocolate is definitely a New York tradition.'

I laughed. 'Well, I am a bit cold, and I do like traditions.'

Blake bantered with the street vendor a little. He had that effect on people; he was able to talk to them like they were old friends.

We walked until we came to the Saks building.

'Wait, hold on,' he said as he put one hand over my eyes and one arm around my back to guide me. This was adorable. He really wanted me to get the full experience. I slowly shuffled my feet as he positioned me in front of the window, then took his hand away and said: 'OK, open your eyes.'

I did. It took me a few seconds to process what I was seeing. In the first window was the setting of a Victorian living room, or parlour, as they must have called it then. There was a Christmas tree in the corner and on the wall a sign that read, *'Twas the Night Before Christmas*.

Blake stood beside me and said, 'It's a story, each window is a scene from *'Twas The Night Before Christmas*.

My eyes watered over. This was breathtaking. I stepped closer, completely hypnotised by it. In the centre of the parlour was a fireplace, with 'stockings hung by the chimney with care'. The stockings must have been true vintage pieces with red and green patterns, not the commercial Christmas stockings you get now, but actual socks. The green garland above the fireplace was simple and thin, but also vintage-looking. The tree was decorated with hand-made ornaments, each different from the other and made of wood or paper. There were a few glass ornaments, but not many as it would have been a luxury to have those during that time period. A small toy train and tracks went around the bottom of the tree. An old wooden vintage train set circled around intricately wrapped presents with red, green and gold paper and velvet ribbon. There were only a few presents, maybe five in total. The large winged-back chairs were set before the fire-place with a cosy blanket throw across the back of it. A small table near the chairs had an old book on it, *'Twas The Night Before Christmas*.

I looked at Blake, and smiled. 'It's the loveliest thing I've ever seen.'

'I'm glad you like it,' he said. 'Come on, let's see the whole story.'

'Wait,' I said.

He stopped and looked back at me.

'Thank you, Blake. For all of this.'

'It's my pleasure,' he said as he put his elbow out for me again. I encircled my arm around his, took a sip of my creamy hot chocolate and continued on.

The next window was the children's bedroom. They were snug in their beds and wore adorable nightclothes in a wrought iron bed. Sugar plum fairies hung from the ceiling, and sprigs of holly from the corners. The next window had a white powdered rooftop with smoky chimneys, featuring the man himself. There was a large sled being driven by Santa Claus, as it landed on the roof. He wore the iconic Victorian dark maroon suit, not the bright red and white one, common today. He had rosy cheeks and a thick white beard and next to him was the large velvet bag full of intri-cately wrapped gifts. The reindeer were so lifelike and each one wore Christmas bells. I stared for a long time. It was pure Christmas magic.

The next window was again the parlour scene, only this

time Santa Claus was in it and he was adding more gifts under the tree. A man dressed in a nightcap and nightclothes peeked in at him from around the corner. The store really went out of its way to make this classic Christmas story come to life, and I was grateful to have the opportunity to see it.

I looked at Blake and he looked at me. We locked eyes for several moments. 'So, is it all you hoped for so far?' he asked.

'It's more than that. I never dreamed it would be this way. I've heard about this kind of thing and have seen pictures, but experiencing it in person doesn't compare.'

'I'd love to show you more Christmassy stuff, if you would let me while you are in town. I wish we could keep today going for longer, but I really do have to get back to my project. Would you allow me to walk you home?'

I tried not to sound disappointed. 'I'd love that. It's not too far from here. Just a few blocks,' I said.

We walked back through the length of the park and at one point, Blake gently reached for my hand. When we came to the north end and exited back onto the streets, I felt like we had entered a different world. I'd almost forgotten that I was in the city because the nature and tree lit paths of the park had made me feel like I was in a fairy tale.

We finally got to Sarah's condo and stepped under the long red awning that covered the path in an archway to the front door.

'This is it,' I said.

'Madeleine, are you free tomorrow night?' Blake asked then. 'I'd like to take you to dinner.'

'Yes, I would love that,' I said, hardly daring to believe it.

'Great. Pick you up here at 7?' Then he looked down at me and continued,

'Madeleine, what is happening here? This is so unreal. I've never connected with anyone this instantly.'

'I ... I'm not sure.'

Then he leaned in and hugged me. A soft, gentle hug, because the doorman was watching.

'I'll pick you up tomorrow, OK?' he whispered.

Then we parted ways. He stood there watching until I went inside, feeling like I was walking on air.

Upstairs, I opened the door of the apartment to find Sarah at the kitchen table, piles of paperwork spread out before her. She looked exhausted. I must have been glowing because as soon as she looked up at me she raised an eyebrow.

'What happened to you? You look almost ... hypnotised,' she said.

I skipped over to her. 'I met someone ... a guy.'

'What? You've been in New York less than twenty-four hours and it's the holidays. How?'

We both laughed. Then I told her everything. Of how I had sat in front of the museum at lunchtime and met Blake. I explained the rest without leaving out any details. I continued on about the museum tour, and the buffet picnic and the lights and the window displays, followed by the hand-holding walk through Central Park. Sarah was astounded.

'Wait, stop,' she said. 'Let's move onto the couch. I need to get away from this work space.' Then she went into the kitchen and opened a bottle of red wine and brought two glasses to the couch. 'Is this guy for real? I almost feel like you made him up. No one is that perfect.'

I laughed. 'No, I did not make him up. And yes, he does seem too good to be true, so much in fact that there's a problem.'

'Well, that's a relief,' Sarah laughed.

'It's just that, I can't help but think he's pulling some trick or something. Maybe he's just trying to get me into bed. He's so romantic and seems so honest. Every time he says something about his feelings for me, I can't enjoy it because I feel like there's some sort of ulterior motive.'

Sarah sighed and rolled her eyes. 'When you said there was a problem, I thought you meant with your perfect man. But there's no problem there. Just an issue you made up in your head.'

I sighed. 'Maybe you're right.'

'I know I am. Trust me. So, what are you going to wear to dinner tomorrow night?'

My eyes grew wide. I hadn't even thought that far ahead. 'I have no idea.'

'Come on, let's see what you brought.' Sarah stood up and went into the guest bedroom where I had my stuff.

We threw open the closet and I tried on every outfit I owned. It was a complete fashion show because with it being cold outside, I had to try on every outfit and then put on my coat and boots to see if everything went together.

'I don't like anything I have. I just don't have the right clothes for freezing weather,' I groaned.

'Come on, I do.' Sarah grabbed the wine and glasses and led me to her room.

We went through the whole thing all over again with her clothes. I tried on every dress she owned. I found a festive red one in a fitted style that went to just above my knees. It was off the shoulder with quarter-length sleeves made of silk. This made it elegant, but not over the top; the perfect balance.

Sarah clapped her hands. 'That's the one. It's perfect.'

The next day, while I spent a lovely morning wandering around Manhattan, Sarah had a break for lunch so I met her at a little café near her office. She was on her phone most of the time, still conducting business, so I was glad when it was over. I wanted to prepare for tonight anyway.

In the afternoon I went home and took a long hot bath and relaxed. Around six o'clock, I began to get the jitters. What if Blake didn't show up? I took a deep breath and allowed myself to trust this man. Trust that he would show and not stand me up. I went ahead and got dressed and at seven o'clock sharp, the doorman rang up. Blake was downstairs waiting for me. I breathed a sigh of relief, grabbed my coat and went down.

He stood in the lobby and I was taken aback at how I felt as soon as I locked eyes with him. He stood there, his tall figure towering in the brightly lit lobby. He wore an elegant black suit and his woollen pea coat. He topped it off with a red silk scarf around his neck, the perfect complement to my dress.

His eyes were wide as he looked me up and down.

'Madeleine, you look stunning,' he said as he greeted me with a light hug.

The doorman stood next to me and held out my coat, offering to help me put it on.

'Allow me,' Blake said.

He slid my coat on and then planted a light kiss on my cheek. 'Shall we?' he asked as he offered me his arm. I looped my arm in his and he led me outside.

A black car was waiting for us. I was confused as I thought we would surely be walking. A nice surprise.

He opened the door and I got in. As the car drove, we made light banter in the back seat, talking about what we did with our day. We weren't in the car long and arrived a few minutes later at our destination.

I stepped out and nearly gasped out loud. The Plaza Hotel.

A visit there would be a treat for anyone at any time, I knew, but at this time of year it was doubly astounding. The entrance was beautifully decorated with holly wreaths and delicate lights. It was intricate and elegant, and again had that classic 'old New York' feel I'd so longed for.

Blake put his arm around me and said, 'You mentioned you wanted an old-fashioned Christmas experience. There's no better place for that than this hotel. It hasn't changed much since it was built in 1907.'

I looked up at him. This was perfect. He looked down at me and grinned that brilliant grin, before putting his hand on the small of my back and leading me inside.

The lobby was alive with festive cheer, with several Christmas trees elegantly decorated. There was a table with a toy train, of the vintage kind, surrounded by vintage toys. The lobby was buzzing with people enjoying the holidays, everybody beautifully dressed and being fussed over by attentive waiting staff beneath sparkling chandeliers.

I was in complete awe of the glamour. I really did feel like I had stepped back in time.

Even with me in heels, Blake still towered over me. As we stood there in the lobby, surrounded by all this festive beauty, he looked down, and then in one unexpected motion he kissed me.

'I'm so sorry, I couldn't help it,' he said, pulling away quickly.

I didn't want him to stop, and while I loved his politeness and hesitation, I wanted to keep kissing him. So without a word, I reached up on my tiptoes and put my arms around his neck. His body was so warm it was like having my own personal heater. I tilted my head back and this time it was a longer, deeper kiss. He was so strong he almost lifted me off the ground. I was floating now, and it was magical.

Right then I forgot all about my ex-boyfriend and any mistrust I had in Blake. It had all vanished in just twenty-four hours. Walking around New York, exploring a new place was exactly the kind of thing I needed to get a different perspective of how my life could be.

Blake and I had the most festive silver-service dinner in the Palm Court in the true Christmas tradition, turkey roast and vegetables with brandy, and for dessert we shared pudding and a cup of nutmeg.

At the end of the night we said our goodbyes at the door of Sarah's condo. He never made me feel under any pressure to carry things further. It was almost the way old-fashioned courting should be.

'So, see you tomorrow night?' he suggested with a grin. 'I was thinking maybe ice-skating at the Rockefeller this time.'

I grinned. It was like this guy could read my mind. 'Yes, I would love that.'

Blake leaned in and planted another kiss on my lips. He was gentle about it. It was slow and romantic, full of feeling and it made me feel a bit dizzy.

The next day I went for a daytime walk through Central Park by myself. Reliving memories from the day before, I was in a great mood and I smiled and said hello to every passer-by, so much so that eventually people started avoiding the crazy-looking Irish girl.

When I got towards the middle I saw the museum and remembered the pretzel stand so I thought I would grab one. Exiting the park, I crossed the street near the building and suddenly saw Blake sitting on the steps.

An attractive female beside him.

I stopped in my tracks, feeling so duped. I couldn't believe it. Was this what he did all day? Was this his pick-up spot? Did he even work in the museum at all? I was furious but even worse, my heart was breaking a little.

I watched as they talked to each other. They seemed very comfortable together and smiled a lot as they chatted, very much like we had only two days before.

I debated whether I should go up to him or not – confront him, or should I just let it go, walk away and never talk to him again?

After a few minutes of staring and not knowing what to do I watched as they both stood up. It was unbelievable; they were going inside! This *was* his thing. This is what he did.

My despair quickly turned into anger and I stomped off in their direction. I stood at the bottom of the steps as I watched them disappear into the museum together. They were laughing and talking loudly. I willed him to turn around and see me. Just then Blake turned in the doorway.

He locked eyes with me and smiled in recognition. My eyes darted immediately to the woman and then back at him. Seeing my discomfort, the smile disappeared from his face. Turning quickly, I raced down the steps and back into the park. I wanted to disappear as soon as I could in case he was coming after me. I didn't want to hear his pathetic excuses.

I ran all the way home. I was in disarray. Sarah was at

work and I had no one to confide in. Everything suddenly felt grey to me. The cheery Christmas tree in the living room taunted me.

I fell asleep on the couch and woke up a few hours later. It was dark and the only light that filled the room was the light from the tree. I looked around. It didn't look like Sarah had come home yet. I checked the time and it was only seven o'clock. It felt so much later. The embarrassment of what had happened earlier flooded back.

I sat up and remembered myself. Why was I letting this get me down? Yes, I was hurting, but I had come to New York to enjoy myself. I wasn't going to let a player destroy my dream getaway. What would I be doing right now if I had never met Blake? I would probably be ice-skating at Rockefeller Center, under the giant tree. It was exactly what he'd suggested we do tonight. He knew me well, or I should say he knew how to woo clueless New York tourists like me well.

I pulled myself together and decided to go anyway. I would put all thoughts of him out of my mind and continue as if I had never met him. I washed my face and got changed into a comfortable pair of jeans and a sweater, perfect for ice-skating.

I headed downstairs to the lobby where the doorman stopped me.

'Miss,' he said. 'You have several messages from a Mr Blake.' He handed me a few small notes.

'Thank you,' I said, grabbing them and walked out the door. As soon as I saw a street rubbish bin, I tossed them. I didn't open them. I didn't need to.

I walked all the way to Rockefeller, careful to walk on the side of the park opposite the museum. I moved through the bustling streets of Fifth Avenue, taking my time strolling along and window-shopping.

I finally arrived at Rockefeller Center. I could see the tree as I approached the plaza, but getting up close to it was beyond words. I tilted my head back, staring up at the massive tree in the centre of the plaza above the ice rink, mesmerised. It was even more glorious in person. There must've been a million lights on it. The entire plaza was decorated for the holiday season; beautiful life-sized angels blowing trumpets and giant painted nutcracker soldiers all lined up. Below on the ice rink, people were skating and full of cheer and laughter.

I sat down on a nearby bench and gazed at the tree. Its beauty and romance seemed only to mock my sadness. I thought of Blake again, wanting to cry. I was only kidding myself with all these distractions. It wasn't working. It was then, right in that moment of thinking about him that I heard a familiar voice.

'May I?'

I looked up to see Blake towering over me. He was gesturing at the empty space beside me on the bench. I didn't say anything. He sat anyway.

'Madeleine, I've been trying to get hold of you all day. The doorman wouldn't let me up no matter how much I pleaded with him. I tried for an hour at least,' he said.

I just looked at him and my eyes watered over. His sincere way of talking to me was enough to make me feel over-whelming sadness. I wanted things to be as they were before. But they couldn't; I did not trust this man. I don't think I trusted any man at this point.

'Why did you run off like that today?' he asked.

'I watched you, on the steps. Talking to that girl and then I saw you bring her back into the museum, just like we did. Is that what you do to pick up women? It works. It worked on me, I was stupid enough to fall for it, just like the girl today was.'

I could barely get the words out. My voice was shaking. Blake's eyes were wide. At first I thought they were wide at having been caught.

'Madeleine, that's not what that was – at all,' he said. 'You've got it wrong and I'm sorry if what you saw hurt you. That's the last thing I would ever want to do, but if you would just let me explain …'

'I don't see the point in an explanation. I could never tell if you were lying.'

'That is true,' he said. 'Would you like to meet her then?'

'Meet who?' I asked.

'The woman you saw me sitting with earlier. That's the only way I can prove that I'm not lying about it. She's at my apartment right now,' he said.

'What? She's in your apartment?' I repeated, suspiciously.

'Yes, I couldn't make it home for Christmas this year so she came here so that I had some family around.'

'Family?'

'Yes. She's my sister.'

My heart sank. I couldn't say why but I believed him. Now I felt like a complete idiot. I was kicking myself for acting so rashly earlier. Sarah was right about me. The problem wasn't this man. It was me. The break-up had left me a paranoid mess. I let my head collapse on his shoulder.

'I'm so sorry. I feel so stupid,' I said.

'It's OK. Don't be. Actually I'm kind of glad it happened.'

'What? Why?'

'Because I wasn't sure if you felt anything for me. When we look at each other I can feel a connection, but you haven't said anything … about what you really think or how you might feel. But seeing your reaction today … now I know for sure you feel something too. And that I might be more than just your New York Christmas guide.'

I sat in silence and processed what he had said. He was right. Perhaps I needed this to bring me to that next level. This entire thing had been a roller-coaster for me.

'So, we're OK?' he asked.

'Yes, we're OK. And I'm sorry,' I said, feeling stupid again.

He held my shoulders and turned me toward him. 'No need to apologise. I want you to be comfortable with me, Madeleine. I know this is crazy and we only just met, but I think we might have something here. I know it. I knew it when I saw you for the first time. You're the best Christmas present I could have asked for. Maybe this was meant to be.'

I looked up at him, my eyes watering over. This dear sweet man was all I could ever hope for, and he was pouring his heart out to me. Then he leaned down and kissed me.

'Now, I seem to remember I promised you ice-skating.'

And when a few minutes later Blake took my hand and led me out onto the ice rink, I looked around again at the twinkling lights on the tree, and the scene around us, unable to believe that I was actually here and this was really happening. Everything felt so surreal. And impossibly romantic.

But then the most magical thing of all happened.

Out of nowhere, it began to snow. Small perfect snowflakes fell on our faces, and we laughed amongst the beauty of it all.

This New York Christmas was perfect, even better than I had imagined, more than I could have ever dreamed of.

And as Blake leaned down and kissed me, I knew I wanted to experience it over and over again.

Winter In Venice

Chapter 1

'She is beautiful, no?'

'What?' Max shook himself out of his daze. He was huddled uncomfortably at the back of the water taxi, trying to ignore the swaying of the little boat and the lapping water of the canal only inches away. The driver waved with both hands at the scenery around them, seemingly unperturbed about steering the vessel. 'The city, Venice. She is beautiful?'

'Oh. Yes – of course.'

The Italian man beamed and went back to zooming along the canal. Max tightened his grip on the wooden seat and tried not to show his extreme discomfort at being forced to ride in this treacherous little bucket. Instead he focused his attention on Naomi, who was gazing around at the city in pure delight.

If this makes her happy, then it will be worth it. Max tried to keep that thought in the forefront of his mind. It would be worth the long flight, the chilly December air, and yes even the endless network of canals, if only his wife enjoyed their trip.

It was a much-needed getaway for both of them. They hadn't had a moment to themselves, let alone a whole weekend, since the birth of their daughter eight months prior. Max loved baby Julia and adored being a father – he wouldn't trade it for anything in the world but in truth, the craziness of having a newborn in the house was taking its toll on their marriage.

Julia had only just begun to sleep through the night, and Naomi's constant fussing over the baby was hard to take. She was reluctant to leave her alone with a babysitter for more than a few hours; the fact that he'd convinced her to leave her with her parents for a whole weekend was a minor miracle.

But she'd agreed – reluctantly, but even so – and Max had put together a romantic weekend getaway as an early Christmas present for her. He knew she'd dreamed of visiting Venice all her life.

As for himself, he had no love of the water, no taste for Italian food, and no knowledge whatsoever of the language or history of this odd little place. But if the break could help them reconnect as a couple – no demanding infant in the background, no baby paraphernalia to cart around everywhere – then it would be well worth the discomfort.

He snuck another glance at his wife. *So far, so good.*

She'd nearly had a change of heart at the last minute,

fretting over how Julia would manage on a full weekend without her. Luckily, Naomi's mother had all but shoved her out of the door of their home. 'You need a break,' she'd said firmly. 'You have a husband, remember? Spend some time with him. Try and remember what your relationship was like before the baby came along.'

'But what if she misses me?' Naomi protested feebly, and her mother waved a hand in dismissal.

'There's such a thing as being too attached, darling. She'll be fine. She has to learn to spend a little time away from you sooner or later. What will you do when she goes to pre-school? When she has friends and wants to go to a sleepover? Do you want her to be so attached to you that she can't function on her own?'

Naomi hadn't liked that very much, Max could tell, but she didn't really have a reply. And so, taking wheeled suit-cases packed with warm clothing and rain gear – Max had read that Venice could be rainy this time of year – they took a taxi to Gatwick and set off for Italy, Naomi fretting about what she was leaving behind, and Max thinking warily about everything that lay ahead.

Their hotel was on the water – *right* on the water, as was everything in Venice, with guests stepping out of water taxis onto a dock with an awning and large double doors welcoming them into the lobby.

The concierge checked Max and Naomi in quickly and summoned another employee to help them carry their luggage up the stairs; apparently there was no lift in the building.

Their room was small but cosy, and there was a little kitchenette with a coffee maker and a microwave. The wooden headboard and dresser were ornately carved and there was a vase of perky fresh flowers on the nightstand.

Max stowed their suitcases and checked his watch; they'd arrived in the late afternoon, and there was still some weak winter sunshine outside before the sun set. 'Well. We're here. Shall we head out for a bite of dinner?' Travel always made him hungry.

But Naomi was already on the phone. 'I'm just going to call Mum and Dad really quickly and check in on Julia,' she explained, covering the mouthpiece with one hand. 'It'll only take a minute.'

Max nodded and stifled a sigh. *She's going to be calling multiple times a day*, he thought gloomily. *I'm going to have to work hard to keep her distracted.*

Naomi was making cooing noises into the phone, talking to their daughter.

He could tell when her mother came back on the line because the cooing stopped and his wife said reluctantly: 'Well, I know it's still early but I just wanted to— oh, the flight was fine. Did she sleep through her afternoon nap? Oh, that's good.' Max thought his wife almost sounded a little disappointed to hear that Julia seemed to be doing fine without her.

When Naomi finally put down the phone he suggested

brightly that they find a place to eat but she still seemed worried and distracted.

'Mum says she slept this afternoon but I can't help worrying – I mean, we'll be gone for four nights, and what if she doesn't sleep through the night for any of them? Maybe a full weekend was too much too soon, Max. Maybe we should have stuck to just a night in London in case something goes wrong and she needs us ...'

He stifled a groan and wrapped his wife in a hug. 'Look, you're an amazing mother, and it's brilliant that you love our daughter so much. I do too. But your mum will take great care of her! I'm sure she's thrilled to get some grandma–granddaughter time in. In the meantime, let me spoil you, OK? A night in London is nothing out of the ordinary. You've always wanted to visit Venice and I want us to really make the most of this weekend.'

'Well, OK.' Naomi melted a little in his arms, returning his hug. She smelled like vanilla and pears – the perfume she'd worn since they first started dating over six years ago.

Max breathed deeply of her scent and promised himself that he would make sure she enjoyed herself with the most perfect, romantic vacation possible. *Even if we do have to go everywhere in a bloody boat.*

He couldn't actually understand why he feared the water so much. When people asked, he usually told them that as a toddler he fell off a dock into a deep lake while at a family reunion. Unable to swim, he would have drowned if an older cousin hadn't quickly pulled him out.

In truth, though, the story was a lie. Max had never fallen off a dock and never even come close to drowning; in fact, he'd taken swimming lessons and learned to swim perfectly well.

He just didn't like water, or boats, or being piloted everywhere in one of these low-riding gondola things that Venetian tourists seemed to view as so romantic. All the same, there was no way to get from their hotel to the restaurant he'd selected from the guidebook unless they went via water, and so again they climbed into a water taxi and set off.

The driver chatted to them in a mix of English and Italian. Max truly only grasped every other word the guy was saying, so he tried to smile and pretend he was too wrapped up in the city sights to talk.

Naomi leaned forward to talk to the driver, asking him about sights as they glided down the Grand Canal and asking him how to say basic words and phrases in Italian.

Finally they reached the area of the restaurant and disembarked from the water taxi.

There were only a few other diners – apparently a Thursday evening in December was not the busiest time in Venice for tourists – and Max and Naomi were given a quiet table with a nice view of the canal.

Nice if you enjoyed looking at the water, Max thought bleakly, and turned his attention to the menu.

Once again, his lack of Italian was flustering him. He read through the dishes suspiciously. Culinary exploration was not one of his strong points; in fact, when he and Naomi had first started going out, it had been a bit of an inside joke between them.

After a while, though, it turned into a slight sore spot. Naomi loved ethnic foods, trying new recipes, and sampling new cuisine at new restaurants. For Max, the definition of 'trying a new food' meant using a different brand of ketchup on his burger. He preferred good old English cooking – burgers, meat-and-potatoes, that sort of thing – and tried new stuff only with the greatest of reluctance.

As far as Italian food went, spaghetti and meatballs were about as familiar as he got with the cuisine. *Antipasto*? That sounded like something that would require an antacid later on. *Secondi*? He didn't know what it was, but it sounded like a side effect of a bad illness. *Brioches*? Were they made of shoe leather? There were plenty of other items on the menu that he couldn't even pronounce.

When the waiter finally appeared to take their order, Max explained haltingly his trouble with the choices. The waiter smiled and explained several of the dishes.

Finally, Max settled on polenta with grilled meat and vegetables. The way the waiter explained it, the polenta sounded like a kind of cornmeal porridge, which seemed like a weird choice for a dinner item, but he supposed it was better than pumpkin ravioli or calf liver and onions, both of which the waiter explained were Venetian specialities and seemed to think were very fine dishes.

Max ordered a bottle of red wine for the table while

Naomi picked out her own meal – some type of fried sardine and onion dish, risotto, and vegetables. It didn't sound in the least bit appetising to Max, but he wasn't about to admit that.

The food arrived quickly and they tucked in. Max decided the polenta wasn't half bad; at least there was a generous helping of meat to be had, though he couldn't help wishing for a bottle of ketchup to smother it in. He poked through the vegetables and wondered idly if Italian supermarkets sold anything like Heinz; he could buy a bottle and carry it around with him.

Dessert was at least a touch more familiar; Naomi ordered tiramisu, that strange, spongy creation which looked like cake but was soaked in espresso and a dark cocoa powder that made his nose feel itchy.

For himself he managed to order, of all things, a small plate of fried doughnuts and a cup of coffee. The doughnuts were suspiciously filled with raisins and bits of orange, and the coffee was extremely strong, but at least it somewhat resembled something he might find back at home in England.

He was pleased at least to see that Naomi was enjoying the meal, though. She'd *ooh*ed and *aah*ed at every dish the waiter presented and blissfully downed two glasses of wine.

They'd lingered over their meal for more than two hours; now she seemed quite ready to return to the hotel for an early bedtime.

'Great food,' Max exclaimed, more enthusiastically than he felt, as he paid the bill and then hailed yet another water taxi. *How many more of these meals will I have to eat? Not to mention get water taxis ... Let's see, tomorrow is Friday and our flight leaves Monday morning ...*

The driver helped them into the boat and they sat down at the back, Max somewhat awkwardly, Naomi leaning her head on his shoulder.

'This was a good idea,' she surprised him by saying. He put one arm around her shoulders and squeezed gently, forgetting momentarily the uncomfortable rocking of the boat.

The sun had set, leaving Venice dark and quiet for the night. City lights reflected on the canal and lent the scene a sort of peace that even Max could appreciate. Bright lights twinkled here and there; the city was getting ready for the Christmas season.

Back at the hotel they hung up their coats, scarves and gloves and turned down the bed. After the earlier flight and the heavy dinner, Max was ready for an early bedtime.

Naomi's hand wavered momentarily over the phone, and Max hesitated, holding a spare blanket. Then she let out a massive yawn, covering her mouth in surprise. 'Oh my goodness! I don't know where that came from.'

'I do,' he said smiling. 'You're just worn out from the journey and all the excitement of finally being here.'

'I suppose that is it,' she agreed.

Max duly spread the extra blanket over the bed for added warmth and watched with relief as Naomi switched off the lamp and curled up in bed, phone call forgotten.

He switched off his own bedside lamp and curled up next

to her, breathing in her vanilla-pear perfume and stroking her hair as she snored softly.

Maybe Venice can work its magic on us yet, he thought sleepily, before he too drifted off to sleep.

Chapter 2

Lucy stared forlornly out the window of the plane. They were descending into Venice and in the late afternoon sunshine she could see the city laid out below her, full of promise.

But she didn't have eyes for the snow on the cobbled rooftops, or the maze of canals in the place of city streets. She was too wrapped up in her own thoughts to notice any of those picturesque details.

She exited the plane with the other passengers and collected her luggage mechanically, moving through the airport terminal with a heavy heart. She flagged down a cab that would take her as far as the outskirts of the city, and from there she needed to get a water taxi to take her to the hotel for the night. After the flight from Dublin, she needed a hot bath, a simple meal and a long, deep sleep in a plush bed.

At the Piazzale Roma – the main transport hub of the city – her water-taxi driver helped her load up her luggage and steered the little boat quietly along the canals of San Marco, sensing she wasn't in the mood for small talk.

Reaching the stop-off point which was located a couple of blocks away back from the Grand Canal, Lucy got out near Rialto bridge and dragged her single suitcase along the cobbled streets to the hotel.

She checked in and accepted her room key with a smile and a nod, trudging quietly up the stairs to her room and dropping the suitcase on the floor.

One year.

It seemed so much longer. Only one year had passed since she and Dominic had enjoyed the weekend of their dreams here in Venice.

Gliding along the canals, drinking too much wine in trattorias, taking in the theatres and the opera of the festive season – it had been a magical time, full of romance.

Then towards the end, they had capped it all by stealing away to a quiet corner of the city – a tiny bridge off a sidestreet, away from the hustle and bustle of central San Marco.

There, on the picturesque wrought-iron bridge and above the inky black canal waters, they had marked their initials on a metal padlock and hung it from the rail of the bridge, sealing in a promise of their love in this most romantic of cities.

What a difference a year makes, Lucy thought forlornly. Maybe the trip had been *too* romantic, too perfect, because not long after they returned to Dublin everything seemed to start going downhill.

For starters, they'd got into a fight at a friend's party on New Year's Eve over a simple misunderstanding made much worse by the copious amounts of intoxicating champagne. Then Lucy suffered from a cold on and off for the rest of the winter, and feeling rundown only made her more irritable, which led to more fighting.

Spring was supposed to be a breath of fresh air, but a promotion at work meant more hours away from home, which Dominic resented. Once summer came she thought they might get away for a mini-break to make up for all the stress, but then he was busy with family issues. By the time autumn arrived there was barely a shred left of the relationship they had once had, and one day Dominic announced out of the blue that it was over.

He was moving on, and so should she.

In retrospect, Lucy supposed she shouldn't be surprised. But she was still hurt. How could someone just walk away so easily, without putting up a fight? Surely everyone had a bad year now and then, and it was worth sorting through it all to save your relationship.

In any case, Dominic was gone, and Lucy was back in Venice, alone.

She shrugged off her coat and scarf, hanging them over the back of a chair, and slipped her tired feet out of her boots. When she and Dominic had come here last year, she'd packed two suitcases full of clothes – gorgeous dresses, cashmere scarfs, plenty of jewellery, and of course silky negligées to wear underneath. Now she had a single suitcase with a few sweaters and pyjamas in it. What was the point in dressing up, when there was no one special to see it?

Lucy slowly got ready for bed, changing into cosy flannel pyjamas and brushing out the knots in her hair. *Once this weekend is over, I'll feel better,* she promised herself.

Eating Ben & Jerry's in front of the TV and crying on the phone with her friends wasn't helping her feel better about her break-up, so she was trying a more radical plan.

She would unlock the padlock from the bridge, thereby unsealing their promise of last year. Maybe then she could finally move on with her life and accept that Dominic was gone for good.

Chapter 3

In the morning Lucy located a café and sat down for a lonely breakfast. The skies were grey with the promise of snow, much as they had been this time last year.

She ordered a cappuccino and biscuits and gazed out the window of the café. San Marco was twinkling with holiday lights; festive greenery hung from balconies and decorated windows and shop fronts. All along the canals glowing decorations were reflected in the water. Venice was well and truly ready for Christmas.

Other tourists were enjoying the morning, gliding down the canals in gondolas or hoofing it on one of the narrow cobblestone side streets. Some were shopping, enjoying an early morning cup of coffee, and others had their heads down, chatting on cell phones and planning out their day. Lucy watched idly as they passed her by. There were people walking alone, but there were many couples or families out and about too. It gave her a small pang to see so many carefree people happily striding by, when she herself felt so down in the dumps.

She sipped her cappuccino and considered what she should do over the next two days. She truly adored Venice and would love nothing more than to spend more time exploring it, so she had booked her return ticket for Monday morning.

That gave her plenty of time to hit the major sites – St Mark's Square, perhaps a concert at the Basilica – and maybe just float around the city a bit on a gondola, looking at all of the lights and enjoying the gentle chatter of other tourists. It would be a nice, relaxing, and well-deserved weekend break.

Since the sun was peeking weakly through the clouds and the temperature seemed fairly moderate, Lucy decided to make her first stop the Piazza San Marco – St Mark's Square – for a refreshing stroll and some more people-watching. She didn't fancy lingering outdoors in the cold but as she was bundled up in a wool coat and cuddly scarf, she thought a little walking about wouldn't hurt. Besides, she wanted to get a closer look at the architecture of St Mark's Basilica. She and Dominic had briefly visited it last year, but once was not enough.

Her memories of that visit with Dominic stabbed a bit. They had strolled through the square, surrounded by the cooing of pigeons and the lightly falling snow, admiring the cathedral but mostly admiring each other. *Well, this time I'll be alone, so maybe I'll get a better look at the details,* Lucy thought ruefully.

And the Basilica was magnificent, even if she had no one to share the view with. The murals on the outside and the gleaming domes were beautiful. She stood for a moment on the stones of the piazza, contemplating the work that must have gone into planning and building such a magnificent structure.

Other tourists nearby were talking about the cathedral and snapping pictures, and she amused herself by watching them, too.

One couple in particular caught her eye. Something about them reminded Lucy of Dominic and herself on their prior trip; something about their cosy posture that said clearly 'we're head over heels in love'.

The girl had red hair tumbling down under a knitted hat and was wearing a bright red pea coat that complemented rather than competed with her hair. The young man was clearly enamoured of her, though he also seemed a bit distracted. Lucy looked closer. Not distracted … nervous? Suddenly he slipped down to one knee in the crowd, and Lucy realised what he was about to do.

A proposal! The romance of it touched her as much as it hurt, and she turned away quickly, partly to give the young couple their privacy, and also to spare her own feelings. She wouldn't deny that when she and Dominic had visited the city, she'd secretly hoped it might lead to a proposal. Clearly, it wasn't meant to be.

Lucy decided to warm up a little by touring the inside of the Basilica. The interior was just as impressive; gleaming gold and bronze mosaics on the ceiling gave the cathedral a warm, shimmering appearance. Between the mosaics and the enormous paintings everywhere the eye could travel, Lucy had the feeling of being inside of a Fabergé egg. It was incredibly beautiful and a little overwhelming. She found a pew away from other groups of tourists and sat down to admire the interior of the cathedral.

She was still musing about Dominic when she had the oddest feeling of being watched. Turning, she glanced around, but there were so many other groups of people that it was hard to tell if anyone in particular had been looking at her.

Nonsense, she thought sadly. *You're so lonely that now you're imagining you might bump into a friend, at least for the duration of your trip. Snap out of it!*

She looked back up to the religious paintings on the ceiling and resolved to put the feeling behind her. If someone could put so much effort into a project of this scale, I think I can manage the very tiny project of rebuilding my love life, she thought resolutely.

And with that notion, she decided to put Dominic out of her mind for the rest of her trip.

She would enjoy herself, unlock that padlock, and fly home again ready to start over fresh and enjoy her newly single life.

Outside the cathedral Lucy had to make a decision about what tourist site to visit next. The Basilica tour guide had recommended the Doge's Palace, across the Square, but she wasn't altogether interested in another tour of rooms and historical artefacts.

Instead she decided to take a boat tour. She'd heard that the slow-moving vaporetto on the Grand Canal offered a great water tour of the San Marco, and somehow she and Dominic had never got around to taking one last year. It would be nice to see the city during the daytime, when she could really peer at the sights.

She bought a ticket and a hot chocolate and took her seat, with her guidebook at the ready. The views were pretty decent: she could see the bridges on the main canal and the side streets, including Rialto bridge, which was decorated with festive lights for the season. Gradually she stopped thinking about everything she saw in the context of whether she and Dominic had seen it the year before; she was simply enjoying the colourful buildings and festive displays as they slid by, simply because they were beautiful – not because they evoked any particular memories.

The water bus ran around the city for about an hour. Finally Lucy collected her guidebook and empty cup and stepped off to plan the next part of her day. She fancied going out to Murano Island to visit a glass-blowing studio, and since the next water bus wasn't leaving for nearly an hour, she decided to grab a quick bite of lunch first.

There were plenty of cafés and small restaurants offering both traditional Italian lunches and more standardised tourist offerings, like miniature pizzas. Lucy chose a hot sandwich and another frothy cappuccino and watched the tourists around her while she ate. She'd always enjoyed people-watching, and it helped to distract her from the fact that she herself was alone.

Finally it was time to board the water bus and head out to Murano. Lucy was happy to see that there weren't quite as many tourists out here; the island was in fact much quieter by comparison to San Marco, though there were still some tourists here and there exploring on foot. She wandered the streets until she found a quiet glass-blowing shop that appeared to be open, and ducked inside.

The man in the workshop was skilfully blowing and moulding glass before the delighted eyes of a few other tourists. Lucy watched with wonder as the man shaped the molten glass into a vase. The tourists broke into applause, and the man smiled. Lucy lingered on for a while to listen to him explain his craft, the history of glass-blowing in the city, and the time that went into crafting each piece.

In display cabinets there were glass vases, abstract sculptures and glassware for the kitchen; Lucy marvelled at the work that went into each piece. Ultimately she left without purchasing anything; she certainly didn't need anything for herself and she was terrified of something breaking in transit back to Dublin. *Maybe another time,* she thought wistfully, giving the colourful, fragile pieces one last look before exiting into the street.

Almost before she knew it, the sun was setting over the island and it was time to take the water bus back to San Marco. By the time Lucy reached her hotel, she was famished, and she was happy to pop into a small trattoria down the street for her evening meal. *I don't think I'll ever tire of the food here,* she thought as she dug into a fragrant bowl of pasta and washed it down with a glass of wine.

By the time Lucy returned to her room and crawled into bed, it was fully dark in Venice, and the city was slowly quietening down as people returned to their homes or hotels for the night. Somewhere in the distance Lucy thought she could hear Christmas carols playing in Italian.

'Goodnight, Venice,' she mumbled sleepily, burrowing deeper into her blankets. For the first time in weeks, she was looking forward to the coming weekend.

Chapter 4

Scott checked the pocket of his coat for what seemed like the hundredth time.

Still there.

He patted his pocket and zipped up his coat, stepping out of the hotel lobby into the brisk December air.

Rachel was waiting for him outside. Her red hair was gleaming under a knitted cap and she was wearing a red woollen pea coat that made her look as though she belonged on a Christmas postcard.

Scott stood back for a moment, silently admiring his girl-friend as she chatted to an older woman in fluent Italian. Rachel was obsessed with Italy – the language, the art, the food, everything – so of course when everyone else chose to study Spanish or French in high school, she picked Italian.

She'd even spent a college semester abroad in Italy as an exchange student. Her efforts were paying off now; she'd been eagerly chatting to everyone she met since they'd touched down from New York on Thursday night. She seemed to be having the time of her life.

Everything is going according to plan, Scott thought with relief. After all, when your girlfriend is obsessed with all things Italian, what better place to whisk her away for a romantic vacation … and a Christmas proposal?

He'd spent nearly six months planning everything out. Step one: find the perfect ring, a combo of diamonds and emeralds that would appeal to Rachel's non-traditional tastes. Step two: book the perfect hotel in Venice, a five-star affair with a gorgeous view of the Grand Canal. He wanted their long weekend in the city to be one of utmost luxury; nothing less would do. Step three: choose a romantic site for his proposal. Venice had such a reputation as a romantic city, he was sure he'd have no shortage of memorable spots to choose from, so he planned to take Rachel on an extended tour of the city and just wait until the mood felt right. They had plans to visit the Basilica, have a romantic dinner or two, and perhaps tour the canals, so he was confident the perfect magical setting for a proposal would present itself in no time.

But first, they needed to get breakfast. A small café near their hotel offered piping hot cappuccinos, pastries and more for a tasty Italian breakfast. They sat at a small table by the window, looking out at the festively decorated streets, sipping their coffee and chatting about their plans for the day.

'Where do you want to go first?' Scott asked, still absent-mindedly fingering the ring box in his pocket.

'Oh, I don't know.' Rachel nibbled at a pastry, her eyes alight with happiness. 'There's so much to see! Did you have a preference?'

'I was thinking St Mark's Square,' he said casually. 'It's pretty mild today, so it's a good day to be outside. And after that we could tour the Basilica, since you did say you wanted to go there.'

'Oh, I'd love that.' Rachel gestured expressively with her hands when she was excited; just like an Italian, Scott thought. 'We should go to the sung Mass there on Sunday. I hear it's amazing.'

'We will,' he promised. They finished breakfast and went outside to navigate their way to St Mark's Square. Scott hoped he was keeping his excitement under wraps; he didn't want Rachel to have a hint of the surprise that was waiting for her.

They were able to zigzag their way to the Square on foot, crossing small canals via ancient stone bridges and finally emerging into the crowded piazza. It was full of tourists and pigeons, exactly as it had looked in hundreds of postcard-worthy pictures that Scott had seen online. Weak winter sunshine peeked through the clouds to illuminate the masses taking pictures of the Basilica or each other.

The Basilica was an impressive sight even to Scott, who knew little enough about the history of the place. The sheer size of the structure and the murals on the front of the building were enough to make anyone pause for a second look. Rachel was fairly glowing with excitement, rattling off a steady stream of facts about the architecture and construction of the cathedral. Scott looped an arm through hers as they walked, meandering slowly through the crowd. He loved her intelligence and enthusiasm for the world, and was happy to listen to her talk.

Rachel trailed off and leaned her head on his shoulder, smiling. Scott gave her a quick kiss on the forehead. 'What are you thinking about?'

She snuggled closer to him. 'How nice it is to be here with you.'

'Yeah?' He gave her an affectionate squeeze, and she grinned up at him.

'Yeah. I love it here. This is the best Christmas present ever.' She stood up on tiptoe and gave him a kiss.

He kissed her back, not caring about the crowds of tourists around them. For a moment it was as if everyone and everything else faded away, and it was only the two of them, arm in arm in this romantic city. Rachel's eyes sparkled as she turned away with a contented smile, gazing at the spires of the Basilica.

The perfect moment ...

'Actually, there was something else ...' Scott started to say, kneeling down on the cobblestones and feeling for the ring box in his pocket.

Splat! Suddenly he felt something wet land on his head.

Horrified, he quickly stood up as Rachel turned back to him. He touched one hand to his hair and stared at the white smear on his fingers in disgust.

'Eww!' Rachel exclaimed, quickly pulling tissues out of her coat pocket. 'Is that ...'

'Stupid pigeons.' Scott wiped at his head and looked around the square for the offending pigeon, but they were all busily cooing at tourists trying to get scraps of food.

'Come on,' Rachel said, already tugging him toward a café on the edge of the piazza, 'you can duck in the bathroom and get cleaned up, and I'll get us something hot to drink. It's kind of cold out here anyway.'

'OK,' Scott said reluctantly, fingering the box in his pocket. He let her lead him across the crowded stones through even more flocks of pigeons. In the café, he popped upstairs to the tiny bathroom and quickly cleaned up, mortified and irritated in equal measure. So much for a romantic moment.

When he emerged Rachel had ordered two hot coffees to go. They headed back out into the piazza, and Scott hopefully slipped an arm around her shoulders, but the earlier magic was lost.

It was late morning now, and St Mark's Square was filling up with winter tourists taking pictures and talking loudly in a mixture of languages. It was difficult to have an intimate conversation with all the noise and bustle, and Scott soon gave up trying.

When they had finished their coffees they entered the Basilica, and for a moment left the hustle and bustle of the outside masses behind. Stepping into the cathedral was an experience that Scott could only classify as otherworldly; the paintings stretched up the walls and all over the ceilings of the domes above, combined with swirling mosaics and inlays that made the entire interior seem to spring to life.

Rachel pointed out several of the paintings. 'St Mark's Basilica was constructed in the eleventh century,' she whispered. 'The paintings and mosaics were constructed and touched up over the centuries. Very little of the original mosaic tiling on the ceiling is left – probably only a third – due to restorations. If you look up to the roof you can see scenes depicting the life of Christ and the lives of the patron saints of Venice.'

Scott admired the scenes overhead. Every available nook and cranny of the walls and the ceiling was covered in one Biblical scene or another – some that he recognised, and some that he didn't. The press of tourists meant that they had to move fairly quickly through the church interior, and soon they were back out in the Square.

Rachel hooked her arm through Scott's and laced their fingers together. 'So, where to next?'

'You're the tour guide,' he said, and she grinned a little.

'True. How about a tour of the clock tower? One should be starting soon. We can get a good view of San Marco from up there.'

'Sounds good to me,' Scott said, wondering if the clock tower would provide him with a good place for a proposal. Surely a quiet spot overlooking all of the city would be romantic enough for that?

Unfortunately, the stairs were steep and crowded with

tourists, and their tour guide kept up a brisk pace as he told them about the history of the construction of the piazza, the Basilica, Doge's Palace, and the clock tower itself.

'The clock tower, Torre dell'Orologio, was designed by Maurizio Codussi and took a period of ten years to complete, beginning in 1496 and ending in 1506. The wings were added later on, perhaps by Pietro Lombardo. You can see the original workings of the clock, which was wound manually until 1998; now it runs off electricity.'

The tour ended on the roof, with a magnificent view of St Mark's Square. Scott didn't regret the tour for a second, but with all the people around there was no way he could propose. Rachel was clearly enjoying herself though, even if she was distracted by all of the chatter around her. She conversed for a moment in Italian with their tour guide and turned back to him. 'He says that if we love the view here, we should go to the Campanile. It's the tallest building in the city.'

'Off we go, then.' Scott let Rachel lead the way as they completed the tour and bounded away to the Campanile, where they climbed yet more steep stairs to reach the top. The view, however, was reward enough: at 325 feet tall, the bell tower offered them an amazing view of the city, even more so than what they had seen from the other one. All of Venice was visible from here, and even Rachel stopped talking long enough to be enchanted by the sight.

Snow dusted the rooftops of Venice like powdered sugar. Holiday decorations could be seen strung in streets and along canals; here and there a brightly lit Christmas tree was visible. From up so high the people of Venice looked like brightly coloured ants, rushing here and there in the streets. Scott's stomach rumbled, and he realised it must be dinner time; many of those people below were likely rushing off to eat.

With this in mind, he and Rachel descended the steep flights of stairs back to street level and set off in search of a restaurant.

It wasn't hard to find one, and once they were settled in and dining on appetisers of fried meatballs and calamari, waiting for their *Secondi* to appear, Scott started to relax. This day certainly hadn't lent itself to the perfect romantic moment, but it was only Friday afternoon; he had two more days to make it happen. He'd already sought out a charming restaurant and a gondola ride, both of which he imagined would be perfect settings for a proposal that would surprise and delight Rachel.

The waiter arrived with part of their order, and she chatted to him in Italian. Scott sipped contentedly at his wine. Rachel was having a blast, and he had to admit that he was having fun, too. He just needed to be patient and wait for the right moment. In a city so famed for romance, surely it couldn't be far away?

Chapter 5

Naomi woke up slowly, stretching languorously.

The winter sunshine was barely peeking around the curtains of their hotel room, and she snuggled deeper under the fluffy duvet. Max was still sleeping, blissfully unaware of the world, and she smiled to herself. Poor, dear Max.

She knew he was probably dreaming of being back at home in England, where he didn't have to travel by boat and where Frosted Flakes and bacon sandwiches were easy to come by.

The fact that he would go to such lengths to treat her to a dream holiday in Italy when he was so clearly out of his element spoke volumes about how he felt about her.

She stole a quick glance at the clock and bit her lip, feeling momentarily guilty for having not called before she went to bed for the night.

What if Julia fussed, or had trouble sleeping, or wasn't feeling well? What sort of mother didn't check up on these things?

Almost as if he could sense her consternation, Max woke up beside her, stretching and groaning. Naomi smiled as she rolled over to face him. He always looked so rumpled when he woke up – hair sticking up in multiple directions, pillow creases on his face – and somehow she found it charming. He looked so relaxed and unassuming, much like he had in college when they had first started dating. She leaned over now and planted a quick kiss on his forehead. 'Good morning, sleepyhead.'

'Morning.' He rubbed the sleep out of his eyes and looked around. 'Mmm. What time is it?'

'Eight o'clock, aka time to rise and shine and get some breakfast.' Naomi threw back the covers and raced to the bathroom for a hot shower. Max protested weakly from the bed, laughing. 'Not fair. You had a head start.'

Naomi laughed and pulled a fluffy towel down from the rack. Her guilt over not calling home was fading a little. Julia was in the most capable of hands, she reminded herself, and after all, she had to admit spending time alone with Max was a luxury she'd sorely missed.

She'd got so used to building her daily routine around the baby that she'd forgotten what it was like to spend a romantic evening with her husband and wake up slowly, on her own timetable, the next morning.

It was rather a lovely feeling.

Once they had both dressed for the day, in warm sweaters and coats, they set out to find breakfast. Naomi was thrilled to get a chance to experience a real Italian menu, though she could sense Max's trepidation.

To say he wasn't big on trying new foods would be putting it nicely, but luckily a traditional Continental breakfast didn't veer too far from what he was used to eating back home. At the café near their hotel they ordered frothy cappuccinos and plates of flaky pastries filled with sweet cream or chocolate. There was fruit, yogurt and muesli on the side, and hot chocolate. Max seemed pleasantly surprised, and Naomi found herself relishing her breakfast without having to worry about feeding the baby.

After breakfast they set out to see the sights. Naomi had read plenty of guidebooks on Venice before they had left, taking meticulous notes in a small notebook to carry in her handbag, but nothing could have prepared her for the reality of the city.

The narrow stone side streets felt almost like hidden passageways, beckoning to visitors with the promise that they might lead to some secret location. Even with the winter chill, the canals were a sight to see, with gondolas gliding past and colourfully attired gondoliers calling out to each other as they went. Everywhere there were strings of Christmas lights and oversized decorations for the upcoming festivities.

Wandering through the streets and over the stone bridges that crisscrossed the canals, Naomi felt like she was melting away into another time and place entirely. Shop windows with signs in Italian and English advertised blown glass, Venetian masks, and leather goods. They stopped to browse in a few shops and when Naomi admired a hand-blown glass Christmas ornament, Max promptly bought it for their tree back home. She eagerly pressed her face to the windows of other shops, admiring the handiwork within even though she couldn't decipher most of the signs.

There were plenty of other tourists about, but as she strolled hand in hand with her husband, Naomi was starting to feel like it was just the two of them. Max seemed happy to find plenty of streets that could be walked rather than toured by boat, and he was starting to relax.

Italian music drifted from shops and trattorias as tourists entered or exited, holding the doors open just long enough for the sounds and smells within to escape onto the street. There was an intoxicating blend of spices, perfumes, leather, food, and wine in the air, and it fuelled Naomi's excitement at seeing the city.

According to her guidebooks one of the must-see attractions in the city was the Piazza San Marco, or St Mark's Square, which was bordered by several attractions: St Mark's Basilica, the Doge's Palace, a historic clock tower, and a bell tower of impressive height, the tallest building in the city. Naomi had planned ahead and booked a multi-attraction ticket and tours, so they could take in all of the sights in one day. She had no intention of missing out on anything so magnificent; after all, who knew when they might be able to take a trip like this again?

Chapter 6

As it turned out, the tours were every bit as amazing as promised online. The Square was packed with tourists and with flocks of pigeons; Max snapped a few shots of Naomi trying to coax one onto her outstretched hand, laughing as it flew away, disgruntled, because it realised she didn't have a snack for it. They lined up with other tourists for the trip through the Basilica and were rewarded with hearty neck cramps from gawking at the mosaics and paintings inside.

'When we get back to the hotel, I'm wrapping a hot towel around my neck,' Naomi said with a laugh. Max wrapped an arm around her as they moved leisurely across the Square to the clock tower, where their next tour awaited. 'Maybe the front desk could recommend a spa or something? You know, one of those places that does couple's massages?'

'You'd be up for that?' Naomi looked at him in surprise. Normally any mention of a new activity would have him wrinkling his nose in suspicion. But he nodded. 'You'd enjoy it. And I would ... try to enjoy it!'

Naomi nestled closer to him as they joined the line for the Doge's Palace. She couldn't even remember the last time they'd been able to do something like this – well over a year ago, she supposed, before the late stages of pregnancy and then the baby left her essentially housebound. She was startled to realise she was truly enjoying herself, not worrying about Julia. She snuck a quick glance at Max, who only smiled. She smiled back a little. Was he thinking the same thing – that they were long overdue for this kind of date? As if to answer her question, he pulled her close and gave her a quick kiss.

Their guide was enthusiastic about her subject, and gave them a richly detailed rundown of the history of the Palazzo Ducale. Even Max looked interested as she explained that the Palace was the hub of political power in Venice from the ninth century onwards, and its proximity to the Basilica was no accident, but rather a result of the intertwining of church and state in Italy at that time. Gothic arches and an impressive array of sculptures, paintings and frescoes covered the inside of the Palace. The tour wound through multiple floors, through state rooms, criminal courts, cells, cramped administrative offices, and finally outside to the Bridge of Sighs.

'Why is it called that?' asked one of the tourists, and the guide explained that the bridge connected the interrogation rooms of the Palace to the outside world. Built in 1600, the bridge earned its name from Lord Byron centuries later based on the somewhat romantic notion that it offered convicts their last view of Venice before entering their cells; prompted by the beauty of it, they would sigh over their city.

'Of course,' she added, tapping on the stone bars on one of the bridge's tiny windows, 'there wasn't a lot to back up that notion. By the time the bridge was built, there wasn't a lot of criminal traffic going in and out of the Palace. And with the small windows and the roof, there wasn't much you could see of the outside city. But it makes for a very poetic name, in any case.'

Following the tour of the Palace Max and Naomi joined the line leading into the Torre dell'Orologio clock tower. The stairs inside the clock tower were steep, and Naomi marvelled at the idea that for years someone had actually climbed the tower on a regular basis to wind it up. Thank goodness for the modern marvel of electricity.

If she thought that tower was steep, however, the Campanile bell tower was even more staggering. The guide explained the story of the tower's 1902 collapse and rebuilding, and pointed out the view of the Dolomite Mountains in the distance. Naomi sighed with delight as she leaned on the railing, surveying Venice below. It looked to her like one of those miniature Christmas towns that people assembled on their mantels in December, complete with tiny people, glowing shop windows, and snow-powdered rooftops. She could almost picture the spot where a tiny horse and carriage would travel, laden with packages to be delivered to homes in the city. Her mother loved to create such miniature cityscapes in her home every Christmas; she was probably setting one up now, or shopping for new pieces with baby Julia in tow.

The thought of her daughter made her start suddenly. She looked quickly at her phone. Time to call and check in! She slipped the phone back into her bag and joined the crowd of tourists edging their way slowly down the steep stairs.

Night was falling in Venice, and while another city might have quietened down with the dying light, San Marco seemed even more beautiful now as the Christmas lights blazed to life. The Basilica was gloriously lit up, and everywhere Naomi looked festive displays were being lit up in the darkness. The city looked like a romantic postcard at night.

Unfortunately, the dying daylight also meant the temperature was dropping, and Naomi and Max hastily moved on from the Square to find a restaurant. Naomi hadn't noticed her stomach was growling; now she realised they had skipped lunch in the excitement of the tours. It didn't take long to find a little trattoria that wasn't too crowded and sit down to order their dinner.

Max let Naomi take the reins in ordering, and she found it hard to pick just a few dishes. There was calamari, a favourite of hers already; pumpkin risotto and seafood risotto; seafood dishes she'd never even heard of, including squid ink and cuttlefish; and of course plenty of tempting noodle and vegetable dishes, often with seafood in the mix. Max visibly paled at the mention of the squid ink but bravely ordered a tamer seafood dish with crab meat and vegetables. Naomi finally settled on her order and also asked for a bottle of wine for the table; the waiter produced one with a flourish, along with two very generously sized wine glasses.

The concept of lingering over a meal at a restaurant had always seemed a little odd back home since Julia, but somehow here in this ancient and magical city it seemed that hurrying through the meal would be an affront to Venice itself.

Max and Naomi ate slowly, talking about everything they had seen during their tours. By the time dessert had been served, drunk the last of the wine, paid the bill and got ready to leave, they had been at the restaurant for nearly three hours.

It was only once they had returned to their hotel room that Naomi realised she hadn't called her parents to check in on Julia. While Max brushed his teeth in the bathroom, she guiltily dialled her mother's cell phone.

She answered after several rings. 'Naomi! How is Venice?'

'Beautiful,' she answered truthfully. 'Amazing. We're seeing so much. And the food is incredible.'

Her mother chuckled. 'And how is Max coping?'

Naomi laughed a little, remembering her husband's face as they perused the menu at the restaurant. 'Well, he's a little alarmed by some of it, and he doesn't like the boats. But he's having fun. How is Julia doing?'

'Oh, she's as perky as ever! We're out shopping for Christmas decorations now.'

'You remembered to bundle her up?' Naomi immediately thought of a dozen other things to ask: *Did you pack her favourite stuffed animal? Do you have an extra soother in case she loses hers? What about a bottle? What about ... did you ... what if ...*

But her mother seemed to anticipate the questions. 'She's wearing her favourite teddy-bear coat, I packed Mr Hippo in her changing bag, she has an extra soother and a bottle of formula, and she ate and got a clean nappy on before we left the house. And we'll be home in plenty of time for a little pre-dinner nap. Don't worry, Naomi, she's doing fine! Concentrate on enjoying yourself. Your weekend will be over far too soon.'

'I suppose you're right,' Naomi said, giving her 'I love you's and hanging up. Max emerged from the bathroom and collapsed onto the bed. 'Oof. I'm worn out from all that walking. How's Julia?'

'Apparently she's doing great,' Naomi said, fiddling with her phone. She felt torn – on the one hand she was obviously glad to hear that her daughter was doing well, but on the other she still felt bad for being so far away. And yet, she'd truly enjoyed her day, and knew this entire trip would have been impossible with a baby in tow. 'You're still up for more sightseeing tomorrow?'

'Of course,' he said quickly, trying to look alert and failing utterly. She leaned down and kissed him. 'Get some rest. There will be plenty of time to make plans in the morning.'

Max fell asleep almost immediately, and Naomi slipped

under the blankets. For a moment she debated leaving the phone on in case her mother tried to call, but then she resolutely turned the ringer to the 'silent' mode. *Mum's right*, she thought sleepily, pulling the blankets up to her chin. *This weekend will be over in a heartbeat. I'm going to enjoy it while I can.* With thoughts of decadent desserts and twinkling lights still filling her head, she drifted off to sleep.

Chapter 7

Lucy woke on Saturday morning feeling strangely refreshed. She wasn't sure what had changed overnight, but somehow as she stretched and stood in front of her window, gazing down at the canal below, she felt lighter, brighter, and full of excitement for the rest of the weekend.

She chalked it up in part to the delightfully fluffy mound of blankets and pillows on her bed – a good night's rest always made her feel so much better about things – and partly to her visits to the Basilica and Murano the day before. She couldn't exactly explain why, but seeing something so magnificent made her feel a little better about her own small problems. Even if her relationship had crashed and burned, there was still so much beauty to enjoy in the world, so why should she mope? She felt ready to get out and enjoy herself.

She hummed a little as she dressed, pulling on warm black pants and a black turtleneck sweater with her boots and coat. She slightly regretted not bringing anything more colourful with her; she'd been in a bit of a funk when she packed. She pulled her blonde hair up into a French twist and added her everyday diamond stud earrings. On impulse, she popped down to the front desk and asked for the nearest chemist.

Twenty minutes later, she stood in front of the glass window of the shop, surveying her reflection as she applied red lipstick from a freshly purchased tube. She looked over her appearance with a small amount of satisfaction. The lipstick seemed to make all the difference in the world. She no longer saw a sad post-break-up woman in the mirror; now she saw a sassy single gal out to have a fun holiday weekend in a foreign city. Just this thought excited her.

She had a new sway in her step as she popped into a small coffee shop for a frothy hot coffee and biscotti. The only Italian she knew was '*grazie*' but she grinned nonetheless as she thanked the girl at the counter for her food. Sipping the coffee and munching on the crunchy-sweet biscotti, she set off down the street to the nearest dock to catch a vaporetto.

Lucy made it a point to visit museums and art galleries in any city she visited, and her main destination today was the Gallerie dell'Accademia – an amazing collection of artwork that spanned back over centuries, and included work by the sixteenth-century Venetian painter Titian – followed closely by a trip to the Peggy Guggenheim Collection, which boasted a dazzling array of more modern art by American and European artists alike, including Picasso and Jackson

Pollock. She was certain the museums would hold her for most of the day. After that, she could spend her Sunday doing a bit of leisurely souvenir shopping – what better Christmas gifts to bring home than genuine Italian stuff from Venice? Then, she thought sadly, she would return to the bridge and do what she came here to do.

The Gallerie proved every bit as involved as her guide-book had promised, and the hours flew by as she toured the various rooms. The tour was guided, but the group that day was fairly small, and so she was able to linger and enjoy the various pieces of art. At one point she thought she saw a man who reminded her of Dominic in one of the adjoining rooms, and for a moment she wished he could be there to share the tour with her, but she quickly pushed that thought aside. *Today is for me to enjoy the present, not linger on the past.*

In one of the rooms, surveying Giorgione's *Tempest*, Lucy found herself near an English couple. She commented casually on the artwork and hearing her Irish accent, they immediately introduced themselves, and the trio quickly fell into small chat about all they'd seen in the city.

'We're here as an early Christmas present to ourselves,' the man who was called Max explained, beaming at his wife. 'It's our first outing since our daughter was born.'

'Oh! You have a daughter?' Lucy had always loved the idea of having a little girl. 'How old?'

'Eight months.' His wife, Naomi, was clearly a proud mum, pulling up pictures on her smartphone to show off.

Lucy made appropriate compliments on the little girl's cute looks and wide smile. 'Is it hard to be away from her?'

Naomi hesitated for a moment. 'A little,' she confessed. Max looked like he wanted to say something but wisely didn't, and Lucy guessed that it was harder than the mother wanted to admit. She tactfully changed the subject. 'What's been your favourite sight in Venice so far?'

'I think the bell tower at St Mark's Square,' Naomi said dreamily. 'The view makes you feel like you're looking at a postcard. It's such a romantic city.'

Yes, it is, Lucy thought with a pang. She couldn't help envying the couple a bit for their romantic trip. It was clear they were relishing the time spent together, without the demands of parenthood to interrupt their time together. She supposed that *was* one perk to the single life – no worries about other people imposing on your routine, especially 'people' of the nappy-and-bottle variety.

Naomi was asking Lucy about her own trip to the city, and she struggled for a moment to explain what she was doing there. She finally settled on the generic half-truth 'it's a gift to myself' rather than explaining that she was there to forget about love lost. It seemed like too sad a tale to share with strangers, especially those celebrating their own happy romance.

She had a bit of time in between tours to grab lunch, and found herself munching on a hot panini and coffee at a tiny café. Afterwards she joined the tour through the Guggenheim collection and quickly lost herself in room after room of art. The variety presented made it impossible to get bored, and the tour almost seemed to end too quickly.

Outside, the weak afternoon light signalled the close of day. Tourists were moving in groups to find dinner, attend an evening Mass at one of the city's cathedrals, or rent a gondola for a private cruise up and down the canals to view the holiday lights.

Not quite yet ready to move on to dinner so early, Lucy opted to hire a gondolier and relax on the canals.

She was glad she'd bundled up warmly, because the air off the water was definitely cold. However, the view of San Marco at night by boat was worth the chill. One of Lucy's favourite childhood memories was that of piling into the family car with her parents and siblings, and driving around their hometown to look at the Christmas lights on homes and businesses. Lucy and her sisters had given imaginary ratings to the displays as they passed and debated seriously about the merits of each, awarding scores to the decorations based on imagination, colourfulness, and sheer size of the displays.

Some of their favourite houses went all out, with all of the trees in the front gardens ablaze in ropes of lights and lighted figures across the driveway and even on the roof. As a child Lucy had found it delightful; now she thought about how much work those displays must have entailed.

The ones in Venice evoked a similar feeling of awe.

Large lighted stars hung above her, seemingly suspended in thin air. Strings of lights outlined windows and doorways or encircled trees on balconies. Here and there a business had a brightly lit nativity or other display in their shop windows. Most of the bridges, too, were brightly lit for night, and the cathedrals all featured lighting of their own. Christmas music floated down the canals from nearby businesses; though most of it was in Italian, Lucy recognised the tunes and hummed along.

Her good-natured gondolier hummed too and occasionally sang along to the tunes.

By the end of her forty-minute boat ride, Lucy had pretty well lost all feeling in her nose and fingertips, but her heart and soul felt warmer. She asked the gondolier for a nearby restaurant recommendation and thanked him warmly, rubbing her hands together as she walked down the street. The joyful Christmas spirit combined with the obvious magic of the city was improving her mood more and more with every passing hour.

She ducked into a trattoria playing Italian sacred festive music; Lucy recognised the tunes of 'Silent Night' and several other hymns that had played on heavy rotation during her childhood. She smiled at the thought of how she had squirmed through Mass services at church while thinking ahead to opening presents!

The waiter brought appetisers and wine and soon returned to the table with a hearty order of seafood risotto, crusty bread and marinated anchovies. Lucy ate her fill and lingered at the table afterward, enjoying a strong cup of espresso despite the late hour. She nibbled her tiramisu and asked the waiter to add an extra bottle of wine to her order; she could take that back to one of her sisters in Dublin as a Christmas gift.

Satisfied and laden down with a bag containing her wine, Lucy strolled slowly down the street, lost in thought. She felt almost giddy from the fun of the day and of course, the delicious food. She was so lost in thought (and more than a little tipsy) that for a moment, she imagined Dominic standing at the corner of the narrow street, waiting for her.

She sighed to herself and continued walking.

My imagination is just not going to let me be, she thought ruefully. *Now I know what unrequited love means.*

Even a full day of great fun and good food can't get a person out of your head. You still see them everywhere you go.

Chapter 8

Back at the hotel Lucy tucked the wine safely in her suitcase, and drew a hot bath scented with plenty of lavender and chamomile.

Soaking blissfully in the bubbles, she considered what to do the following day.

First, a lazy breakfast. Second, shopping; she was already compiling a mental list of things to look for in the little shops: a leather-bound journal for Dad, some blown-glass trinket for Mum (maybe a Venetian mask or a paper-weight?), perhaps a knitted scarf for her younger sister.

And of course, if I find some little things for myself, too, that wouldn't be half bad.

Her eyes fell on her smartphone, sitting on the bathroom counter. It was tempting – oh so tempting – to call Dominic's number, just to see what he was doing. They hadn't spoken since the break-up, but that didn't mean she couldn't call just to say hi. She might get his voicemail, and then that would solve a lot of the awkwardness of having an actual conversation. And wouldn't he be surprised when he heard she was calling from Venice.

She composed a message in her head:

Hi, Dominic, I'm in Venice and I was just thinking of you – remembering all the fun we had here last year. God, no – that was far too needy. Maybe: *Hey, Dominic, was just thinking of you and wanted to wish you a Merry Christmas.*

Too casual? What about: *Hi, Dominic, hope you're doing well. Maybe we could grab a coffee some time and catch up?*

She half reached out for the phone before she pulled her arm back. *Nope. Don't do it.*

This trip was about getting over heartbreak, not inviting it back in. Besides, she wasn't sure what might be worse – having to talk to Dominic and dealing with a stilted conversation, or leaving a message that he might not return.

After all, it was possible he didn't want to speak to her at all, and calling him might just confirm that for good – something she'd rather not deal with, in all honesty.

Or, he might return her call with some news about a new girlfriend – something she *definitely* didn't want to hear about. At least if she didn't call, she didn't have to face the complications of a conversation. Dominic could stay safely tucked away in her memories and one day he would be just that – a memory.

Lucy finally drained the bathtub and wrapped herself up in a fluffy robe before settling down in bed with a magazine. She was drowsy from the wine and the warm water, and it was easy to put Dominic out of mind and curl up to sleep.

She dreamed that night of standing on the bridge last winter with Dominic in the snow, hand in hand as they locked the padlock.

But in the morning she didn't remember her dreams, and she whistled cheerily to herself as she got ready for another day.

Chapter 9

Saturday morning dawned colder than the previous day, but Scott wasn't daunted in the least. He'd already bounced back from the disappointment of his failed proposal at St Mark's Square, and he'd moved on to an even better idea: a romantic candlelit dinner near Rialto Bridge, followed by a stroll along some of the quieter streets nearby.

There, under a starry sky, away from all the hustle and bustle of the tourist crowds, he would get down on one knee and propose to the love of his life. He could already picture the scene in his head; he'd replayed it a dozen times since he got out of bed that morning.

But first, the day ahead promised plenty more sightseeing in the historic city. Rachel, enamoured of Italian art, was eager to tour the Gallerie dell'Accademia, which boasted centuries' worth of Italian paintings, frescoes, sculptures and more. For his part, Scott didn't really know the difference between the various periods and styles of painting, nor did he understand the political significance of some of the pieces, but Rachel was having fun and for her sake he made an effort to have fun, too. It was hard to concentrate on the tour, though, when he kept thinking forward to the table he'd booked for the evening.

Even as they sat at lunch, he was only half-listening to Rachel as she chattered on eagerly about the art they'd seen. Inside he was playing out the proposal as he intended it to happen:

First, they would go to the restaurant. Scott had found one near the impressive Rialto bridge; if you sat near the windows you had an excellent view, and for the festive season the bridge was lit up much like the rest of the Grand Canal.

They would enjoy a lovely dinner, then take a walk across the bridge and enjoy the sight of the holiday lights across the Grand Canal. Perhaps, if the mood struck them, they would take a gondola down the canal and marvel at the lights from the water.

Then, they would take a quiet walk through the less-populated city streets. Then, on a quiet bridge, away from the crowds, Scott would get down on one knee, pull out the ring, and …

'Earth to Scott.' He snapped out of his reverie to see that Rachel was staring at him, looking slightly bemused. He realised she must have asked a question, and he felt his ears reddening a little. 'Sorry, babe, I was lost in thought. What were you saying?'

She smiled and said, 'I was suggesting we do a little shopping today. Instead of hitting another museum. I could tell you were a bit bored with the last one.'

Scott winced a little. 'Was it that obvious?'

She laughed out loud. 'It's OK. I know I'm the one who's crazy about Italy; I know you're not as big a fan.'

'We can do whatever you want today,' he promised, and meant it. He wanted her to enjoy herself, and more importantly, he wanted her to be in good spirits for their dinner date. He patted his coat pocket once more and followed her out of the café and through the city streets.

Shopping proved to be a bit of an interesting experience. Rachel was clearly enjoying chatting with the shopkeepers in Italian, and she found several small items that she wanted to purchase: a leather bag, a cashmere scarf with a gossamer texture and a price tag to match, and some beautiful tiny glass birds, which were wrapped carefully and placed in a sturdy box for safekeeping.

By the time they had finished touring the shops and returned Rachel's purchases to the hotel, it was time to get ready for dinner. As usual, Scott was astounded by how a few simple changes could turn Rachel from a daytime tourist into an evening beauty.

She emerged from the bathroom with her hair swept back up from her face, showing off a pair of diamond earrings he had bought her for her birthday. She'd added a little make-up but not much – she didn't need it – and swapped her sweater for a silky, low-cut black top. She'd kept the warm black pants and boots, though, and bundled up in a thick scarf, gloves and coat.

'It's freezing out here!' she exclaimed, as their water taxi took them to the restaurant. 'I'm so glad we're not going on a gondola tour tonight.'

'Yeah, me too,' Scott echoed, privately disappointed. *Well, there's always tomorrow.*

As promised, the Rialto Bridge was aglow with lights that changed colour as festive tunes played over the water. Scott and Rachel *ooh*ed appreciatively at the sight and hurried into the restaurant to their table.

The waiter frowned when Scott mentioned his reservation. 'We seem to have had some issues with our booking, sir,' he said, and Scott's heart sank. 'Somehow there are mix-ups with the seating. That table is not available this evening.'

His expression made it clear he wasn't going to offer any further explanations or help, so Scott tried politely, 'Could you find us another table then? I promised my girlfriend a romantic dinner tonight.'

The man looked irritated at this request, as though the endless romantic trials of visiting tourists were of no concern to him. However, he consulted his book and grouchily conceded that he did have an available table.

'This way,' he said, marching off briskly without a backward glance, and Scott and Rachel glanced at each other in concern. Nonetheless, Scott was determined to make the most of the night, and they hurried after the man to the table he indicated.

Scott thought that it was almost as if the guy had deliberately selected the worst table in the restaurant. Tucked into a dark corner, it offered no view of the bridge whatsoever, but a very good earful of the clamour from the kitchen.

He reached under the table and squeezed Rachel's hand in apology. 'I'm so sorry, I didn't know this would happen. Do you want to go somewhere else?'

'No, this is fine.' She busied herself studying the menu. Scott also buried himself in the menu, and when a waiter appeared to take their order, they decided to start with a round of appetisers. This waiter also seemed a little on the surly side, but Scott decided it could just be the busy evening – the restaurant was packed – and tried to brush it off.

Wine appeared on the table in short order, and Scott and Rachel tried to strike up a conversation. It was difficult to chat quietly with the din of their fellow diners and the noise from the kitchen, and after a while they fell silent. Some time passed before it occurred to Scott that their appetisers had yet to appear. He finally caught the attention of their waiter and inquired about their order, only to be met with a terse, 'I'll check' before the man disappeared without a second look.

Scott glanced at Rachel, but she was carefully studying the other diners, trying not to let on that she was disappointed. After what seemed like forever, the waiter finally returned with a plate of bread and olive oil and fried meatballs – all rather lukewarm now, after what Scott suspected was a long period sitting on a side counter waiting to be served. They picked half-heartedly at the food and waited for their Secondi to come.

The second round of the meal came out with decidedly more speed, but when the waiter set Rachel's dish down in front of her, she said something haltingly in Italian. The waiter did a double-take and apologised curtly, whisking the dish away. Scott didn't need a translation to know that whatever the man had brought out was definitely *not* the risotto dish she'd ordered.

Next the waiter brought out another dish, but after a couple of bites she had to signal him back. 'Sorry,' she said, 'it's just that this has cuttlefish in it, and I asked for the chicken.'

This time the waiter was duly embarrassed, and muttered several apologies as he took away her plate. In the meantime another order had arrived – polenta with porcini and sausage – and Rachel nibbled at it a bit while they waited. She urged Scott to go ahead and eat his, but he felt bad eating when she was having so many issues with her own order.

Finally the waiter brought out fresh risotto with chicken, and Rachel dug in. By now Scott's own food was growing cold, but he ate as much of it as he could anyway. When Rachel finished eating he leaned across the table and whispered, 'Do you want to order dessert?'

'No thanks!' She shook her head and glanced at the kitchen, as though expecting to see the waiter again. 'No, this was terrible. Let's just go.'

They paid and left, Rachel shivering in the cold. Scott quickly abandoned the idea of either a gondola ride or a walk; he guessed she wouldn't enjoy either, and after their disastrous meal, he felt terrible that he hadn't planned out better entertainment for the night.

Back at the hotel, he scrolled through internet listings of local late-night happenings while Rachel warmed up with a hot shower. When she emerged, wrapped up in a cosy robe, he queried, 'Would you want to go out again? We could catch a late-night movie, maybe, or go to one of the local bars for a drink?'

Rachel made a face as she crawled into bed. 'Ugh, I don't think so. I'm so worn out, and it's so cold. Let's just stay in for the rest of the night, OK?'

'OK.' Scott closed his laptop and decided to take a quick shower to warm up, too; Rachel was right about the temperature outside. By the time he emerged ten minutes later, however, soft snores could be heard coming from Rachel's side of the bed. Stifling a sigh of disappointment, he switched off her bedside lamp and crawled in beside her.

The ring box was still waiting in his coat pocket. Scott thought sadly of his ruined evening and wondered if the following day would provide any better chances for the proposal he wanted to make.

Come o*n, Venice,* he thought desperately, *show me a little romantic magic before we go home.*

Chapter 10

On Saturday morning, Max and Naomi got off to a sluggish start. Max noticed happily that she was relaxing more with each passing day; today she slept much later than usual, and seemed happy to cuddle in bed rather than rushing to get up and out of the door. He took it as a good sign that the beauty of the city was working its magic.

He didn't want to say it out loud and spoil the mood, but he missed mornings like this – just the two of them, cuddled up in bed, then perhaps picking out an activity for the day. No baby needing to be fed, clothed, changed and coddled; no schedule that included mandatory feedings and naps. Just he and Naomi, the way it used to be.

Part of him felt so guilty for even thinking that, though. Of course he loved Julia – until she was born, he hadn't quite understood how people fell head over heels in love with infants, but one look into her serious green eyes and he was a goner.

He adored his daughter, loved playing with her, napping with her on his chest, dancing around in the living room holding her and listening to her laugh. He looked forward to many years of firsts – first day of school, first pet, first date, first car – and to many father–daughter chats. He was thrilled with his daughter, and thrilled with what a wonderful mother Naomi was to their baby.

He just missed having his wife around, too.

He sat in bed and watched her put on make-up in the bathroom mirror. It seemed like so much of her energy these days went into the baby, not into herself. It wasn't just their relationship that had been put on the back burner; he realised that now, a bit belatedly.

Little things like putting on mascara in the mornings, picking up a novel she wanted to read – they had gone out the window in favour of feedings, changings and caring for Julia. Max realised a bit guiltily that his wife didn't have a lot of time for her own interests any more and he wondered if maybe he should be chipping in a lot more than he was. Either way, he wanted to do something to help make it up to her.

So, while she was busy getting ready for the day, he popped down to the hotel reception desk and asked the manager on duty to help him find a good couple's massage therapist in the city. 'I don't speak Italian, so perhaps you could set something up for us? Preferably with someone who speaks a little English?'

The manager seemed only too happy to help, and

promised to have something lined up for the afternoon, after they came back from their museum tour but before dinner. That treat all taken care of, Max went back upstairs to collect his wife and whisk her off to tour the art galleries.

The first one was full of classical Italian art from the past several centuries, and Max looked around with amazement at the extensive collection. He didn't necessarily know anything about the artists featured – none of the names jumped out at him – but even so it was hard not to be impressed with the huge collection. Their tour guide was fairly chatty but also let them have plenty of time to study the pictures on their own.

In one of the rooms, he and Naomi struck up a conversation with an Irish girl visiting the city – from Dublin, as it turned out. 'Oh, we're from Newcastle,' Naomi explained. 'So we're used to this cold!'

The woman laughed. 'At least the city isn't flooded,' she said. 'It happens from time to time. I've been lucky, though; both times I've visited it's been dry.'

They chatted for a while about everything they'd seen so far, and Naomi asked if Lucy was travelling solo or with a partner. For a moment the woman looked sad, but she laughed. 'No romantic trip for me, I'm afraid. I'm just taking a little break as a Christmas gift to myself.'

After the galleries, Max and Naomi found a nearby café where they ordered miniature pizzas and drinks for lunch.

Naomi checked her phone, scrolling across the screen to check the time. Max could see that she was calculating the hour time difference between them and whether it was too early yet to call home, and he said quickly, 'I have a surprise for you.'

'Oh?' Naomi was distracted enough to put the phone back in her bag. He nodded, encouraged. 'Remember I mentioned that massage yesterday? Well, I asked the hotel manager to book us one. I've got the paper in my coat pocket with the address; we can have a water taxi take us straight there. Our appointment is at two o'clock.'

'Really?' He'd expected her to be excited, but he hadn't realised she would light up so much at the idea. She quickly checked the time. 'Oh, we should leave now! We don't want to be late.'

At her insistence Max hurried through the rest of his pizza. *That wasn't even half-bad*, he thought reluctantly. *Maybe Italian food is growing on me.*

The directions were clear enough to follow, and the water taxi easily deposited them outside a luxurious-looking day spa. To Max's relief, the masseuses who were handling their appointment both spoke fluent English, so at least he didn't have to feel awkward about *that* part of things.

If Max tolerated the treatments – he thought they were a little frilly, to be honest – he could tell Naomi was beside herself. They started out with a foot bath and moved through a series of massages and body treatments, rubbing in fragrant oils that Max supposed were relaxing or calming. Naomi certainly looked relaxed, and he settled down onto his treatment table, feeling a touch better himself.

By the time their hour session was up, Naomi was practically radiant, and Max could definitely feel that the kinks in his neck were long gone.

She was beaming as they glided back down a canal to another restaurant for dinner. 'Have you ever felt so relaxed before?' she said dreamily, and he couldn't help but grin. He supposed he hadn't, but better than that was seeing how relaxed she was. It was like her old self was coming back – the one who wasn't constantly stressed and fussing over the baby.

Dinner was the usual mix of terrifying choices, but somehow Max didn't care so much. He discovered that he could in fact order pasta with a tomato and meat sauce, and did so without caring if it looked too English. He didn't even know the names of the dishes Naomi ordered, though he could smell seafood in at least one of them. When dessert came around he even tried a bite of her tiramisu, though he still thought the espresso and chocolate was too strong.

They finally left the restaurant late and went to hail a boat to take them back to their hotel. Max noticed all the gondoliers lining up outside nearby and on impulse said, 'Shall we take a detour?'

Naomi was snuggled up tightly against him. She followed his gaze, looking delighted. 'Are you sure? I know you don't like being so close to the water ...'

'I can put up with it.' *I think.*

Max asked the gondolier to take them on a short tour of the canals, and off they went, poling out into the Grand Canal and taking in the sights of San Marco by night.

Naomi sighed contentedly. The lights strung up along buildings and over bridges reflected on the lapping waters of the canals, leaving the whole city aglow. It was hard not to feel festive, gliding under lit snowflakes and stars and listening to classic Christmas hymns sung in Italian playing through loudspeakers on Rialto Bridge and in shops closing up for the night.

Max tried carefully to avoid looking down at the water as they glided along. He found that if he just kept his eyes on the level, looking at the colourful paint of the buildings or at the lights overhead, he could almost forget they were in a glorified canoe.

Naomi seemed perfectly content. Out of the blue, the gondolier gently sang something Italian in a baritone voice, and although Max couldn't understand a word, he thought he could sense some of the joy in the man's voice.

The gondolier ended their tour right at the dock of their hotel, and Max released a breath as he climbed out of the shallow boat. A dock wasn't solid ground, but it sure beat a gondola for stability.

Upstairs he shrugged out of his heavy clothes into pyjamas and listened as Naomi drew a bath and changed into nightclothes. To his surprise and delight, she emerged from the bathroom smelling like her perfume and wearing a silky black slip that was definitely not intended for sleeping in. Apparently she'd forgotten all about calling home promptly each evening, and once she'd climbed into bed he forgot all about it too.

Later that night he woke up for no reason, startled out of a dream, or maybe hearing some noise outside the hotel. He got up quietly and went to the bathroom to get a drink of water, and when he came back he lay propped up on one elbow, studying his wife.

For the first time in over a year, she seemed totally at peace, breathing softly, her hair spread out over the pillow.

It was a good idea to come here, he thought, satisfied, as he curled up next to his wife. They hadn't had so much quality time together since the baby came, and he thought it was worth every moment spent in those darn boats.

A feeling of extreme contentment spread through him as he listened to Naomi's soft breathing, and he eased himself carefully back under the blankets to cuddle up next to her, drifting away to sleep.

Chapter 11

When Sunday morning dawned cold and overcast, with a chance of snow, Scott knew at once that his chances of getting Rachel to take a scenic gondola ride were probably low.

After the crowds, the disastrous dinner, and now with the cold, it was obvious her excitement at visiting Venice was waning. She was already talking about what they might do the next weekend at home, discussing the possibility of a movie and drinks with friends, and his heart sank.

Was he never going to get a chance to propose here?

But when he asked if she was game for a gondola tour on the Grand Canal, to his surprise, she agreed. 'It'll be cold,' he added, almost as an afterthought, expecting her to change her mind. But she just shrugged and said that she would wear an extra layer of clothing.

They attended the late morning Mass at St Mark's Basilica, as he'd promised they would, and they were not disappointed. The sacred chorale was sung in Italian, and echoing off the gilded domes of the cathedral it sounded otherworldly.

Scott didn't know much about Catholicism or how Mass progressed, but he was able to appreciate the obvious meaning behind the service. They emerged onto the steps of the Basilica to a light snow, oversize fluffy flakes drifting down to the stones like tiny down feathers.

He was more than happy to spend a quiet afternoon at the hotel, and when they left for their evening gondola ride, he made sure Rachel had bundled up in extra thermals and a warm sweater. He didn't want anything to ruin the night; this was his last big chance to propose before the weekend was over, and nothing would mess it up if he could help it.

But the line for gondola rides was long, and the gondoliers themselves seemed jaded and in a less-than-cheerful mood. Scott tried to put a positive face on things; Rachel remained silent. The minutes in the queue dragged by, and soon it became apparent that they were going nowhere fast, if they intended to go in a gondola.

After nearly an hour, they finally secured a free gondola, and Scott sat down next to Rachel with relief. At last, they were underway!

Rachel tried chatting a bit with the gondolier, switching from English to Italian, but he seemed dismissive and uninterested in making tourist small talk. Finally she gave up, sitting back and snuggling against Scott to take in the sights.

The view of the Grand Canal was even more impressive

from this vantage point, with views of the buildings and also the side canals and bridges that led off to smaller businesses and homes.

However, after just a few minutes of floating along, their boat came to a halt. The large number of vessels out on the canal for the night had led to a water-locked traffic jam, and now boat traffic was nearly at a standstill as gondoliers and water-taxi drivers shouted and argued with each other.

Beside him, Rachel was shivering. Scott hugged her a little tighter. *This was a terrible idea,* he realised, listening to their gondolier mutter to himself in his native language. English or Italian, the tone was the same with a complaint, and it was clear to Scott that the man was not having a good night.

The ride was supposed to last about forty minutes, though Scott knew he could pay for a longer stretch of time if he wanted. However, by the time the forty minutes were up, it felt as though they'd been in the boat for hours. As soon as the gondolier pulled up at a dock, Rachel nearly bolted out of the boat, and Scott hastily paid the man and followed her.

From the set of her shoulders and the way she walked, Scott could tell his girlfriend was dejected. He could also tell she was freezing, and when she ducked into a small café and ordered hot chocolate he asked the waiter to make it two, and followed her to a quiet corner table.

They sat in silence for a moment, warming their hands on the cups and sipping their drinks without speaking. Scott finally reached out to touch Rachel's hand. 'Babe, I'm so sorry for how this weekend's been going. It seems to have just got worse and worse as it went on.'

'It's not your fault,' she said gently, wrapping her hands more tightly around the cup to steal its warmth. 'I guess I thought Venice would be so much more ... magical, I guess.'

'We've just had some bad luck, that's all.' Timidly he asked, 'Do you want to try and find something else to do for the evening ... maybe sit by that café orchestra in Piazza San Marco?'

Rachel shook her head firmly and she looked sad. 'No. The city was fun at first, but like I said I'm a little ... disenchanted by now,' she admitted. 'It's cold, people are in a bad mood, and there are so many tourists. It just isn't the romantic getaway I thought it would be.'

'Yeah, I guess I'm bummed too,' he admitted. *For more reasons than one.*

Rachel drained the last of her hot chocolate. 'So while it's been fun, I think I'm ready to go home.'

'Me too,' he agreed half-heartedly, even though he didn't feel the same way. He quickly finished his hot chocolate and they returned to their hotel by the fastest route possible, avoiding the packed Grand Canal.

In the lobby, Christmas music was playing softly, and Scott took a moment to admire the nativity scene by the front desk. He hadn't paid it much attention before, but now he thought wistfully of the romantic Christmas break he'd planned and how things had run downhill so fast. There didn't seem to be much for it but to admit defeat and head back home.

Maybe I can arrange a really romantic proposal back home, he conceded. *It won't be as good as Venice, but it will be better than nothing.*

Scott climbed into bed as quietly as possible, thinking Rachel was already asleep, but to his surprise she rolled over to face him and said quietly, 'Remember our first date?'

Scott was surprised by the question. 'How could I forget?' he said, snuggling up to her. He had planned the day for nearly two weeks, down to the restaurant reservation, tickets to a movie starring her favourite actor, and dessert at a local hotspot he knew she'd been dying to try.

It had taken no small shortage of planning and a considerable chunk of his wallet, but he'd managed to pull off the best first date he could imagine, and Rachel had been delighted.

Now she rested her head on his arm, closing her eyes. 'And remember when you put together that surprise birthday party for me at that new nightclub, and I had no idea you'd invited my best friends because they were all sworn to secrecy?'

'It wouldn't be a surprise otherwise,' he protested, and she smiled.

'You always go to such lengths to make things perfect,' she said sleepily. 'But I'm happy just spending time with you. Isn't that enough?'

'I guess,' he said reluctantly, nuzzling her cheek.

She opened her eyes and gave him a wry look. 'It's not, though.'

'It's not that,' Scott sputtered, trying to put his feelings into words. 'It's just that … well, I feel like you deserve the best of everything. And I know how much you love Italy, and Venice is supposed to be such a romantic city … and I wanted you to really have the time of your life on this trip. That's all.'

'I did have a lot of fun,' Rachel said, rolling over to tuck her back against him. He curled around her, enjoying the softness of her skin. 'But I've had fun because I was here with you. It wouldn't have mattered if it was a five-star trip if I was alone. Everything – the dinners, the bell tower, touring the Basilica – it was all amazing because I was sharing it with you.'

Scott buried a sigh in her hair. 'I've had an amazing time with you, too. I just wish I could have created more perfect romantic surprises for you. That was part of the whole point of coming here.'

'Well,' Rachel said, sounding suspiciously less sleepy, 'I have a little romantic surprise of my own …'

'What's that?' Scott ran a hand down her side, lingering on her hip, and was surprised when she suddenly pulled his hand around to rest on her stomach.

'I was going to wait to tell you until we got home. I was surprised you didn't say something about me skipping the wine and the seafood.'

For a moment Scott could only stare down at her in shock, and she rolled onto her back, peering up at him in concern. 'Babe? Say something. You're worrying me.'

Scott racked his brain, thinking of the perfect most romantic thing to say. Instead all he could blurt out was, 'I can't believe you climbed all those stairs in the tower yesterday!' and Rachel started laughing and pulled him down for a kiss.

Chapter 12

On Sunday morning, Max and Naomi decided to attend the late morning Mass at St Mark's. Max had attended a few Masses as a child and Naomi had attended more than her share throughout her childhood and teens, but there was something different about standing in a cathedral, listening to a carol sung in a foreign language. It gave a person chills, and yet at the same time it was beautiful. The voices of the choir echoed off the domed roofs and filtered back over the assembled worshippers in the pews.

After the Mass they walked slowly through St Mark's Square, under a cloud of softly falling snow. There were fewer tourists out today, and fewer pigeons due to the weather. Max noticed a young couple also walking through the Square, and pointed them out to Naomi. 'Don't they kind of remind you of us, before we got married and had Julia?'

Naomi looked at the pair and smiled. The girl was

bundled up against the cold and clearly not enjoying it; she pulled her hood up over her red hair in a bid to stay warm. The boyfriend kept one arm protectively around her. 'We were always glued at the hip,' she mused. 'Whatever happened to us?'

'We got busy,' Max conceded. They stopped at a café for coffee and took a quiet table where they could watch the falling snow and talk. Naomi wrapped her hands around her coffee mug and studied the scene outside without speaking.

'Sometimes I think you don't worry about Julia like I do,' she said suddenly, and almost immediately her cheeks reddened, as though she hadn't really meant to speak out loud and was embarrassed that she'd done so.

Max was a little startled, but he thought guiltily of how often he wished they could have more time apart from the baby. 'It's not that,' he began. 'It's just that I miss you – I miss *us*, before we got so wrapped up in real life – and now you're so wrapped up in being a mum, it feels like we don't get much time together. And I don't like that. I miss my wife.'

To his utter bewilderment, Naomi suddenly started to cry. Alarmed, Max patted her arm and fished in her bag for tissues, unsure of how to react.

She dabbed at her eyes, trying to wipe away the tears without disturbing her make-up. 'I just get so worried about her! I'm afraid to be a bad mother. I'm constantly thinking, what if something happens, and I'm not there? What if she needs me, and I'm busy doing something else? It feels so – so selfish to have fun!'

Max blinked, still unsure of how to respond to this sudden outburst. 'But I am having fun, and now I feel terrible for it!' she continued, sniffling. 'I'm enjoying spending time together, just the two of us. I enjoy going out for dinner, and sleeping without listening for a baby monitor. I like getting dressed up and going out, instead of packing a nappy bag. This whole weekend, it's been—' she flailed her arms a bit as she tried to find the words. 'It's been brilliant, and I don't want it to end. But I feel like a bad mum because I'm not checking in on my daughter every few hours.'

'I don't think that makes you a bad mum,' Max said cautiously. He still wasn't sure if this was his cue to say something, or if he should let her keep talking. She didn't respond though, only sniffled, so he kept going. 'I think you're an amazing mum to Julia. And I love you for it. I wouldn't want you any other way. But you need to take care of yourself, too. And I don't want us to be so wrapped up in being parents that we forget about each other. That was the whole point of this trip – for us to reconnect.' He grabbed her hands in his own and gave her a pleading look. 'Please don't feel bad for that. I don't want you to feel bad, I want you to be happy.'

Naomi sniffled and nodded. 'I am happy,' she admitted. 'This whole trip has been so lovely. I just … I'm torn. I feel guilty for not missing Julia more, and I feel guilty for being away from her, and I feel guilty for ignoring you …'

'You can be all those things. It's normal, I promise. I feel them too.'

'Really?' Naomi looked doubtful, but Max nodded. 'I miss her, and then I feel bad for not missing her enough. And I feel bad because I don't think about how you're feeling sometimes.'

Naomi wiped her eyes and drained her mug of cappuccino nearly in one swallow. She set her mug down with a sigh. 'Today I woke up glad that I'll see my daughter tomorrow, and then I felt sad that it's our last day in Venice.'

'Then we should enjoy it,' Max said firmly. 'Tuck the phone away in your bag. You know your mum is perfectly capable of handling anything that comes up.'

'I know but . . .'

'So let's get going. We can tour the city, eat as much Italian food as we can, and go home tomorrow happy and contented. How does that sound for a plan? C'mon. We might only get this one chance to explore the city. Let's make the most of it.'

Naomi seemed to finally make up her mind. 'OK,' she said, tucking the phone in her bag. She gave Max an apologetic look. 'Just don't get upset if I check it now and then throughout the day.'

'Promise,' he said, grabbing her hand. 'C'mon. I know you have a notebook full of destinations and notes tucked away in your bag; tell me where we're going today.'

Chapter 13

They started with a map of the city and no real destination. It was cold out, but they were dressed warmly and there were plenty of cafés dotting the streets where they could buy hot coffee, hot chocolate or a snack to eat while they warmed up.

The snow was falling only lightly, drifting past them without a whisper. They started out from their hotel and began wandering across the map, exploring tiny side streets and playing a sort of treasure hunt game. Could they find the narrowest lane in the city, Calle Varisco? Could they find the house labelled '1'? They also looked for street addresses that reflected their birth years and anniversary year. All of this was marked down with a pen on the map.

When they had crisscrossed the city, they ended up near Rialto Bridge. Naomi's notebook listed the Rialto food market as an interesting place to linger, and while Max had no interest in the actual food on offer (lots and lots of seafood), he did find it interesting to see the cultural side of the markets. He hadn't put a lot of thought into the lack of farmland available or how most Venetians got their food, and a look at the market gave him a greater appreciation of the many types of seafood up for grabs at local restaurants. *I still want English fish and chips when I get home,* he thought with amusement as a vendor showed off fresh squid.

After that, tired of walking, they decided to hop on a water bus and cruise the Grand Canal for a daylight look at the city. The snow had stopped by now, and they had a nice view of the hotels and other businesses lining the water, along with glimpses of some of the side streets and canals. It was nearly dusk now, and the Rialto Bridge was well lit up for the night. Further down they spotted the Bridge of Sighs – somehow less impressive now that they had heard the story of its name – as well as a myriad smaller bridges, quiet and deserted in the gathering dusk.

Rising above all they spotted the bell tower and clock tower in St Mark's Square, and the spires on the cathedral. Max checked his watch. 'If we're ready, we can get through a quick meal and make the late Mass. You up for it?'

'Definitely.' Naomi's eyes were sparkling.

They grabbed food at a small takeaway café nearby – more pizza for Max and a panini for Naomi – and then headed into the Basilica with the other tourists and worshippers who were joining the Mass.

They were in for a treat. They'd been expecting a regular

service, but tonight there was apparently a visiting choir who would be singing the Mass. The voices that rose up to the gilded domes filled the cathedral with the same spine-tingling sound they'd heard that morning, yet somehow it seemed even more impressive at night.

Outside, the Basilica was flooded with light for the night-time hours, and Max and Naomi took a moment to admire it as they stood in the piazza. Finally the cold got the better of them, and they all but ran back to the hotel, laughing at their own attempts to hurry without slipping on the fresh snow.

Back at the hotel Naomi made a quick check of her phone. 'No calls,' she said happily, and stowed it away again.

Max plumped up a pillow and handed it to her. 'Aren't you going to call and check in?'

She thought about that for a moment. 'I don't think so – not today,' she said at last. 'It's our last day and I'll let my mum do what I asked her to do – watch Julia. And I'll enjoy us for one more night before we go home.'

'Speaking of the night – look at this.' Max turned off the lamps and opened the curtains, gesturing out of the window. Naomi joined him and gasped a little. They could just see down the canal to Rialto Bridge, and it was still lit up with an ever-changing rainbow of Christmas lights, even at this late hour. Very faintly, they could hear the stream of a jazzy-sounding Christmas carol drifting down the water.

'It's magical,' said Naomi. 'Like something you see in a movie. And we were lucky enough to see it in person.'

They stood in the window for a while longer, holding each other and not speaking. Sometimes, they both realised, you didn't need words to express a feeling.

Just being in the moment and sharing it was enough.

Chapter 14

On her last full day in Venice, Lucy slept late.

She indulged a little, ordering room service so she could linger in bed a while longer, watching a local English-language morning news programme and nibbling on a croissant. Finally she took a hot shower and dressed for the day.

She made sure to pick out the nicest outfit she had and tied a scarf around her neck. She wanted to see the morning Mass at the Basilica, and afterwards, she would do a bit more sightseeing in the city and go to dinner.

Then return to the bridge, do what she came here to do and go home.

After the late Mass she found a café where she could get a quick snack – more coffee and croissants sounded just about right – and then set off to do her shopping. She wandered through the Rialto food market and was fascinated by the variety of items available for purchase, but declined the vendors' enquiring nods regretfully. Unfortunately she had no way to take home fresh squid or crab meat in her suitcase, however delicious they might be. She would have to settle for one more evening of stuffing herself with local delicacies before heading home.

After the food market she spent some time admiring Rialto bridge from the windows of a local café, where she snacked on deep-fried meatballs, olives and bread drizzled with plenty of olive oil and herbs.

The waiter who dished up her antipasti had plenty of suggestions for where to shop on her last day, along with a warning that if something seemed cheap, it probably was: 'Many shops import goods from China,' he explained, 'so stay away from the cheap stuff. Real Italian quality, it will cost you. But it's worth it!'

Lucy kept his warning in mind when she caught a water bus out to the island of Burano. She wanted to take a peek into the Church of San Martino, which looked positively rustic after the decadence of the Basilica, and the Oblique Bell Tower.

She also hoped to see the school of lace-making, where she was told a few dedicated Venetians hung onto the craft of making fine lace by hand. She was impressed by the number of hours that went into the craft; for herself, she'd never had the patience for fine handicrafts, so she couldn't imagine spending hours and hours on one tiny piece.

Besides the church and the lace-making museum and school, Burano boasted rows of colourful houses along the main canals that looked even prettier with a dusting of snow on the roofs. They reminded Lucy of colourful cupcakes with icing on top. Too soon it was time to board the bus back to San Marco, and she looked one more time at the colourful waterfront as they sailed away.

Back in the city, it didn't take long to find all manner of shops with tempting things that she knew her family and friends would love. Leather goods, Venetian masks, handmade chocolate and more – it was hard to pick out just a few things.

Finally she settled on a tooled leather journal for her dad, one which she knew he would enjoy writing in and would look lovely sitting out on his desk. He prided himself on keeping a neat and tidy study and this journal would fit right in. There were lovely cashmere scarves and tiny blown-glass paperweights for her mother and sisters.

She picked up an extra blown-glass necklace charm for herself – a souvenir of her trip – and finally returned to her hotel as dusk fell and the shops began to close up for the day. In the distance she could hear the bell tower chiming out the hour, and she knew it was time to find something to eat – her stomach was rumbling even louder than the chatter of passing tourists.

She tucked her bags safely away in her room and went down the street to a cosy restaurant that was just gearing up for the dinner rush. There were lots of other tourists out and about at this hour too, but Lucy had no trouble getting a small corner table and her dinner arrived quickly.

She had a little trouble choosing what to order – there were so many delicious things to choose from, and this would be her last dinner in Venice – but finally she picked out fried crab and pasta with an anchovy and onion sauce. Fried doughnuts and strong coffee for dessert prepared her for the walk ahead of her, to find that cursed bridge.

Unfortunately, there was one small detail Lucy had overlooked in her planning: she couldn't remember where, exactly, the bridge was located.

She had a map of Venice and she thought she knew the name of the area, but now she realised that she was somewhat off on the name. It hadn't seemed important at the time – why would it be? She wasn't planning on going back there – but now she belatedly realised that she had a bit of a search ahead of her.

It took the better part of an hour, but eventually she had circled several possible bridges on the map and was methodically setting out to each one.

The first bridge was a bust; not only did it not bear any locks at all, it was made of solid stone whereas the one she wanted was wrought iron. Another had some padlocks on it, but it was so close to the busier tourist districts that Lucy was almost certain it couldn't be the right one. Nonetheless she checked each of the padlocks, wanting to be certain.

It was getting late now, and it was getting cold too. Lucy was discouraged, and she muttered under her breath as she marched to her last location. *Stupid romantic ideas, stupid lock, stupid bridge in the middle of this stupid city ...* She thought she might start crying if she got mad enough, and she took a deep breath to calm down. It was just a symbolic thing, after all. Nothing to get all worked up about.

When she turned onto another street, suddenly she knew she was in the right spot. She walked to the middle of the bridge and gazed out over the quiet water. If she closed her eyes, she could picture it all: standing here with Dominic under a snowy sky, their breath coming out in puffs, writing their initials on a lock and then locking it around one of the metal rails on the bridge. What a silly, romantic, yet lovely thing to do.

She opened her eyes and knelt in the fresh snow, feeling for the lock. There were a few on the bridge, and her fingers were getting cold when she found theirs. Feeling in her pocket for the key, she was about to unlock it when she heard footsteps crunching in the snow.

Lucy dropped the lock and stood up. There was a man standing at the foot of the bridge, hesitating. 'Hello?' she called out cautiously.

'Lucy?'

Lucy froze to the spot. *It can't be! There's no way ...*

But even while her brain was denying it, her eyes confirmed that Dominic was, indeed, standing in front of her now. He walked hesitantly onto the bridge, shoulders hunched up in his coat against the cold.

Chapter 15

They stood looking at each other for a long moment, neither sure of what they should say next.

Then they both started speaking at once. 'What are you doing here?' she blurted out, even as he started to say, 'I was hoping I'd catch you …'

Embarrassed, they both stopped. 'You go first.'

'No, you go ahead,' she said quickly, and he shuffled his feet in the snow.

'Maybe we could go somewhere warmer to talk? There are a few places around the piazza open late.'

'What are you doing here, Dominic?' she demanded, remembering her original question.

In answer, he took a key out of his pocket. 'I was hoping to persuade you not to use this.'

She stared at his key for a moment, then took her hand out of her own coat pocket and opened it to reveal a matching key. They stood silently, looking at each other and at the tiny keys that had once meant so much.

Lucy closed her hand and thrust the key back into her pocket. 'Why are you here?' she repeated defiantly. 'You broke up with me, remember?'

'I do. But I made a mistake.'

'And now what? You fly halfway around the world to stop me unlocking our old padlock?'

'That sort of thing usually works in the movies,' Dominic said, looking desperate. She snorted, and he burst out suddenly, 'Look, the real reason I flew here was that I was too stubborn to call you and admit I made a mistake. I thought you'd laugh or hang up on me, and I hoped eventually you'd be the one to call, and then I wouldn't have to hurt my own stupid pride by begging you to take me back. But obviously that didn't work, and when I found out you were coming here – well, I knew what you were planning, or thought I did, and I hoped I would catch you in time to stop you. And to tell you that I still love you, and I want to give us a second chance.'

She stared at him for a moment. 'I almost called you,' she said finally. 'I've missed you. I thought unlocking the padlock was the best way to let go of our past together and move on.'

'I don't want to let go of our past,' Dominic said, moving closer to her.

There was just enough moonlight peeking out of the clouds to show the blue of his eyes and the gleam of his hair.

He took Lucy's hands in his own and drew her close. 'I made the biggest mistake of my life when I let you go. But I want you back, if you'll have me. I think we can give that promise a second chance.'

Her heart soaring, Lucy looked down at the padlock on the bridge, and then up at Dominic. Around them the snow had started again, softly.

'I think so too,' she whispered, leaning in to him. His lips brushed hers, and for a moment she forgot all about the cold.

Only for a moment, though.

'I think you're right,' she said, leaning back from him. 'We should definitely go somewhere warmer to talk about this. Preferably somewhere serving hot chocolate.'

'I know just the place.' Dominic tucked his arm through hers and pulled her closer as they walked slowly over the bridge, their bridge.

She leaned in to him and as the snow fell, touched the key in her pocket once more.

I think I'll hang on to this, she thought, *but not to unlock the padlock.*

I'm going to tuck it away somewhere to remind me that even when it seems impossible, miracles can still happen.

Chapter 16

Dominic and Lucy spent the next hour sitting in a small café, drinking hot chocolate and mostly ignoring the plate of fried doughnuts that they'd ordered.

What started out as awkward small talk quickly turned into rapid-fire chatter about everything that had been going on in their lives since the split.

And more pertinently, how Dominic had come to find her in Venice.

Lucy had been on his mind ever since that disastrous night when he said he wanted to break up. OK, so he *had* wanted to at the time – they'd had a terrible stretch of months, and it seemed like they fought more than they enjoyed each other's company. There was the nasty blow-up at Mick and Jenny's party and then a general period of friction that he honestly couldn't put down to any single thing. It was as if they had just stopped 'clicking'.

Oh, and that ridiculous summer barbecue at his parent's

house. Even now Dominic cringed. He shouldn't have bad-gered her to go. He still wished she would make more of an effort to get along with his parents, and he did *not* think his mother was overbearing – well, maybe a little bit, but not enough to warrant a fight – but he had to admit that if he hadn't pushed Lucy to go when she would clearly rather stay home ...

Weeks of rehashing all their arguments from the past year only seemed to bring him back to the same conclusion, time and time again: they didn't have any major problems, they just happened to make very big mountains out of totally manageable molehills. They were both strong-willed – some-thing Dominic loved in Lucy, as much as it often irritated him – and neither was willing to back down when they thought they were in the right. They'd had too many com-plications thrown at them too quickly, and they just weren't good at working through them. But breaking up? That had been a stupid move, too impulsive and too unthinking. And afterwards, he couldn't figure out how to talk to her without admitting he felt like an idiot.

So he said nothing. His friends assured him she would reach out first: 'Women can't help it,' his best mate Tom said reassuringly, while they were out drinking and playing pool one night in a bid to help Dominic get over his misery. 'She'll want you back, but she'll try to play it casual. She'll call and act like she just wants to say hello, or she'll make up an excuse to come to your place – she'll say she left a jumper there or something. And there's your chance to charm her and show her that you want her back. Seriously, everything will come together.'

But how wrong his friend had been. Lucy didn't call, and she didn't turn up unannounced at his apartment. Dominic had spent a night hopefully going through drawers and wardrobes, thinking maybe he could find a wayward jumper or a lipstick and use it as an excuse to call her, but none surfaced. For a moment he was even tempted to head to the shops and buy something just so he could pretend it was hers, but he knew instantly that she would see through him, and then he would look like an idiot *and* a fool. That combo was too much for his pride.

But as the weeks went by and Dominic got more desperate, he finally decided to casually mention her to some other mutual friends – just to see how she was doing, he told himself.

Instead, he got the shock of his life.

'Lucy? She's great. Going to Italy next week, I heard,' Mick said when they met up to watch the football last Saturday. Dominic felt his mouth go dry. He didn't need to ask what part of Italy; he knew Lucy well enough to know exactly where she was going: Venice, where this time last year they had pledged to love each other forever.

If he knew Lucy's mind – and he thought he did quite well – she wouldn't be content just to move on from a break-up. She would need to get rid of any romantic symbols that lingered on as a reminder of their relationship. It seemed extreme, but somehow he wasn't surprised by the realisation that she intended to unlock the padlock in Venice and throw it into a canal to sink into oblivion. It was just the sort of strong-willed thing she would do.

It took only a little prying to get more details on the dates she intended to be gone – Mick and Jenny typically kept an eye on her flat whenever she was away, watering the plants and feeding her fish – and within mere hours Dominic had in his possession a ticket to Venice.

All the way en route, his nerves were jangling. He supposed he could have just *called* her, but what if she didn't want to talk to him? No, if ever there was a time to pull out all the stops with a big romantic gesture, this was it. And if flying to a foreign city to declare your love for someone didn't count as a big romantic gesture, then Dominic honestly didn't know what did.

It was a gamble, of course, that he wouldn't catch up to her in the city, but he was pretty sure he knew how she would plot out her trip. According to Jenny she was flying in on Thursday night and leaving again on Monday morning.

Dominic guessed she would spend Friday sight-seeing, probably catching up on the major attractions. She'd been particularly impressed by St Mark's Basilica last time, he remembered, so it was almost certain she'd go there. She also loved art and he remembered regretfully that they hadn't made time to visit the museums during their trip, so she would likely spend Saturday touring the art galleries and culture hotspots.

He had a hunch she would wait to retrieve the padlock

until the last day. It would be her farewell to the city, and to that chapter in her life. In Lucy's mind, it would be the final touch to her trip, so it made sense that she would save it for the very end.

Dominic wasn't senseless enough to try to catch Lucy anywhere on Thursday night; he knew she was flying in too late to hit any tourist destinations. Instead he set out on Friday morning, trying to put himself in her shoes and guess where she'd go first.

It was impossible to find her among the tourists in St Mark's Square. He thought he caught a glimpse of her inside the Basilica, and quickly shrank back behind a pillar. He wasn't ready to talk to her just yet, and by the time he got up his courage and looked for her again in the crowd, she was gone.

The next day he bought tickets to a couple of art gallery tours in the city. Browsing through one long collection of classical art, he again thought he caught a glimpse of Lucy, chatting with a couple. Was it possible she came with friends? he wondered. Then she parted ways with the couple, and he decided she must be alone.

Dominic almost decided to approach her outside the museum, but he lost his nerve. For a moment his impulsive trip began to look like a bad idea. What, exactly, was he supposed to say to her when he materialised out of thin air? *Hi, I've been semi-stalking you around Venice in the hope of persuading you to get back together with me ...* Probably not the best opening line.

And so he had decided that the best possible place would be their bridge.

Thank goodness, he thought now, sipping his coffee and staring at his beloved, it had worked.

Lucy was telling him that she had stepped down from her newly awarded position at work. 'I thought I liked it,' she confessed, 'but the hours were terrible and the extra stress wasn't worth the pay. I wasn't seeing my family and friends as much as I wanted to. So I kicked myself back down a level.'

'I'm sorry,' Dominic said, and meant it. He knew how much the promotion had meant to her when she got it.

But Lucy shrugged. 'You know, I was annoyed for a while. And then I started thinking about it, and I realised I didn't care that much about the job itself. I just wanted the extra cash, and I realised I valued my free time more than the money. Lesson learned, I guess.'

Dominic told her about his endless struggle to find a way to get in touch with her and reconnect, and Tom's terrible advice. Lucy laughed and told him about the night she'd nearly phoned him from her bathtub. 'To think I was going to tell you I was in Venice just to see what you would do,' she said, giggling, 'and you were here, too!'

Eventually the café owner made it clear he was ready to close up shop, and Dominic and Lucy left, strolling hand in hand through the quiet streets of San Marco. Even the gondoliers had mostly disappeared, leaving any late-night wanderers to find their own way around on foot.

They weren't really walking in any particular direction,

but soon Dominic and Lucy wound up in a deserted St Mark's Square. If the piazza was picturesque in the daylight, it was beautiful at night. Deserted save for one or two other hardy souls braving the cold – and devoid of the flocks of pigeons that called it home during the day – the square now had a romantic ambience, like a piece of the city carved out of ancient times and deposited into modern Venice. It was well-lit, even at night, along with St Mark's Basilica and the towers at the edge.

'When we were here last year,' Dominic said, 'remember the café orchestras that played here in the evenings?' Though the cafés in question, situated right on the edge of the square were long closed by now. 'We danced in the piazza. Remember?'

Lucy nodded. They were surrounded by tourists, but it had felt like they were the only two people there.

Dominic took her hand and gently led her out into the square, and they began slowly waltzing in place to an imaginary orchestra. 'I think we should have a tradition,' he whispered in her ear. 'We should come back here every winter, or as many winters as we can possibly manage. And we should visit our padlock on the bridge, and dance here in the square, and eat fried doughnuts until we burst.'

'That sounds good to me,' Lucy said dreamily, snuggling into his coat. She suppressed a yawn, and Dominic hugged her. 'Aw, you're tired. I'll take you back to your hotel.'

'I'm not that tired,' Lucy started to protest, but a jaw-cracking yawn cut her off, and she admitted sheepishly that she was ready to drop.

Back at the hotel Dominic sat gingerly on the foot of her bed. 'How soon are you flying home?'

'I'm supposed to go tomorrow,' she said, shucking her boots and coat.

'Do you think you could change the flight?'

'I'd imagine so. Why?'

He got to his feet, a slow grin spreading across his face. 'Because I have a few days off, and we're here in the most romantic city in the world, and I think we should make the most of it.'

'I like the sound of that.' Lucy looked at him speculatively. 'Are you going to stay? Here, tonight, I mean?'

'Are you inviting me?'

In response she smiled and scooped up her pyjamas from her open suitcase.

'Tell me if I need these,' she asked coquettishly.

Without another word, Dominic took them from her hands and dropped them back into the suitcase, pulling her down on the bed next to him.

'I guess that would be a no then,' Lucy said, smiling as she kissed him, and reached to flick off the lamp.

Chapter 17

When morning dawned, Lucy went online and rescheduled her return flight.

Dominic left to gather his things and check out of his hotel and returned an hour later, scrubbed up and ready for the day.

He still wouldn't tell Lucy what he had in mind, though he insisted she check out at the front desk and bring her suitcase.

Then they boarded a water bus out to an island close by.

To Lucy's surprise and delight, Dominic had taken the liberty of calling ahead to the island's lone but massively exclusive hotel, the Cipriani and making a reservation for the two of them.

At this time of the year, the luxurious hotel was well decorated for Christmas, but luckily was not brimming with guests, with most people opting to stay in the busier and less expensive hotels in San Marco.

As the older woman at the front desk explained, most of the island was now a dedicated nature reserve, with some hiking available to tourists. Obviously in this weather walking all over the island wasn't high on most visitors' priorities but from the wink Dominic gave her, Lucy guessed he didn't intend for them to spend a lot of time out and about anyway.

The windswept little island seemed almost bleak in the December light, yet there was a sort of peacefulness to it. She could easily imagine returning here for a future getaway, though perhaps in a warmer month.

'Do you really think we'll spend every winter in Venice?' Lucy asked, snuggling closer to him.

Dominic shrugged. 'I hope so. But I don't think superstitions should change our fate, though. I think it's up to us to decide our future.' He stopped and looked down at her, tracing her chin with his thumb. 'And I for one am very serious about our future. I want to make sure our love stays locked in place forever.'

'I want that too,' Lucy whispered. He tipped her chin up for a kiss, and she melted into him, forgetting all about the cold.

The flight from Venice back to England had to be rerouted due to weather, and when Max and Naomi finally arrived home late that night they were exhausted.

Max was thrilled to be home, but he would be most thrilled once he was tucked into his own bed.

Naomi's parents were up waiting for them, but baby Julia

was tucked safely in her cot, sleeping. Naomi beamed down at her daughter despite her fatigue. 'She's such a good sleeper,' she whispered proudly to Max, who smiled and rubbed her back.

Naomi's mother poked her head into the bedroom. 'You know,' she said, a hint of a smile on her lips, 'she's done so well this weekend. Why don't you leave her here one more night? That way you can get some solid sleep after your flight, and unpack at your leisure tomorrow.'

One more night without baby in tow sounded heavenly, but Max could see Naomi wavering. He held back, waiting to see what she would say.

To his surprise, she tiptoed out of the bedroom with a reticent – but exhausted – smile on her face. 'You're sure you don't mind?'

'Absolutely not,' her mother said, looking as surprised as Max felt.

Naomi gave her a quick hug. 'Thank you! We'll come over tomorrow afternoon to pick her up.'

They collected their coats and went back out to the cab waiting for them at the kerb. *Did I really just hear 'tomorrow afternoon' from my wife?* Max wondered.

As if reading his thoughts, Naomi grinned sleepily at him. 'I hope Mum is up for a lot of babysitting. I'm getting kind of used to these baby-free nights.'

'I'm absolutely assuming that is the jet lag talking,' Max said in amazement, and she laughed and leaned against him, snoring almost before the cab pulled out of the driveway.

Chapter 18

On Monday morning, Scott was reluctant to drag himself out of bed. He was still beaming with the news of Rachel's pregnancy, and now he noticed that she had an extra glow to her as well.

He rubbed her stomach affectionately as she lay in bed. 'Good morning to you too,' he whispered, and she laughed as his breath tickled her skin. 'Are you a he or a she? Either way, I hope you get your mom's brains, because your dad doesn't have a lot going for you in that category.'

They dressed and ate breakfast in their hotel room, with Scott springing down to a café for a large bag that included everything from pastries to muesli.

'You're eating for two now,' he reminded Rachel, and finally she laughingly told him to stop hovering over her while she ate.

'Finish packing. I can feed myself just fine,' she said, planting a kiss on his cheek. He quickly turned his head to plant a deeper one on her lips. 'Are you sure you're fine? You don't need anything else? Is the baby moving yet?'

'Goodness no, I'm only eight weeks along.' Rachel tucked herself up into a comfortable cross-legged position on the sofa. 'Eat, and pack. We want plenty of time to get to the airport. I imagine it will be busy today.'

Soon enough they were packed and checked out of the hotel.

Scott handed Rachel gently into a water taxi, fussing about the weather until they were safely back on dry land and bundled into a cab. She leaned into him in the back seat with a contented sigh. 'Venice was lovely. But I think home sounds even lovelier.'

'Actually, I agree with you.' He wouldn't have thought it twenty-four hours ago, but now Scott couldn't think of anywhere in the world more appealing than their cosy apartment back in New York. He was already thinking ahead to everything they would have to do to get ready for the baby. He supposed this meant cleaning out the spare bedroom so Rachel could turn it into a nursery.

Maybe that can wait until after Christmas.

There wasn't too much traffic on the roads, and soon enough they were unloading their suitcases at the airport. Scott checked everything in and they moved through the security lines to board their flight.

Scott kept one hand tucked firmly in Rachel's, and the other he jammed absentmindedly into his coat pocket.

His fingers touched the ring box and he froze. In all the excitement of Rachel's announcement, he'd completely forgotten about the original reason for their trip. Now they were mere minutes away from going through the metal detectors, and the box was still sitting unopened in his pocket.

A bored-looking official was checking passports at the top of the line.

He took Scott's passport and studied it with a glazed expression. 'Any liquids/metals or anything to declare?'

Scott stood stock-still for a moment, the man staring blankly at him. 'Yes,' he said, his voice sounding foreign to his own ears. 'Yes, I do have something to declare.'

He turned around to face Rachel. Other passengers in the line were staring, some curious, some clearly irritated at the hold-up, but he ignored them all.

Rachel was staring at him, puzzled, as he took her hands. 'Rachel, you are the best thing that has ever happened to me. You're beautiful, intelligent, funny, and have a gentle soul. You're everything I could want in a partner, and now I'm blessed enough to learn that you'll be all that and more as the mother of my child.

'I brought you to Venice because I thought there was no more romantic place in the world to ask you to marry me. Obviously that didn't work out the way I'd planned, but I'm not about to leave before at least giving it my best shot. So with that in mind ...' Scott heard audible gasps as he dropped to one knee and pulled the ring box from his coat pocket. 'Rachel, will you marry me?'

A woman in line let out an excited squeal, and Rachel burst into tears.

He quickly stood up and caught her as she grabbed him in a hug, nodding and trying to wipe her tears away with her coat sleeve. He pulled a wad of tissues from her coat pocket and handed them to her, to the happy clapping and cheers of the passengers in line behind him.

Rachel slept through most of the flight home, and when they landed at JFK, Scott quickly collected their luggage and hailed a cab, settling her in the back seat where she dozed off again. When they got home he made sure she was settled on the couch with a hot cup of cider and dumped the suitcases in a corner. They could unpack tomorrow, or the next day. He didn't see any reason to rush.

Their Christmas tree was all set up in the corner of the living room, and he plugged in the lights, bathing the living room in a soft glow. Scott sat down next to Rachel, and she snuggled into him. She was still admiring the way the stones in her ring sparkled, and he laced his fingers through hers, admiring the stones too. 'Do you like it?'

'It's perfect,' she whispered, leaning back into him. They sat still for a moment, admiring the tree.

Finally Rachel broke the silence. 'Are you hoping for a girl or a boy?'

'I don't really care,' Scott said after a moment's thought. 'You?'

She shook her head. 'I'm happy with either one,' she said. Then after another moment she said, 'Promise me something.'

'Anything.'

'When we're getting ready for the baby – fixing the nursery, whatever ...'

'Yeah?'

'Don't try to make it perfect, OK?' She rubbed her stomach, smiling a little. 'Let's just enjoy these moments together and not worry about how they happen.'

'You got it.' Scott kissed her. 'Merry Christmas, my perfect wife-to-be, who wishes for imperfect but totally real and romantic moments.'

Rachel smiled. 'Merry Christmas, my perfect husband-to-be, who will never stop trying.'

After a few moments, Scott could tell by her breathing that she'd fallen asleep. Gently he prised the cider mug out of her hands and placed it on the coffee table, then picked her up and carried her into the bedroom, tucking her gently under the blankets. She twitched and sighed in her sleep, smiling a little to herself.

'Merry Christmas,' he said softly, pulling the blankets up over her shoulders. 'And here's to years of imperfectly wonderful Christmases ahead.'

And here's to the romance of Venice, he thought as he went back to the living room to unplug the tree lights. He smiled a little to himself as he tiptoed back into the bedroom. *I guess the best romantic moments happen when you stop looking for them.*

With Christmas hymns still echoing in Italian in his head, Scott snuggled up to his fiancée and drifted off to sleep.